LILIES, DIAMONDS, AND FROST-KISSED MIDNIGHTS

A Story of Healing, Forbidden Love, and the Secrets that Refuse to Stay Buried

NEWPORT DIARIES
BOOK III

REBECCA ROYCE

This book is a work of fiction. Names, characters, places, and incidents are the products of the author's imagination or used fictitiously. Any resemblance to actual events, locales or persons, living or dead, is entirely coincidental.

Lilies, Diamonds, and Frost-Kissed Midnights: A Story of Healing, Forbidden Love, and the Secrets that Refuse to Stay Buried.

Ebook 979-8901220016

Paperback Print 979-8-90122-002-3

Hardback Print

Copyright @ 2025 by Rebecca Royce

Cover art by Mibliart Designs

Print Cover Art by Mibliart Designs

Content Editing: Jennifer Jones at Bookends Editing

Copy Editing: Jennifer Jones at Bookends Editing

Final Proof Editing: Viv Jackson

Formatting: Ripley Proserpina

Published by Rebecca Royce

www.rebeccaroyce.com

T he weather was cool, perfect, and the landscape so beautiful. I blinked. No, that was only in my mind. It was muggy and raining today. The ocean was beautiful, but it was so far away from where we were and no one brought us there ever. I blinked again. My mind was also muggy, to match the day's weather. They'd injected me again after my outburst the day before. Was it the day before?

I rubbed my eyes and moved from the window. I knew I had eaten breakfast. What was I supposed to be doing now? I wasn't sure. Looking around, it came to me too slowly. I was in the kitchen. When we were in the kitchen we were either supposed to be cooking or cleaning. No one was cooking, and I'd never be in here alone to do that, so it wasn't lunch time yet. That meant it was cleaning time. There were no dishes. So process of elimination... I had to mop the floor. Aha. Yes, the mop was out. Somehow I had managed to do that much.

That was good.

I grabbed the cleaning device and started to rub it against the floor. Humming to myself, I wondered if I could go back in my mind to that first thought, where the weather was cool, perfect and the landscape so beautiful. It was a fictional place I'd never seen, but it had to exist somewhere on this planet.

I rubbed at my neck. Why did I still look for it when I knew it was gone? My necklace that I had worn everywhere, the beautiful pink pearls that Jeremy Lent had given me in the Hamptons was gone. They had ripped it off my neck during check in here. My earrings too were no longer mine. Gorgeous sapphires that Phoenix Lent had picked out for my birthday. Fortunately, they had let me take them out or I might now have permanently ripped earlobes. Jeremy had wanted me to feel strong with that necklace. Without it... I wasn't feeling that way at all.

When I could think about them I had to add their last names or I couldn't manage to make them real. Barrett Lent. Julian Lent. Jeremy Lent. Phoenix Lent. They had been my boyfriends. Plural. Their family lived in secret like that, and they wanted me to be with them as their love. But they were gone. Like the whole world was gone and I was on this island, somewhere in the Caribbean, no one knew exactly where, but we knew we weren't in the United States anymore, and no one was coming for any of us. Particularly me.

My family had dumped me here. I would stay until I was eighteen, and given that I could never think clearly, thanks to the drugs they constantly injected us with to keep us docile, I couldn't fathom what would happen then. One girl had turned eighteen last week. They had packed her up and sent her on her way. But where?

I hadn't known her very well, not like I had gotten to know some of the girls.

Like I'd conjured her, Betsy Roberts came into the room. She smiled at me; her pupils were huge, probably matching my own.

"Need some help? Mrs. Brown told me to make myself useful somewhere. I'd rather make myself useful with you."

I smiled. She was so nice. Blonde haired, blue eyed. She was here, she had told me once, because she had stolen her father's car after he beat her up and joyridden herself down to the beach. That had earned her a placement here. His beating had earned him nothing. But that was how it was for the very rich, and one thing about this place was that it absolutely cost money to keep us here. My family was paying this place to abuse me. I really had no idea why. I might never know because I couldn't imagine I would seek them out when I was eighteen to ask. More like I would hide somewhere they could never find me.

"Hey," she spoke again. "It's hit you hard again. I'm sorry. Give me the mop. You keep mopping the same place over and over. I'll do it while you just let it pass, okay?" She squeezed my arm. "Don't worry. A year from now you won't be so hit by the drugs. They'll affect you but you'll be so used to it that you won't even notice."

I shook my head. "A year from now I'll be gone. I won't be here. I don't think. What month is it?"

She tilted her head. "Good question. I think it's February. I know Christmas passed and it's been enough time since then that I don't think it's January but not March yet. I think it's February. Let's go with February."

"I turn eighteen in September."

She frowned. "I guess that's true. And I like having you here so much." She sighed. "I'll have another year. I'm just sixteen."

Her lip was split from where one of the teachers had struck her. The sight of it made my cheek throb, and I remembered—I'd been struck too. They'd pumped me full of whatever they used to keep me quiet after I'd challenged the way they were treating a twelve-year-old, and they hit me in the process. I was probably bruised, but I'd never know. There were no mirrors.

But I would guess my hair looked pretty similar to Betsy's. They'd shaved all of ours when we first got here and kept doing it on a schedule. Let it grow a little and then cut it again. I hadn't had my second shave yet, so I had a thin layer of fuzz that barely counted as "length." She did, too. I never saw anyone with it longer than this, so my next shave was probably coming soon.

"Are you in some place good? Wherever you are?" She sounded wistful. "I sort of miss that. Now I just feel nothing."

Okay, I really had to focus. She was doing my mopping, and she had been nice to me from the second I got here, which wasn't true for every girl in the place. There were cliques even in a place like this. As though forming groups to exclude was just something women did in general, wherever we went. Even into the mouth of hell.

"I was for a second, I think. But now I'm just lost. What kinds of things would you daydream about?"

I would scrub the counters. We always had to do that when we mopped, so I would work on that. Certainly, I could handle that much. I picked up the spray bottle that made the whole room smell like vinegar and started to scrub.

She laughed. "Well, when my mom was still alive, we used to go to Hawaii. I daydreamed about that. I'm going there when I turn eighteen. I don't care what I do or if I have to live on the beach. I'm going there."

Personally, I would be okay if I never spent another minute on an island. Betsy and I were part of the dead-mother club together. That was a phrase one of them had used. I didn't know who had made it up or if it had already been a thing. Actually, huge numbers of us here were part of the dead-mother club.

"That sounds really nice." It wasn't for me to comment on the validity of her daydream. Okay, my head was certainly getting clearer if I could think that word.

"Will you go back to New York and the boyfriend you left?"

I'd managed to still not tell anyone about how the Lents lived. Would I? They had promised to follow me. They had promised wherever I went there they would be. "You know the first month I was here I was absolutely convinced that he"—*they*—"would come and rescue me like some kind of fairytale prince on a horse."

"Really? I never had a boyfriend so I didn't get to have that thought. I believed my dad would change his mind. Or my sister would find me. I guess we all have rescue fantasies."

I sighed. "I don't know if he would want me back." There, I spoke it aloud. "I think maybe his not coming might mean he's done."

Her face fell. "I'm sorry about that. I mean, maybe it's just too much time separated. We can't really expect the people in our life to wait for us."

No, we really couldn't. Even if I would have waited for them. I wasn't going to fit in their life anymore. Not like this. Just the idea of my walking back into Pullman was a joke unto itself. With my hair like this? Even Bethany who had been kind and cared that I'd nearly been raped by my aunt's boyfriend wouldn't touch me with a ten-foot pole now, and I wasn't sure I would have anything to say to anyone anymore.

"Done, I think." I stepped back.

"Watch it." She smiled. "It's wet."

We both stared at the kitchen together. It was clean. She nudged me. "There you are. Don't do that again, what you did. We can't save each other. All we can do is each learn how to shut the fuck up and put our heads down so we don't get extra dosed or beaten. That's all we can do. Don't try to save anyone else, Altheia. It's pointless, and I hate having you put in solitary."

I hated it too. I'd spent about a quarter of my time here in solitary. Everyone was put in solitary when we first arrived. Like it was an initial lesson or something. I'd cried the whole time. I didn't have tears anymore. For the first time in my life, I wasn't even holding them back and privately doing it. I absolutely had no more tears. It was a bit of a relief, actually.

Then there were the rules I'd broken. The ones no one had bothered to explain. That was when I first met Betsy. She was being sent to solitary too, for messing up her chores. And now this, my punishment for standing up for the child.

I would probably do that again. I wasn't sure I could ever be the type of person who wouldn't. I hoped I couldn't be. But this place broke us. That was what it was meant to do. They didn't reform us, they destroyed us and then sent us back out into the world at eighteen. Here on this Caribbean island where the whole world got to forget I existed.

⚜

MY BUNK WAS the third in a line of twenty. The room that we slept in was poorly ventilated and at one time must have been a large storage unit. Now it was used to store us. I rolled over, feeling my top bunk mate, Sally, roll over too. She was also not asleep. But we wouldn't talk. None of us would say a word. If they caught us speaking, it meant dosage and solitary. My hands started to shake, which must have meant that my extra dosage was wearing off. There was what they gave us every day and then there was the additional "you're in trouble dose." Neither was great, but this one made me feel like I was going to go into withdrawal when it stopped.

Maybe I actually was. Maybe this was how Phoenix Lent felt all the time. In constant need, like he was always at risk to go into withdrawal.

I hadn't really understood it. I'd never done drugs or really seen them until I watched him take it up his nose at the last party. The last one I would ever attend. Even when I got out of here I absolutely wasn't going to go to parties ever again.

I sighed as the memory came back in pieces. That night, Maggie had drugged me. She was obsessed with Jeremy Lent because he'd slept with her once—long before he'd ever known me—and she'd slipped ecstasy into my drink. Boy, had that hit me hard. I'd admit, the high felt good for a while, but the crash was brutal. Never again.

In that haze, not thinking straight and loving Phoenix Lent as much as I did, I made a choice. I took the large bag of ketamine out of his possession and let the police think it was mine so he wouldn't get in trouble.

I rolled over to put my head face down in the pillow. Why didn't I just throw the thing on the floor?

My family had taken every part of my life and used it against me. They'd made me out to be a criminal. And here I was. With a judge's permission.

Alone. And powerless. The way I had been since my mom had died when I was eleven.

"Hey." Sally jumped down on quiet feet. "Mrs. Hollister is snoring in her chair. I think she helped herself to some whiskey again tonight. Let's get out of here for a bit."

I loved how dangerous Sally could be. Betsy must have been on the same page because she swung her legs out of her bed. Well, if they were going, I was going. Sally. Betsy. Dora. Casey. And me. Maybe everyone else was asleep, or maybe they were smarter than we were.

On silent feet, I followed them from the room into the hallways. There were cameras, but we knew no one watched them at night. Why bother? There was a chaperone in the room with us meant to notice if we got up at all. Why pay staff they didn't need to do that job?

I really didn't know where Sally meant to go, but I was

game. Last time it had been helping ourselves to cheese. There was no dessert here, but cheese was heaven.

We only got it on special occasions. There had been cheese on Christmas, before our special Christmas beating. I rubbed my hands. I was covered in scars from rulers and horse crops. I might never be able to go to the beach should I actually be able to tolerate one again.

But I almost turned around when I saw where she was headed. It was Mrs. Oates' office.

"You can't be serious?" I was glad Dora asked Sally so I didn't have to.

Sally turned around. Both girls were beautiful. Sally with her dark hair and dark eyes, Dora with her light brown hair and green eyes. Sally came from Wisconsin and Dora from Arizona. They'd never have known each other, probably, if they hadn't done something to earn their family's disdain.

"I am. They're letting twelve-year-olds in here now. Alatheia spent a week in solitary. I want to see what's happening in the world. I want to know what Oates is doing, what she is planning. I think that is important for all of us." She stared at me. "Don't you, Alatheia?"

Well... I certainly didn't want to discuss it in the hallway. We were out here. We might as well go in. I nodded, and she continued on her way, all of us following her. It meant a beating if you were called into Mrs. Oates' office. I had never seen or heard Mr. Oates, so I didn't know what his deal was. Maybe he didn't exist. Maybe she thought it made her seem more official to be a Mrs.

The headmistress was forty-something years old and very severe. Had she always been perfect for this job or fit herself to it after she got on this path? I really didn't know.

"What are you worried about?" I asked Sally once we were inside.

"I'm worried this is like a growing business or something.

And don't you think it's weird that no one ever comes here to investigate? Like, people leave. They must tell their families how bad it is here. No one comes to look? I mean... I can't believe my family actually knows what is happening. They think I'm being fixed." She tapped her foot. Sally had a legitimate drug issue before she was sent here. Out of all of us, she had actually done some pretty messed up things. Like breaking and entering in a dentist's office. The dentist was her mother, but that didn't really matter in the long run. I had committed burglary too. In my aunt's house, to get a folder about myself. What would Kit do with all of that information now? It didn't really matter, I guessed.

I looked around the office. That was ultimately the issue. She didn't believe her family would do this to her if they knew. I thought mine might have done it earlier if they had. Maybe they did know. Actually, no maybe about it. My family was one hundred percent on board with this. I was sure of it.

I hated it in here. Mrs. Oates' office was a nightmare incarnate; even during the day it was a dimly lit room with dark wooden walls that seemed to absorb the light. This was where hope went to die. I'd never appealed to her for help, but I knew other girls did. They begged. She didn't give an inch. The heavy, imposing desk dominated the space, covered in papers . Harsh portraits of stern-faced figures glared down from the walls. I didn't recognize them. Her relatives?

This place was the heart of the prison masquerading as a school.

"Sally, do you really think she is hiding her secrets in here? Her plans just out where we can find them? And really, what will we do if we do find them?" I lifted an eyebrow.

Casey pointed at me. "What she said."

"Well, maybe I just wanted to play on her computer for a while." Sally grinned. "I mean fuck it, I want to see what's happening in the world."

She jumped down to sit in the big, stiff-looking chair, and I couldn't help my own smile. Betsy grabbed my hand. "I know you're shaky. Take it easy, okay? If you get dizzy, sit."

"Thank you. I mean it. Thank you."

My friend nodded. "We knew you were one of us the second we saw you. The cool girls here." She winked. "Or maybe not. Maybe we are just all really fucked up."

Casey groaned. "Don't listen to her, Alatheia. She's from Florida. All that sunshine made her a constant optimist. We people from Maine know better."

Sally had gotten the computer on. "Any of you a hacker?" She looked around but none of us volunteered that information. Phoenix was a hacker of sorts. That didn't matter right now. "Boo. You all suck." She shrugged. "Not that I am. I was going to be a ballet dancer." That made her snort. "All right, what should we do? Oh, YouTube. I want to see some of that dancing Gus Monroe is doing."

"No." Betsy laughed, nudging her out of the way to enter the URL. "You can have your dancing in a second. Let's do something snarky. Oh, the *Poor Relation*. They posted. A lot, actually."

What? Now that wasn't possible. I was the Poor Relation. That was my creation, my baby. Betsy clicked on the link, and I watched the latest video. It had been uploaded the day before. There was the other Poor Relation, not Gretchen but the guy I had invented who was like her but not. She wanted him to be the Real Deal. He was arguing with someone. He had to find Gretchen, and she wouldn't talk to him. She was off somewhere, and he was lonely without her, needed her. His aunt, who only cared about what he could do for her, wasn't interested.

I had absolutely not written this, although I liked it. And the movements of the characters were different than I would have done them. Not bad. Just... different.

One of the Lents must have done this. But why? For what purpose? I had never made money on this because only in the days leading up to my being brought here had I even had a birth certificate—albeit a fake one—to use to open a bank account. Not that they needed money. They had somewhere around twenty million dollars each in trust funds. Why do this?

The girls were about to move on when I stopped them. "Let me see that for a second? I am... ah... really into the fandom."

Betsy took her hands off. "Sure. Go ahead."

As fast as I could, I scanned through the comments. People were noticing that the story had changed. They hadn't seen Gretchen in months and the Real Deal was so sad all of the time. They wanted it to move on. What had happened?

I chewed on my bottom lip. Should I do something here? Would it matter? Fuck. No one would notice.

I grabbed the keyboard and typed a comment. "Maybe the real creator is locked in a prison somewhere in the Caribbean and this isn't the Real Deal?"

Without giving it any more thought, I hit send. That might be the last time I ever got to see my own channel.

Sally took the keyboard. "Dancing now."

All right. I stepped back. How bizarre had that been?

"Can you imagine if that was true?" Betsy leaned on my arm. Her hands were shaking too. "If the creator of the *Poor Relation* was here too? I mean we know he or she isn't. They're making content. But it would be fun, right? I bet she could tell great stories."

Great stories? I wasn't the storyteller outside of *Gretchen, the Poor Relation*. Julian was. He had written a whole play. A good one. If he was here he would talk about ghosts. The ghosts we carry around with us. In fact, he'd had the Black

Dahlia as a character and had her tell stories about the ghosts around her in the play.

Who were my ghosts right now? My family. The Lents. The Poor Relation. The life I wanted but would probably never have .

"What ghosts are you guys carrying around with you?" I asked the room.

It was Dora who answered. "Hopefully none. It would be really spooky to be haunted."

"This place could be haunted." Casey smiled. "Can't you see it? Ghosts all over this place."

Sally ignored me. She was stretching her arms, maybe imitating the movements of what she saw on the screen.

It was Betsy who sighed. "I think I carry my mom with me. Her ghost. Do you carry yours?"

I nodded. "I do."

All the frickin time. Why had she done this to me?

It was obvious Betsy was getting tired; she pressed her forehead to my arm. "Guys," I spoke again. "Time to go."

"You go." Sally shrugged. "I'm not done."

All right... that was her choice. Betsy and I left, Dora and Casey right behind us. The snores of our drunk chaperone filled the room, with several others joining her. I climbed into bed. I never wanted to do that again. Not YouTube. My heart raced. I couldn't see the *Poor Relation* ever again. On one hand it was great it continued, it hadn't been forgotten. On the other... what the fuck.

I closed my eyes.

When they found Sally asleep in Oates' chair the next morning it went really badly for her. It would be a whole two weeks until we would see her again, and when we did, she was bruised and couldn't make eye contact with any of us. What had they done to her? She didn't tell us. Just did her chores, took her assigned walks around the property. All the light was gone. That's what this place did. It destroyed us.

✣ 2 ✣

I t was head shaving day. A week after Sally had gotten back and she still wasn't making eye contact with any of us. I sat down next to her.

"I put some extra cheese hidden in the back of the fridge where you can get it if you do kitchen duty tomorrow." I squeezed her knee. "I thought you might like that."

She met my gaze. The first time in a week. "Thank you."

"You're welcome."

Oates stood by the door, and a Ms. Jerald stood with the buzz cutter ready to dish out the act on all of us.

"How long does this take? It's my first time."

Sally touched her dark hair, what was left of it before she would lose almost all of it. "It's fast. Did you love or hate having red hair?"

I blinked. Wow. She was actually talking. "I felt benign about it truthfully. I... I hated the frizz."

"Well, no chance of that now."

That was true. Maybe there was a small pro to this hell. Frizzless existence. We had three twelve-year-olds with us now. Two of them cried in the front of the room. They'd both made it through solitary but still had tears to shed. That was kind of beautiful actually. Maybe they weren't as broken as the rest of us.

"Will you still be my friend when this is over? I mean, I leave a month before you. I'll wait for you somewhere out there on this island wherever we are. And, we can go somewhere together. Some place quiet. I'm a constant problem. I know it. I do it to myself. But I would like to be with you. And then Betsy can come. And Casey and Dora. We can go make a life somewhere."

I nodded. "Yes. Wait for me and I'll find you. Okay? You're not a problem. You're just human. We all are. Of course I'll still be your friend."

"Good." She nodded and put her head on her knees.

Betsy sat on my other side. "Here we go."

One of the twelve-year-olds was brought up. She was new. I didn't even know her name, but they shoved her in a chair, and when they were going to shave her, she screamed. It was a gut-wrenching sound. I'd give her credit. Small she might be, but she was tough. She threw herself over. The girl wasn't going to give in without a fight. They smacked her hard.

I jumped to my feet.

"Alatheia." Sally tugged on me, but I couldn't hear her right then.

Who went around hitting twelve-year-olds? "She's scared," I shouted. "Don't do that to her. Don't hit her." I stormed forward. "She's frightened."

I was yanked back by two of the teachers as they managed to get the twelve-year-old—I really needed to learn her name —back into the chair. Oates stared at me; she almost looked bored.

"Take her to the clinic."

I kicked one of the women holding me. I had never been

violent, but maybe they needed a touch of their own medicine. I got her right in the shin.

That made the other one yank me harder out of the room and away from everyone. We rushed down the hall, and before they strapped me to the table, the one I had kicked—Mrs. Rowing—smacked me hard. So hard I tasted blood in my mouth.

Once. Then twice. Oates came into the room. "Give me the dose."

I spit blood out of my mouth as I stared at her. I'd had no warning I was about to crack up, but here it was. "You are a sick, twisted, sadistic bitch."

"You can call me all the names you want to, Ms. Winder, but no one in the world cares about you. And the only time you will ever see anyone who might is when you are dead."

With that statement she jabbed a needle in my arm. I would think by now that wouldn't hurt, but it did. The medicine burned. Oh, this was the bad one. The really bad one.

"You're not a hero. You're nothing."

Time passed. I was pretty sure.

I was alone in the dark. In solitary you had to earn the right to have them open the window shade. It was closed. I had no idea if it was day or night. And that was okay because I could hardly think at all anyway.

I hummed to myself, a nonsense song that wasn't real. Hadn't Barrett Lent played the piano a lot in the apartment? I'd loved that. The background noise of our life. He loved music. Jazz clubs. Wanted to support music. Hadn't he had a test the last day? How had it gone? I never got a final look at him. He had been grumpy that morning, barely spoken to me. I couldn't blame him. College exams were hard. Or I hadn't blamed him then. I could now. Did I want to? Maybe a little. But that was so unfair. He had no crystal ball to tell him we would never see each other again. You got to be grumpy with people that you loved. We had been that. Now I couldn't feel love. I couldn't feel anything.

Just a vast emptiness filling me and becoming me. I wouldn't help that twelve-year-old now. Why bother? She would probably just end up in here anyway.

My mind drifted. Each of the Lent brothers moved through my vision like they were saying goodbye. I wouldn't see them again. Not until I was dead.

Not that my goodbyes with the other three had been wonderful. Phoenix was out of it and horrified. Jeremy and Julian had been shouting at me from behind where the police had put them. I'd told all three of them I loved them. I had. That was why this had happened to me. I'd known not to say it. Breaking that rule had landed me here. I didn't get to love people or be loved.

I hummed and closed my eyes.

Time passed. I had no idea how much. They didn't open my window. But I heard noises. Male voices talking sternly. A woman sounding downright hysterical outside of my door. I tried and failed to lift my head. I'd had my bathroom break already. What was happening? There were no men here. Not ever.

"Open it now." I didn't know that voice. So I closed my eyes. Whatever was happening was not my concern.

Light burst into the room even getting through my closed lids. I lifted my head. What was happening? I raised my shaking hand to try to block it out.

"This her?" That voice I didn't know spoke again.

I was surrounded on all sides. Everyone was speaking. I knew the voices, maybe, but I couldn't see. I pushed my head back down on my knees. It had to stop. It just hurt too much.

"Stop. It's an assault on her senses." Someone spoke. Another man. Did I know that voice?

"Alatheia, can you hear me?" There was a pause.

"Eric?" Someone asked. Why was everyone speaking so loudly?

"Barrett, get her out of here. Come on. We're leaving."

A woman was screaming. I knew her. That was Oates. I was lifted, and my head flopped forward onto the chest of whoever was carrying me.

"Got her?" A hand touched my arm. "Because I can carry her."

"Jules, I've got her. Move. I want her out of here."

The shrieking Oates again. "You can't take her. We are her guardians here, given the right by her family."

"They don't have custody of her anymore." A new voice spoke. "You have the paperwork. Now move, or I'll make you move."

There were so many people here. Ten? Eleven? Twelve? Everyone was blurry.

"You see, Commissioner, what they are doing here. Surely you can't be okay with this happening on your island. What would the press say?" The voices were following us when we moved. "I want this closed. I would think you would too. These children sent home immediately. The abuse here is abhorrent. Close it and you'll get the money for the casinos from my personal investment fund. Don't and you won't see a dime."

The commissioner must have been the one to have had my door opened. He was big. That was all I could see. "Yes, Stephen. I agree. Yes."

"Alatheia. " Sally's voice. Then Betsy's. "Where are they taking her?"

I reached for them. But it was all too much. My eyes closed. I was just supposed to feel nothing right now. Just nothing.

❧

A COOL WASHCLOTH touched my forehead. "Easy. Too much will be jarring." It was a female voice who spoke this time. It was hard to hear over the rumble of a very loud engine. "You're okay now, Alatheia. You're with us and you're safe."

Safe? What was that?

"So it really was just as bad as we feared? " someone asked. I knew these voices. Didn't I?

"Worse," another answered. "Let her sleep. It's what she needs. Right now, that's what she needs."

I'd listen to whoever that was because it was all I could do anyway. But first I had to ask someone in the room a question. They needed to tell me. Whoever they all were. With my eyes still shut, I managed to speak. "Am I dead?"

A hand came down on my forehead as gasps sounded. "No, Princess, you're not dead. I promise you're not dead."

I wanted to believe him.

I woke up to a beeping noise and kind of a whoosh sound to go with it. My head was clear, but it pounded. There was bright light and much as I wanted to avoid it I really couldn't. Something was poking into my hand.

I lifted my head. This was... a hospital room? The walls were white but with paintings on them that were of various cheerful landscapes. I tried to sit up when a woman came walking into the room. I didn't recognize her, but she wore white and purple.

Her eyes widened. "Oh good. You're up. I was just coming to change your IV. That'll make the beeping stop." She was really cheery. How was that possible? Everything was dark and awful in the world. An IV? I looked. Oh yes, that was in my arm. "Give me a second."

I stared at her. "What's happening?"

"Hello, dear, you're bound to be confused. Here, one second." She fiddled with the IV bag and then quickly changed it out. "Let's sit you up, too. And you're nice and hydrated now, but you must be thirsty, so one more second."

It wasn't like I was going to press the issue. I learned my lesson. Betsy was right. Keep my mouth shut and I wouldn't have to get beat up. It didn't help. I'd done nothing for that girl. Where were they? Had something happened that they'd actually taken me to a hospital? There were images. But I couldn't hold onto them, like they weren't solid.

When she was done with whatever she was doing, she stuck a straw in my mouth and I sipped.

"You're really pretty, aren't you, when you're not in this condition." She didn't phrase it like a question. "And you and my daughter are the same age. I bet you'll be friends."

Friends? "Is she at the school too?"

"Hold on." She placed a gentle hand on my arm before she turned and scooted from the room on white sneakers that didn't make a noise at all. "Dr. Lent," she said as she got to the doorway. "She's up."

The nurse had a southern accent. I hadn't heard one in a while. Dr. Lent?

That was the last thing I heard her say. What?

A second later, a man wearing a white collared shirt with a red tie and blue pants appeared in sight. He smiled at me brightly.

It took me a moment to register who was in front of me. This was Dr. Eric Lent. The youngest of the Lent brothers' fathers. Technically, he was Phoenix's bio dad. What was he doing here?

I tried to sit up fu rther, but it was hard. Too hard. He walked over and pushed a button, bringing the bed to an even higher sitting position. "There. That's better. Alatheia, how are you feeling?"

I stared at him. Okay. Was I to assume this was real and

not some drug fueled dream? I didn't know. But I answered him just the same. "Confused. Not sure I'm awake."

"Right." He sat on the edge of my bed. "That's to be expected. Big time. It wouldn't be weird if you fell right back to sleep in a second. On and off for the next few days. That would be normal and not something to worry about." He patted my hand. "You're awake. It's real. How about physically? I am sure a lot of things hurt. Anything really badly?"

"My head." I stopped. This was too odd. "Aren't you a plastic surgeon? "

"That is the rumor, but lately this is more of what I do, it seems. That's not your problem to worry about. I'll get back to it sooner or later. I'm working with another doctor, he'll be here in a bit, who specializes more in what happened to you than I do. Even though I'm a little out of my depth, I can certainly handle keeping you comfortable in basic ways. Your head hurts. We'll get that taken care of." He took his phone out of his pocket and pushed some buttons. "I'm ordering it now. Listen, for just now, I want you to sleep and rest."

A man who stood in the doorway spoke, catching my attention. "Yes, that's right. Sleep and rest. Coming down is painful, and you'll have to endure it. I'm sorry about that."

Eric stood. "This is Dr. Kirk Trevor. He's a dear friend. And he specializes, fortunately for us, in getting people through addiction issues. Not your fault, but you've been so medicated for so long now on things that you should not have been taking that you're going to have to live through withdrawal from it. After that, he'll help you with the things that have happened. Right now, this is the most important thing. Sleep. Rest. Food when you can stomach it. I'm keeping the boys out because I want you to sleep, and all four of them in a room is a lot. But if you would prefer it, I can let them in."

I didn't understand any of this and I was too blank to try. "What?"

Dr. Trevor patted my other arm. "Too much, Eric. Too soon. For now, you're in a clinic in Louisiana. It's a private clinic. You don't have to be concerned about saying anything or everything here. Every person you see here knows what you know. Okay?"

His words sunk in. "About... about..."

I looked at Eric, and he nodded. "About the Life."

Kirk rose. "You'll be seeing me around a lot. We'll get you up and moving as soon as I'm sure you won't fall over, and then we'll go from there. One boy at a time as long as they understand that if she's sleeping, she stays that way. Even if it's mid-conversation. I hear any of them are keeping her up and they're all out."

"Got it." Eric nodded.

I was glad he did because I didn't know what was going on. "Your sons?"

"Yes, them. Are you hungry?"

Was I? It was Kirk who answered. He was older than Eric. Those details were starting to filter in. Slowly. I still wasn't sure I could pick him out in a crowd. He answered Eric. "Doubtful."

My eyes closed.

The next time I woke up it was dark in the room, and I wasn't alone. In a chair next to my bed, staring at something he was watching on his phone, was Julian Lent. I stared at him. He was skinnier than I remembered and there were dark circles under his eyes. But there they were, the blue eyes I remembered. He had been the first Lent I'd met. He liked books best in the world and had written a play.

How was he here? Oh, that was right. I wasn't... wherever I had been. My mouth was dry.

"Can I have some water?"

He jumped, his phone going flying, but he didn't move

except to stare at me, blinking rapidly before he lunged to his feet and was filling a cup with water from a pitcher nearby.

"Here." He tried to hand it to me, and I legitimately tried to take it, but my hand shook. Badly. Oh this. Yes, I knew this feeling. This was because it had been the bad drug. The one that hurt.

Julian frowned and then grabbed a straw and placed it in my mouth. "Sorry. I'll hold it."

I was grateful, but I wasn't going to say anything else until I got the cool water down my throat. Finally, I could speak. "Thank you."

"Yes, of course, Baby. Of course." He took my shaking hand in his. "How are you?" A nurse—different from the first one—poked her head in, and he looked over his shoulder. "She woke up. I didn't wake her." The woman nodded and left. He turned back to me. "They'll throw me out if I wake you. I won't. Okay? I just want to take care of you. That's all I want."

I was actually able to sit up a little, but it wasn't as easy as it should have been. He helped me, repositioning my pillow. "I'm pretty confused."

"What do you remember?" He let go of my hand to smooth a hand over my head. It was then that I realized my hair had been shaved.

"They must have done that again when I was out of it."

"What?" He shook his head. "I'm sorry. I didn't follow that."

I sighed. "They shaved my head. It was head shaving day, but I got in trouble and then they injected me, and I don't remember them shaving my head, but they must have."

I hoped that made sense because I was in no condition to explain it again.

He kissed my hand, bringing it to his mouth. "Maybe later

you can tell me more. I'm so sorry that happened. Yes, your hair is pretty much gone right now. But it doesn't matter. Okay? It's just hair. It'll grow back."

"Oh." I nodded. "I don't care. Not really." I didn't really care about anything.

He tried to hold my gaze, but I couldn't. I just couldn't. I stared at the wall instead. There was a picture of... Paris on it. I knew the Eiffel Tower even though I'd never seen it in person. Paris in sunshine.

"Thank you for commenting on that post. That was what we hoped. That you would see it. That you couldn't reach us, but you could see it there and we would see it. That was just what we hoped, no matter how improbable it seemed."

Post? "Oh, the *Poor Relation* thing."

"Right." He nodded, still holding my shaking hand. "We don't have to talk about it right now. You can just rest. We can sit here. I can put something on the television. Or my phone." It was still on the floor. "We can listen to music. Or just be silent. Whatever you want. That's what's going to happen. From here on in and forever."

Forever? What was that? "Where are the other girls? What happened to them?"

"What do you remember?" He repeated his earlier question.

"Nothing."

Julian nodded, some of his brown hair falling in his face. "Then let's start at the beginning."

I wanted to listen, but my eyes closed.

The next time I woke I was itchy. So itchy. I sat up, which also made me nauseous. Oh, shit I was going to puke. A bucket was placed quickly in front of me—which was good because I vomited. I hadn't eaten in I didn't know how long, but I had plenty of stomach bile and it was coming up.

Over and over. Finally, when it stopped, I grabbed my arms to rub them where they itched. A cool compress was placed on the back of my neck. "This sucks. I know. Hold on. Let me get the nurse."

I stared at the speaker before I recognized the voice. It was Phoenix. He hit a button and then wiped my forehead. "Are you done? More?"

"Done." I hoped. "I'm itching everywhere."

He nodded, wincing as he did. "It just sucks. Maybe they can give you something."

The nurse arrived. "Phoenix?"

"She's throwing up, and she's itchy."

The nurse's nod was slow. "I'll let Dr. Trevor know." As fast as she had arrived, she left. Everything felt off. Fast. Slow. Fast. Slow. Why wasn't anything normal?

"Why am I itchy?" I rubbed my arms and then started to scratch them. Phoenix grabbed my hands.

"Don't do that, Red. It'll hurt you. Okay? It won't help. You're itchy because you're coming off some class of drugs that are making you itchy. It's part of the withdrawal."

I took a deep breath and brought my head to my knees. This was my favorite place. My safe place. This position. No one could really hurt me when I was like this.

Phoenix patted my head. "This is going to end. I promise. It won't last as long as it feels. One day it'll just be a memory. Something you lived through, not something you are still living."

I lifted my eyes to meet his gaze. It hurt, but I managed it for a second. "You look different." Maybe I shouldn't have said that—*I* was the one who looked different. Probably unrecognizable.

"I'm clean." He answered. "For about four months. Still new, but yes, I would guess I look different. That's why I know how much this sucks." He ran his hand over the back of my scalp. "I love you, and I have missed you so much."

I put my head back on my knees and closed my eyes.

The next time I woke, the room was dark, the lights dimmed to match whatever was happening outside. The beeping was back.

"Alatheia." It was Barrett. He walked over and sat down next to me, but he turned to speak to yet another nurse. "You have to stop that. She can't possibly be expected to sleep through that beeping."

"I'm changing it, Mr. Lent." Her tone said what she felt about his comment. "The IVs beep when they need to be changed."

He glared at her. "Then change it before it starts beeping."

She shot him a look of death and then stared back at me. "Hi there. Can I get you anything?" This one was older, gray-haired with lines around her eyes.

"I wouldn't know what to ask for." I was thirsty again. "I could use a little water, maybe."

Barrett jumped up. He poured the water, grabbed a straw, and came back quickly. "Here. Sip." He didn't try to hand it to me but held it, which I appreciated. The nurse left, and I sat back on the bed. My whole body ached. "Is pain medication one of the things I could ask for or is that not allowed? I don't want to break any rules."

Barrett set down the cup. "I'll tell her you need some. There aren't rules here."

"There are rules everywhere. Even when we don't think there are rules, there are rules. I don't want to break them. I don't want to get in trouble. I don't want to go back there."

He scooted out of the room and came back fast. "They'll give you something. There is no world where you will go back there."

"My family could send me back. They could. Or the place could come get me."

He touched the side of my cheek. "Never. It can't happen."

I didn't believe him.

JULIE... and... the... sip... of... time... clock...

❧ 3 ❧

I woke up to find Jeremy sitting on the edge of my bed. I
stared at him. I was tired but I was... okay. I didn't want
to puke. I wasn't itching. My head was only mildly
pounding. All in all, I hurt but I was... okay.

"Well, the good news, Princess, is that you have a great
shape to your head. I mean I wouldn't necessarily have said
shave your hair off, but we can all see now that you don't have
a weirdly shaped head under your hair."

That shouldn't have been funny. But it was. I covered my
mouth, startled when I laughed. I hadn't expected it. His
words, they were just funny.

"There's my girl." He tugged me to him in a tight hug.
"There you are. It's going to be okay, Princess. I promise."

He smelled familiar. I closed my eyes and breathed. It was
a nice moment, so it was terrible that I was going to ruin it.
"Don't make me promises."

Jer put his head on top of my apparently nicely-shaped
scalp. "Why not?"

"Because they don't get kept. Better if they aren't made."

I expected him to rear back and yell at me. That would be

appropriate but instead he just held on. "Because I promised you that you'd never be taken against your will. And you were. We all promised you that we'd go wherever you went. It took months. So, yes, I get it. You have no reason to think that any promises I made or will make can be kept. But, look at it this way, I couldn't be sicker over it, and I can only get better from here."

I was the one to pull back. Jer's eyes were so tired, his blond hair the longest I had ever seen it. I met his gaze. "I don't want you to be sick over it."

"Well, I am." He took my hand.

A thought dawned on me. "I must really stink. I puked earlier."

"You want to shower? I think they'll let you do that. You don't stink. Are you hungry?"

My stomach made a noise. "I am."

"Good. I'll tell them and I'll ask them about showering." He got up. "Good to see you so alert. You had a rough night, Phoenix and Barrett told me. We rotate about every six hours. Or so."

I blinked. "Did I?"

"Yes. But maybe it's a blessing you're not holding onto memories right now that well. Be right back."

Was it? I put my head on my knee. Yes, I liked it here. Right on my knee. It really worked here.

"Okay." He came back and I was forced to lift my head. "Food is coming, and they say you can shower if I stay in there with you just in case you get dizzy. Okay? The shower is going to take a lot out of you. That is what Kirk says."

I tilted my head. "Sure. I mean, if you're comfortable with that."

"I am. If you are." He lifted an eyebrow. "This is about you."

I rubbed at my face. "Can we talk after? I need to know what happened."

Jer put out his hand and helped me off the bed. "Yes, of course. If you are able to stay awake, we'll talk. If not, you can talk to whoever you want, whenever you want. Not that any of them can match my level of discourse—or my incredible sense of humor."

I laughed, coming to my feet and pressing my head into his arm while the world righted. "I'm okay."

"Yeah? You sure? "

I nodded. "Yes." We walked slowly to the bathroom. "I can't believe how weak I am. I'd have been expected to get up and work when my punishment was over. I couldn't be weak."

"This is because of the detoxing. I think. If they'd kept you on the drugs, who knows what you'd be like. I don't know."

Detoxing. It was strange to think about. "Funny, you know I've never taken drugs on purpose. But I have to withdraw or whatever."

"I do know." He let go of me when he turned on the water and then stepped back. "There are clothes in the drawers. I'll stand back here and wait for you. But I'll just listen and keep an eye if you need me."

I realized there was something I hadn't said yet. "Thank you. For coming to get me. And now this is all a lot of hassle. You should be in school. It's February. How are you here?"

"Shower. Then we'll talk details. And I love you. Please don't thank me. It took too long. So long."

I dropped the gown I was wearing and got under the spray. For a second I just closed my eyes and relished the water hitting my body. We'd had to group shower. For the last four months I'd never been alone in a bathroom. Jer was here but not right next to me. This was a luxury. But soon the fact that I was upright was too much. I'd managed to wash my head where my hair should be and my face, then most of my body before I sunk to the floor.

"I think I need help."

"Here." Jeremy flung the curtain open and then turned off the water. "I've got you. Don't worry." He lifted me up like it was nothing and then wrapped me in a big towel. With one hand, he grabbed something from the drawer and carried me over to the bed.

"You're making this seem like it's nothing when I have to be heavy."

"You've lost so much weight it is nothing. It would always have been nothing. I am mad strong, Princess." He winked at me, which made me smile. In one second, he pulled a nightie over my head. That must have been what he'd grabbed. I looked at it.

"It's mine."

He nodded. "Sure, we brought your stuff."

I was no sooner clothed than the nurse showed up with food, which she set in front of me. It was a rice dish, and it actually smelled really nice. There was apple juice with it and a dessert that looked like it was chocolate.

She was stern when she spoke. "Of course they gave you the good stuff. Don't go too quickly and you don't have to eat all of it."

"I remember you." Jeremy regarded her. "You're the one who was so judgy of my brother. How did you get in here? I think it was pretty clear you are supposed to stay away from the Lents."

She snorted. "The Lents. Oh yes, the right-side-of-the-lake Lents. She's not a Lent."

No, I wasn't. And I never had been. The stern-faced woman strode out, leaving me with my dinner. I sighed. Some of my earlier okayness fled. I hadn't been overly happy, but it was better than this.

I took a bite, then a second one. I could hardly taste it. Jer reached over and opened my juice.

"Sorry about that. She's such a bitch." He shook his head. "She was terrible to Phoenix. I mean really bad, and he was just taking it when we found out. Eric banned her from us. I'll get her away from you."

I shrugged. "It's fine. She's right. I'm not a Lent. I can't imagine what this is costing all of you. In time and money and..."

He kissed my temple. "You're a Lent in everything but name. You'll be one, and I know you're not okay, so we aren't going to do any of this just yet. But you are ours. As much as you always have been. Maybe more."

I would have asked him why, but after sipping my juice and taking one bite of the flourless cake, I was done. Gently, I pushed the tray away and lay back in the bed.

"Still want to talk?"

I shook my head. "I want to sleep. I think."

He put his cool hand on my forehead. "You can sleep. You should sleep."

"I'm hurting."

That made him run out the door again. "She'll take ten times as long as she should, but she'll bring you some meds in a second."

"Thank you." I did want to ask him something. "Are they okay? The girls? That I was with? Are they okay?"

He sat down next to me. "They're not there anymore. The place was shut down. Of course the government knew about it, but they are pretending they didn't. It's in the island's financial benefit to do that. Stephen is throwing money at the island. He stayed to make sure it got done."

I shook my head. "That's interesting, but the girls?"

"Have all been sent home."

I closed my eyes. For some of them that was going to be really bad. But why was I surprised? We were all at the mercy of others. All the time. I drifted off. It was okay if she didn't bring me pain meds. I would just go back to... nothingness.

The bed dipped as Jeremy stretched out beside me. "I'm not supposed to do this. I'll probably get shit for it, but I need to hold you."

I lifted my lids. He did? That was more than okay with me. I rolled onto him, the motion feeling familiar, like something we'd done a hundred times before. "Don't let her make you move."

"She can't make me do anything." He ran a hand over the back of my scalp. "She's only not fired because Eric is patient. We own more than fifty percent of the clinic. We built it."

I smiled. "Well, you paid someone to do it, right? You didn't wield a hammer?"

He snorted. "No, good call. I did not."

I sighed. "The girls aren't going to be okay. They're going back to the places that sent them there. Maybe they'll be sent to other places. It would be like sending me back to my family." In fact, my heart rate kicked up. "Do I have to go back to them?"

"No." He kissed my temple. "You aren't going back. Ever. Kit found your other family. Your father's family. They're problematic but not sending you there. His associate went to court and argued child abuse. You are now theirs. And things are going badly for your family. But we don't need to talk about that now. I know you have a million questions. You should. I'm sorry about your friends. So sorry."

I did have a million questions, but it was like there were too many. It overshot my head. My father's family? Who were they? Where were they? My lids closed. This time it was hearing Jeremy's heartbeat against my ear. It was peaceful. Familiar. It said that for tonight I was okay.

I dreamed.

My mother and I were sitting outside our trailer. She was drinking a Coke, and I was sipping lemonade. It was lovely outside. Cool but not too cold yet.

"Why don't we have any family?" I kicked the dirt, and the smile on her face faded. I'd made her sad. I hated making her sad.

"We have family. I think everyone probably has some family. Maybe not. I am sure there are some people with no family. Anyway, I get what you're asking. We have family but we don't see them."

I stared at her. She was tired. But she was always tired. I couldn't wait to talk to her anymore when she wasn't. I was turning eleven. I wanted to know things. Lots of things. "Where are they? We don't visit them even. Most people go places for Thanksgiving or Christmas. They drive. Wanda went on an airplane once. It's just you and me. All the time." Plus she had started working Thanksgiving and Christmas. It was lonely.

She hugged me to her. "Do you mind it being just you and me?"

"Not most of the time."

Mama laughed. "Well, there is your honesty. Okay. My family is mean. They want things from me I don't want to give them because they are for you. Not for them. They do bad things with those things they want from me. Don't ask me more about that. I won't say. Take that as truth, okay? I even have a twin sister. We look exactly alike. Or we used to. You could be walking down the street one day and see two of us. But she is mean. Like our father was mean. With your daddy's family, it's a crapshoot. Some of them are very good people. Some of them are awful. Most of them are awful and he was hurt by them, deeply. He didn't want them in your life. Maybe someday you could meet his mom. She was better than his dad."

This was more than she'd ever told me. "What was wrong with his dad?"

"He used to beat Daddy. All the time."

I caught my breath. I'd never been beaten. I could barely remember my father. Maybe it was the trauma that kept me from remembering much. But I hated that for him.

Movement began to pull me awake, pushing the dream back. If that had happened I had no idea. Maybe it never did. I couldn't tell anymore. It slipped away before I could hold onto it. When she had died, I hadn't even known she had family. It had to be a dream. I felt myself drifting again.

"How did you pull that off?" It was Julian's voice in a whisper. "They told us no."

"I know they did. But look at her, she's silently sleeping. Her eyes are moving below her lids. She's in REM. She's not thrashing or hurting. She's not crying out. She's just sleeping. It's hard to argue with that. They left us alone." He kissed my forehead. "Climb in this side and we'll switch."

The bed dipped, and I opened my eyes.

"No," Jer whispered. "It's just Jules. Keep sleeping. He cuddles too."

"She knows that," Julian answered.

Jeremy kind of rolled me over to his brother, and I let it happen. This was too nice. He must have just showered because he felt warm. "What time is it?"

Jeremy got off the bed. "Late. It's midnight. Get some more sleep. I love you."

Well, if it was nighttime, that was fine. Hadn't it just been nighttime? Who knew how often I was really up or asleep anymore. Who knew how many rounds of this we had done without me knowing it?

Jules stroked my neck. I didn't see Jeremy anymore. Had he just left or had time passed?

I liked the cuddle, but I was awake. "I thought a lot about your play. When I was there."

"You did?" He didn't stop his stroking.

"I did. I even asked the girls what ghosts they were carrying. I thought about my ghosts."

He sighed. "I was so afraid you were going to be one of my ghosts. We couldn't find you anywhere. Like the world had swallowed you up. I couldn't... never mind. What were your ghosts?"

"My family. Your family. Parts of my life. The *Poor Relation*. Pretty much everything. I wasn't going to go back to New York. I can't let my family near me again. When I turned eighteen I was going to vanish. And I thought... maybe I would reach out as soon as I was safe at some point to see if you had all moved on or you might like to see me again sometime. Somewhere else."

His voice was low. "Oh, Alatheia, we will never move on. We would still be looking."

My eyes closed.

৩৯৩

THERE WAS ONLY SO MUCH I could do in the room. Days later I could stand. I could walk. I could shower. I could eat. And I was going stir crazy.

Phoenix arrived to replace an exhausted Julian. I didn't think he was sleeping even when I wasn't with him, but he stared at me with a smirk. "It's pretty bad once you start to feel better. Come on. You're not locked in. Let's walk to a place I found."

A place he found? "How long were you here?"

Phoenix handed me some slippers and, when I'd put them

on, placed his arm around me, drawing me to him. He was... calmer. Less jittery than I had ever known him. Not to mention he actually seemed to be present mentally when he was with me. His eyes really dove into me, like he saw me very clearly all the time. I didn't know if that was a good thing or a bad thing.

I did know that he was attentive beyond what I could have imagined.

"I was in your room. The same one. For a week. Before they moved me to elsewhere in the hospital. This is detox. That next place is 'okay, let's tackle the addiction.' They'll be moving you soon, too."

I squeezed his waist. "What made you finally decide to do it?"

"What made me finally decide?" He actually sounded confused. "Really? I got my girlfriend arrested. She was sent off and we couldn't find her, and we find everyone. Vanished. It was my fault. I had to get clean. There was no other way. Clean or dead. That was it."

Dead? "Don't say that."

"Well, I preferred clean. So I am. Every day. It's new. I have no answers about it in any way that makes any sense. Not yet anyway. But, I'm here. You got yourself rescued and we are going to get you feeling better."

I'd been avoiding questions. Jer had given me quite a lot to ponder. But maybe it was time to push a little harder. There was only so much I could handle at one time. Processing was slow.

"How did I get myself rescued? You came and got me."

We came to a stop in a room with a view with a lake. I gasped. "Is this the *lake*?" I deliberately emphasized the word.

"This is the lake. Granny thought you would know it from where you were in the journals. This is the good lake." He rolled his eyes. "I hate placing that kind of value on things.

But there it is. The other lake is the problem, where my family who may have kidnapped me and killed people still live. We're avoiding them. Most of them don't come here."

Most? It dawned on me. "That nurse?"

"The mean one? Yes. Distant cousin. Very distant. But this one is ours. Or where we come from. On my fathers' side." He motioned for me to sit, and he sat next to me. "You rescued yourself because you left that message, which only you could have left, and I traced the comment to the island you were on. Then, Kit found out there was a fucked-up school there, which we knew nothing about and showed up on no research, so your family dug deep to find the worst place ever. Getting you out wasn't hard because you don't belong to your family anymore. So we were able to convince your paternal grandmother to let us get you out and take care of you for a while. Stephen sweetened the deal with the island by making it financially better to simply shut down. It took two weeks. Two of the longest weeks during the longest time."

I put my head on his shoulder. "I've lost all time."

"Yeah. I bet." He strung our fingers together. "Ask me. You have questions. Jeremy told you days ago about your dad's family. Ask. You're brave enough to ask. You always have been."

I swallowed. "Who are they? Where have they been?" Something niggled in the back of my mind. I knew something, didn't I? My mother had said something? Or maybe I had dreamed it. What was it? I couldn't remember.

"You'll never believe it, but actually Kit had started to suspect before you were taken because he'd started to look into your mom and who she hung out with. Alatheia, your real last name is Monk."

I sat up. "What?"

He nodded. "Monk."

"As in Murial Monk?" She had been my frenemy for a little bit in that she scared the shit out of me but also was kind of nice to me at the same time.

"Yep. Your first cousin." He shook his head. "She's ecstatic."

"Really?" My mind whirled. "Okay. Too much. I need..."

"Time. Yes. I know." He pressed on my head until I set it down on his shoulder again. "But Alatheia, you are richer than we are. Significantly."

I didn't care about that. At least not now. Murial was my cousin? Davis was my cousin? How... the sibling that went missing. My father was the sibling that went missing. They'd told me about him. They thought he was on an ashram or something. But no it was my dead father.

Phoenix and I sat together staring at the lake. It was huge and framed by towering pine trees, their branches heavy with the weight of winter's chill. No snow but just what looked like a dusting of something. It was afternoon, the sun was starting to dim. Around the lakeshore, big houses stood like sentinels. People not in the know would think that they were symbols of wealth, and they were, but they also hid what happened in those houses. The families created here weren't traditional. One woman, multiple husbands. For generations now. Big enough to hide secrets.

The water shimmered under the pale winter sun not quite gone from the day. It was soothing. It had been days since I'd been randomly falling asleep, but I yawned.

Phoenix squeezed my hand. "Nap if you want to. I did here. A lot."

"You just sat here alone and napped?" I rubbed my nose to his shoulder, almost like I was keening. I couldn't help it. I was so fucking needy.

"My brothers never left me alone. In a good way. They left me alone when I had to lock in and get through things. But they were here the whole time. Waiting for news on you. And keeping me company. I made them promise they would leave to go to you if I wasn't done and ready. They agreed. So we knew we would get to you and I wasn't ever abandoned."

That was so Lent of them.

All of them together against the world.

"You didn't get me arrested and sent off. I chose to grab that bag. I should have thrown it on the floor. I think we can blame it on Maggie drugging me."

He shook his head. "I played a role. One hundred percent I did. And Maggie will no longer be a problem."

What did that mean? "Is she dead?"

"No. It was bad enough when she fucked with you because that pissed off Murial and now that you're her cousin? Forget it. My father bankrupted them and Murial ran them out of New York. Maggie is somewhere else now. You are now Murial's family."

That was sort of... nice? In a weird, disturbing way. Why had we stayed away from them? Why had I been hidden, living in a trailer when both my parents came from money?

It was too much. I closed my eyes.

Barrett's arrival roused me, which was a good thing. I didn't want to sleep all day. He sat down next to me, and I lifted my head to smile. Phoenix was so quiet that I looked over. He was asleep, his head sort of tipped back. He breathed deeply.

"When you weren't in your room you had to be here. His favorite spot. We called this Phoenix's healing spot. He's out." He motioned toward his brother.

I took Barrett's hands in mine. "I'm so sorry we had a bad morning, the day I was taken."

Barrett's head fell forward just a touch like for a second he couldn't maintain it with his neck. "Alatheia, you are never going to know how it haunts me. How that has ridden me every second of the days without you. Why didn't I kiss you and tell you I loved you? Why did I storm out of there? Because I was unprepared for my test, but that isn't your problem and never was. I am so sorry."

I kissed him. "I thought it was a terrible ending for us."

"Not an ending. Never that."

4

I had to make him understand.

"There are always endings. Everything ends. You know that."

He kissed me back, right on the mouth. He was the first person to kiss me like I wouldn't break since we'd been back. I sighed against him. Okay, I liked it. A lot.

"I am so sorry I wasn't there when she dosed you. That you couldn't have reached me if you had tried. I'm so sorry I wasn't there to hear your ecstasy confessions. I hate them a little bit that they all did. I'm so sorry I wasn't there when the police took you. Or any day since. I am so sorry."

I threw my arms around him and held on. He shuddered against me. "What are my ecstasy confessions?"

"That you loved them. You told them."

I smiled, pressing it on the skin by his neck. "You have to know I love you." How could he think otherwise?

He audibly exhaled. "I do now. I love you, too. I love you so much. It's been hell without you in my arms."

"I... I don't know if I should say this."

He hugged me tighter. "Say anything. Anything."

"I wanted you so much when I was in the police station. To be there with me. When it all started to hurt, when the drug left and I was empty. I wanted you."

Barrett was so quiet I wondered if I had made a terrible mistake. But then he kissed my cheek. "I would have done anything for the privilege of being there."

I laughed. "I don't think you can call sitting with me in jail a privilege."

"Sitting with you anywhere is a privilege."

My laugh must have roused Phoenix. He opened his eyes. "Nice sight to wake up to, you laughing. What's funny?"

"Sitting with me in jail as being something he should want."

Phoenix blinked. "Not going to lie, I could think of other places I'd rather sit with you, but sure, we can sit in jail."

I shook my head. They were being ridiculous. "For the first month I thought you would all come get me, and then, when you didn't, I thought we were just done. I was going to call at some point after I was eighteen. But, yeah. I thought it was over."

They both frowned and then Barrett hugged me. "At first we thought they had sent you to a school. A boarding school. That's what you'd always thought so that's what we thought. We looked at every school in the world. Phoenix was occupied and the rest of us don't hack, so my parents were calling on every connection they had to find out where you were. You showed up nowhere. Your family was so smug. Your aunt has left New York to avoid Granny because she camped out outside her apartment. But she was so dismissive. Couldn't be swayed. Even your uncle losing all his funding did nothing. It makes no sense. If you hadn't posted that comment when you did, we'd still be looking. Phoenix was back with us by then, and he tracked it."

I smiled at him. "Thank you. Have I thanked any of you for getting me? I really... can't remember."

Phoenix put his head down on my hands for a second. "No thanks."

"How is this possible that you're all here? You're all supposed to be in school."

Jeremy walked into the room, spotted us, grinned and then sat down next to Barrett. "I'm texting Jules if you are feeling good enough to talk. He should be here too. He's close by. Around the corner, getting coffee."

I shook my head. "Julian shouldn't be caffeinating. He looks exhausted. He should be sleeping."

"Preaching to the choir." Barrett shook his head. "He couldn't really sleep after you were taken, and he isn't yet sleeping."

If we were going to wait for question-and-answer time, then I was going to sit back and enjoy the lake again. It wasn't long because Julian did come tearing in the room. He smiled when he saw me and made Phoenix scoot over a bit so he could sit with all of us. Sure enough, he had a cardboard cup in his hand, and he was sipping coffee.

"Alatheia is worried that you're not sleeping." Jer lifted his eyebrows.

"That obvious? Please don't worry about me, Baby. I am worried about you. But actually I might sleep tonight because you are coming home."

I gasped. "What?"

"Yes. They're releasing you. The stuff you need to do next can all be done outpatient. It's different than what Phoenix had to do. So, you can come home."

I loved the idea of that, but the reality sunk in. "I can't go back to New York. Maybe not ever, guys. I know this is going to be a huge problem. I committed a felony. That much keta-mine was a felony. I only got out of it because I went to that place where they sent me. Otherwise I was going to jail. I didn't complete it. I could be in serious trouble. Fuck. Am I in serious trouble?"

Once my mind started to go it really went. A million worries all at once.

"Hey. " Phoenix shook his head. "No. You're not in trouble. Charges were dropped entirely. Once Kit got involved it was handled. He tried to be involved right away. You're one of us. We take care of our own. Right or wrong we use our influence. Your family isn't the only family to know a judge. And no, for now you're not going back to New York."

Barrett nodded. "Outpatient. You stay here. Come back here for the clinic. We have a big house and a small house on the lake. We're in the small house and you'll be with us." He smiled. "Granny is coming down soon, and then we'll all be together."

Okay. That sounded better. I pulled my knees up and let my head sink down to them. I needed a second like this. I just did.

Jeremy reached around Barrett to rub the back of my head. No one said anything, so they were maybe silently judging me, but I preferred to think that they were giving me a second and that was fine.

After a few seconds, I lifted my head. "Sorry. I guess I do that now. I put my head on my knees."

"I can think of worse coping mechanisms." Phoenix smiled.

"All right. So question and answer. Um. I know I'm a Monk. How are you all here? Shouldn't you be at Pullman and Columbia?"

Julian gave the answer. "Well, Jer and I have graduated. We had enough credits and the school was happy to play ball with my parents, so to speak. We're done. College applications sent in, but we aren't going anywhere until everything is settled and you are fine. Only New York schools, which maybe we'll need to redo if you are really set on no New York."

"Let's wait a second and give her a chance to settle into her new reality." Jer stood. "But yes, we'll move schools. This is about us being together. Not about where."

That was really sweet, only I couldn't have them screwing up their whole lives for me. Maybe Jer anticipated what I was going to say because he lifted his hand up. "Don't say it."

"Okay." I smiled. Yep, he had read that correctly.

Phoenix squeezed my knee. "I have to finish school. You have to finish school. We don't have to finish at Pullman. We can go anywhere. Even online. Whatever happens, we'll do it together."

I loved that thought. It settled my stomach a bit. He and I were both going to have to repeat Junior year. We'd do it as a team.

Barrett shrugged. "I don't like school. I was happy to leave for a bit. I'll go back if you end up in New York, or I'll go somewhere else. None of us could concentrate with you gone and Phoenix going through this time. School is on pause for the Lents. Our fathers, too. They're all here."

"To be fair, only Eric can't work. He has to actually be at the office." It was Phoenix's turn to stand up. "And he seems to be keeping busy. Helping here a lot."

Their lives were all on pause. I hadn't asked them to do that, but they had.

"Okay." Jer made me meet his gaze. "Start talking. What happened with you? Don't spare us details. I want to know how bad it got. I need to know. Please."

It was so unusual for Jeremy to say please. I sighed. "Well, I think you know what happened in New York. I grabbed Phoenix's bag of ketamine. I got caught with it. They left me in a jail cell all night. My aunt gave them permission to conduct a drug test on me which of course was bad because Maggie had drugged me. A detective questioned me, and I didn't tell them anything." I directed that to Phoenix. "I'm not a snitch like Hal was or whatever."

He shook his head, fast. "Red, I would have preferred it if you had told them it was me."

"No, they didn't want to know whose ketamine it was. They wanted to know where it had been purchased from. I didn't tell them. I told them I didn't know. I didn't want you to get in trouble with Joe."

He shook his head. "Joe is no longer a part of my life. But, you had no way of knowing that, and you just kept trying to save me."

"I felt really sick." I'd already told Barrett I'd been aching for him, I didn't need to rehash that right then. "But the lawyer my aunt hired told me they had made arrangements for me to go away to a school for bad kids. They had taken all these parts of my life and lined them up so they fit a narrative. I ran away from home to live with a known drug abuser. I got in trouble in school. I was on drugs. I was carrying a felony's worth of ketamine. They said I could go or I could go to jail." I had to get up and move. I walked over to the window so I could stare at the lake.

Arms came around me. Jer's voice was gentle. "I should not have insisted you talk."

"No, I get it. You want to know. I would want to know." I sighed. "I puked in a garbage can, and then I followed him outside where there two guys with a van. They told me it could go easy or hard but it was going. I told them I wasn't a problem. No one would believe me. And then they drugged me, which was awful because I was already so messed up from the night before."

I loved that his arms were around me right then. They all

moved until they stood facing the window except for Jer who remained where he was.

"I woke up in a strange place. The headmistress was there. She told me the rules. Put me in solitary—everyone starts in solitary. I think you saw it? Were you there?"

Julian kissed my hand. "We were all there. Not that you would remember. Kit tried to leave us home. That was cute he thought that was happening."

I smirked at him. "I love how you put that."

"I have my moments."

"Anyway, they dosed us with things every week. Kept us compliant, but if we needed something else, they did that too. I was always being sent to solitary for standing up for the little kids. And I cleaned and hung around with some girls who didn't mind sneaking out at night to look at YouTube. It's kind of hard to really explain to you what it was like. It was just... horrible. All the time and I was pretty sure that I was never getting out until I was eighteen."

Someone cleared their throat. Kit Lent stood in the doorway. "We have to talk about that. Come see me. The boys don't know about this yet. Bring her home. She's released. We're having dinner. Come to the big house."

Having delivered that order, Kit left us alone in the room. I froze where I stood. I was leaving the hospital. It had been awful going through this, but at least it had been safe.

"What's the matter?" Barrett held my gaze. "You're okay."

"What's out there? Where we're going? Who... will be there?"

He tapped my chin until I looked at him. "Only us. My parents. No one else unless you want to see someone else."

There were enemies everywhere. It seemed everywhere I turned around there was someone new. "This is where the people who hurt Phoenix live."

"I'm not scared of them here." Phoenix ran a hand

through his hair. "It's funny. But I'm less frightened of them right over there, just a few miles away, than in Manhattan. They don't come around here. It's like they know we're here and the fact that we are scares them. Not the other way around. No one saw them coming years ago. But now we're wide awake. It's going to be okay."

Phoenix was not an optimist. If he said that he wasn't scared, then okay. "Truthfully, I'm just waiting for my aunt to jump out of a bush and take me back to that place."

"She can't." Jeremy shook his head. "Granny Monk would eat her."

I laughed. This was all so new. It was going to take some time to get used to.

❧

BARRETT DROVE us to their home. Since he was the only one with a driver's license, that wasn't surprising. We were in a Jeep. I couldn't help my smile. "Do you miss your baby?"

He didn't misunderstand me. "I do. I wish I could bring the car down."

Jeremy looked at Julian, who stared out the window. "We need to get our driver's licenses."

His twin nodded, but Jules seemed pretty out of it. Maybe he would sleep tonight. Maybe I would. Who knew anymore?

I turned to stare at the houses as we pulled up. Of course, they were beautiful. On my left, a small—only relative to the fact that this was the Lents and they always had big homes— stilted house perched above the shoreline. It had a soft gray facade and crisp white trim. A wooden dock stretched from its porch. The guys said that we had the smaller house, so that must be where we were staying.

Further down a path, closer to the lake, a bigger two-story house stood, its beige exterior catching the last of the light. It was getting late. Wide windows framed views of the lake, and the sprawling porch with white railings looked like something out of a painting. Tall pine trees framed the scene, casting long shadows across what must be a well-manicured lawn in the spring. Right now, it was quietly waiting for the spring to come again.

What had Dina called this in her diary? The veil of pines? Or something like that. They were everywhere, hiding this place from the world. Keeping its secrets.

I stepped out of the car and became immediately aware that it was really cold. Or maybe it was only moderately cold, but I was freezing. I had no coat and the top of my head, which had never experienced the cold because it had always been covered in hair before, made it hit even harder. I tucked my arms in front of myself and bent down

"You okay?" Julian put his arm around me, turning me toward the house.

"I'm really cold."

He blinked. "We need to get you a winter coat. You don't have one. We brought all of your stuff here. Jer and I packed it, but I didn't see a coat. I thought for sure you'd have one, but you don't. You were in Chicago before New York. What did you do for a coat?"

"I had one there. They didn't let me keep it. You're not wearing a coat. And you don't seem to be freezing."

He smiled. "I'm cold. But I can't let you think I'm cold."

I laughed, which he must have liked, because he grinned bigger.

"Hey," their mother called out from the porch in her house, where she had suddenly appeared. Or maybe I had simply not been paying attention. "Come eat dinner now. If you go in there, you're all going to fall asleep and want to eat at two in the morning or not at all until tomorrow and then you'll have low blood sugar. Come on. Dinner is on the table."

Jules looked at me. "Can you make it, or do you want me to go inside and grab my coat? I can give it to you."

I shook my head. "It's like ten feet. I'll be fine."

We walked the rest of the distance, the other guys catching up with us. "This must be gorgeous in the summer."

"It's super humid in the summer," Barrett supplied. "Pretty in the spring and the fall. But we don't come here very much."

"Then why have the house?" I asked before I closed my mouth. "Sorry, not my business."

Jeremy turned around walking up the stairs into his parents' house backward. "You've backslid about that. Every-thing is your business. They keep the house because it keeps them essential here, as part of the crowd even though it's highly unlikely they'd ever live here for any length of time."

Daniel opened the door for us. "It got colder today. We have the house because it's a good investment; it gives us some place to stay when we're here, which has happened three times this year; my fathers bought the property; and, frankly, real estate is always a good investment."

Jeremy nodded at his father. "Point taken. But it's also a fuck-we're-rich property to remind everyone here just in case they forget to treat you with respect."

Dan laughed. "Sure. Okay. That too. Come in. Mom drove half an hour and back to get tonight's dinner. She says she's going to cook shrimp tomorrow. So watch out, the longer she stays here the more cooking she will do."

"I would love that." Barrett walked past us. "This way, Alatheia."

I wanted to follow, but I was too busy staring at this house. My breath was taken away by the sheer elegance of the space. This wasn't just some lake house they kept around. Marble floors gleamed under the soft glow of crystal chande-liers, and the walls were adorned with intricate moldings and

artworks that I didn't recognize. More and more I'd acknowl-
edged that my own education about art was very limited. The
view from the huge windows at the back of the house must
be spectacular when it was light out.

The whole moment felt surreal. I just stood there staring.
I'd just been in the fifth level of hell and now I was here? No,
I had to be still on the floor in solitary. I was dreaming this. I
caught my breath. Wow. Life was really cruel. Unless I was
dead. Oates had told me I would see people who cared about
me again when I was dead.

Was I dead?

A hand touched my shoulder. "I know." It was Rosalind.
"Everything is too much. But you're okay. You are."

I swallowed. "I was just wondering if I was dead. But I
thought I would see my mother again when I was dead, and
she isn't here, so maybe I'm just hallucinating?"

"It's normal what you're feeling. Lots of change. And now
this is another one. I would give you your mother in a heartbeat if I could." She hugged me. Her accent thickened as she
spoke. "But you're here with us and we're very glad that you
are. Come on. Food will help. By now the steak is probably
dry and that will certainly tell you that you are in reality
because who would imagine that?"

Eric was pouring wine into glasses, but when he would
have put one where Jer stood and was probably going to sit,
Jer shook his head. "I'm done with that. For now. Maybe
forever."

Phoenix plopped down and then patted next to him. "Sit
here. Alcohol was never my poison. It doesn't bother me."

"I don't want to be out of it." Jeremy sat, too, and I took
the spot that Phoenix indicated. "I don't want to be off
buying beer when someone drugs my girl."

Barrett and Julian seemed to be sticking to water as
well. Wow.

Eric sat down next to Rosalind while Stephen placed food on everyone's plate. "Alatheia, Kit came and got you so we never got to talk. Tomorrow they'd like you back in the clinic at nine. They're going to go over some things with you about your treatment plan. I'll drive you over since I'm taking a shift."

"No, thank you, Eric." Barrett shook his head. "I'm going to drive her back and forth anywhere she needs to go while she's here."

With a shrug, Eric smiled. "Great. Then you can take me tomorrow morning, too."

Since I was absolutely certain that Barrett had meant to get alone time with me, that sort of defeated his point. "Sure."

"Don't do that to him." Rosalind laughed. "Barrett, Eric will take his own car and you'll take Alatheia. That's fine."

Everyone dug in, and I tried to ignore how strange it was to be sitting here like this. Somehow this was less tense than the Hamptons. My first night there with them all at the table had been awful. But then again, the Chinese food for the twins' birthday had been great. So, maybe the Hamptons was the exception and this was more the rule.

"Listen," Kit interrupted. "I want to get this over with."

He did like to make a speech. I'd noticed that about him.

"You said something I overheard about turning eighteen and leaving that place."

That's right, he had interrupted us. I cleared my throat. "They had to let us leave at eighteen."

"They do. But I can't find record of anyone leaving that place, of anyone who actually got out and went anywhere else. That's why I couldn't find it to begin with. I've been going over this with one of my partners and with Stephen all day." He must have just gotten back. Stephen had stayed to see the place closed down on the island. He stared down at the table, not making eye contact with anyone. Kit continued. "And I think people don't leave. I think those girls who aged out, died."

There was silence and then an eruption as everyone started talking at once. My heart rate kicked up so high I could feel it in my ears. What? I had known some of those girls. The room tilted left and then right, but I wasn't going to faint. I didn't do that. It was ridiculous, I was sitting on a chair, but I pulled my knees to lean my head on them.

"Okay. I think that could have been handled better." Was Eric yelling at Kit? "She's fragile right now."

"She needs to hear this. What her family is doing. And why."

"Yes, she does. But if she isn't in imminent danger, maybe it could have waited for dessert."

Yes, Eric, the quiet one, was yelling at Kit. I lifted my head. For his part, Kit looked chastened, his brow downsloped. Eric might not yell very much, but when he did, perhaps it made an impact.

Phoenix had his cheek on my back. I hadn't noticed how he had risen and grabbed me. "No one is going to kill you. We told you that you're safe, and we didn't lie."

"Thank you." I managed to get my knees back down under the table. This was going to be embarrassing later. "But why wasn't I?"

He'd opened this door. I wasn't going to wait to know.

❧ 5 ❧

"**I** am still working out the details. I don't know your
father's story and your Grandmother Monk is not
sharing them if she knows them at all." He shook his
head. "As my mother put it, when we confirmed that you were
her granddaughter, Daisy Monk is a bitch. But right now she
is our bitch and I am not going to mess with her by pushing
too hard."

I sighed. "How did you confirm it?"

"DNA test." Julian met my gaze. "Not to be gross, but we
had your toothbrush."

I was beyond things being gross at this point. "How did
you even know to look at the Monks?"

"I hired someone to look into your mother. There is virtu-
ally nothing about her after she left, but there was plenty
from before. Seems like the rest of your family went to Pullman, but they put your mother in a small girl s' school that no
longer exists. That's why we didn't know her. We knew who
your aunt was and avoided her." He shook his head. "Honestly, I never cared for any of your family."

Rosalind sighed. "Not helpful."

"Right, sorry."

Stephen interrupted. "Your family is in serious financial straits . They're in bed with lots of bad people. Internationally. It's a bad situation. I'd partially funded your Aunt Tricia's husband, but no more, and I'm glad for it. Anyway, Alatheia, they want your money. You're the only one with any left. I hate to tell you, but you paid for your own abuse in that place through the money in the trust that your mother left to cover your education specifically. It was the only thing they could touch it for. Your education or your health."

That was ridiculous. What? It didn't make any sense. None. "I don't have any money. I'm entirely dependent. I am the Poor Relation."

The guys would understand what that meant even if their parents didn't quite get it.

"No," Daniel sighed, taking his turn. "You're not. At the time of his death, your maternal grandfather was worth almost a billion dollars. When he died, that was split four ways among his four children. Each one receiving a quarter of the total. His wife preceded him in death. But your aunts and uncle made very poor decisions. Got in bed with bad people. It's almost all gone. Yours sits in a trust your mother set up for you, set to be yours to access the day you turn eighteen. If something should happen to you before you're eighteen, the trust will be given to a charity to save the whales."

I blinked. "What?"

"Random, right? Unless your mother really cared about whales. She even made provisions for how much a year could be used for your care and welfare. A lawyer in Colorado is disbursing it to your aunt every year. I think she did use it for tuition. Other than that, her own use. The lawyer thought there was also a will giving you to someone other than your mom's family, but he doesn't have it and doesn't know who it was. So, we'll leave that for now. She set it up to protect you from them."

My head started to pound. "I don't understand. We were living in a trailer. We weren't living like she had, what, almost two hundred fifty million dollars."

"She was hiding." Rosalind gave me a small smile. "She was afraid of them. That's why she changed the name. She hid where she hoped they wouldn't find her. Took you away. Never touched it. I can't imagine the strength that woman had. She loved you very deeply. I can tell."

Tears came to my eyes. I thought I was done with crying, but it turned out I just needed the right thing to be said for them to flood my vision again. I wiped at them until Phoenix took a napkin and dabbed at my face. "Of course she loved you."

I sighed. "But she died of a drug overdose and left me to this."

"Still working on that." Kit shook his head. "Anyway, they have to keep you alive until you turn eighteen. Given that you didn't know about the trust, you wouldn't have designated it to anyone upon your death. They could go to court then and make the argument that it needs to go back to the family."

I put my head in my hands. "So, then they sent me off to that place to have it done. No muss. No fuss."

"Maybe it took them that long to find a place like that. Maybe you were just starting to make them nervous. Because you see the one thing that was very clear was that the reason she spent all her time in that other school was because they wanted her kept away from the one guy she couldn't seem to stay away from, Peter Monk." Kit sighed. "Once I read that, I looked him up. Disappeared around the same time as your mom. Red hair. Brown eyes. I went to Daisy and talked to her. She was willing to have the DNA test. He's your dad.

Your mother's family knows that. They can't have you finding that out. We're annoying, but the Monks are deadly to them."

My mind whirled. I was finally starting to catch up. The guys were stunned. All of them silent. "I was seen with Murial. At the museum. She was texting me. The PI. They saw it."

Jer sighed. "They were what? Before they found the death school they were going to kill you themselves? Slip and Fall? Hitman?"

"In any case, you're safe until you're eighteen. They know the Monks know about you, they have taken custody—they're the Monks, they can do that—but they don't know anything about us knowing the rest. That's good. That lets us trap them and destroy them. This is what I do. We're in my territory now. You can trust me on this. They might even actively try to keep you alive now that they know the Monks know, since they're going to gift you money at eighteen too. That's just what they do. Apparently Murial got hers early. I'm not sure why. But, in any case, your family might think they can get that as well."

Money? They were going to kill me for money? I resisted the urge to pull my knees to my face. It was hard, but I did it. Instead, my hands shook. "Did you... did you find my real birth certificate?"

"Oh." Kit nodded. "I did. Once I knew things, it became easier. The lawyer knew. The one you have is fabricated. Your family made your dad's last name Winder lest the Monks ever find out but changed it to make it look like your mom had used her real name. None of that is true. You were born a week earlier. Sorry, you have the wrong birthday every year. But, your real name is Jayne Alatheia Winder. Daughter of Delphine Winder and Peter Winder." He scratched his head. "Nowhere on there does it say anything about Stapleton. Or Monk."

I choked. "Jayne? No one has ever called me Jayne. I promise you that."

"It's probably another level of protection. Give you a first name they never use and call you the middle name." Jeremy played with his fork. "It's smart."

Okay. I was done. "Thank you for all of this hard work. I mean, thank you. And I... I..."

Rosalind took my hand. "You don't have to say anything. Just breathe. I have something for you." She rose and walked into the kitchen, returning with something knitted she held in her hand. "I used to do this a lot as a young woman. I'm worried your head is going to be constantly cold."

It was a pink knitted hat.

I burst into tears. Again. I tried to breathe and wiped my eyes. "Thank you."

"Oh sweetheart. " She held me. "I know how it is to be sold like cattle by family. Like we're nothing. I am so sorry this is your story, too."

"Dad, what happens when she is eighteen?" Jules' eyes were haunted. I could even see this through the blurred vision from my tears. "They'll hunt her."

Kit nodded. "If I haven't buried them yet and sent them to prison, or the poor house, then at 12:01 p.m. on her eighteenth birthday, her real eighteenth birthday, she's going to make a will making sure they don't get the money. I'll let them know at 12:02 about it, and I can't see any reason they'd kill her then. But we'll keep her safe regardless."

Why did it seem like I was always walking from one pain to another?

A thought dawned on me. "There were twenty girls with me. From twelve to seventeen. All of them were set to die? What's going to happen to them now? We sent them home to people who put them someplace to die."

Kit winced. Had he not thought about that? I couldn't get

upset. He was thinking about me. I had been his sole focus; his family was always that way. How could it be otherwise? But they had been my friends.

Panic settled in my stomach. I didn't have contact information for any of them. I couldn't do anything, couldn't warn them. They might just be sent off to other places to die. Nausea hit me, and I dashed to the bathroom, which fortunately was located around the corner in the hallway. I puked up all the dry steak.

A knock sounded on the door. It was Jeremy with a ginger ale that he handed me. "Sip."

"I don't know how I'm going to live with this."

Phoenix appeared in the doorframe. "I'm going to hack into that school's computer system tonight. It's closed, but I can get in. I hope. I'll get the name of every girl who went there, and you can contact them. Okay? We can do that. And they either believe you or they don't, but you'll have tried."

"Like reporting herpes."

I looked up at Jer. "What?"

"They showed us a PSA once in school of how you have to call and tell everyone you've been with if you have herpes. You have to call and report that their parents want to kill them."

I banged him in the shin and he oomphed. "Too far."

"Got it." He kissed my head. "Phoenix will do it."

There were twenty other girls whose parents hated them so much that they wanted them dead at eighteen? Why? Did they have trust fund issues too? I shook my head. I might not ever know the answers. But I had learned before and continued to learn that the very rich were scary bastards. Most of them anyway. They just were. No wonder my mother had run.

THE SMALLER HOUSE was equally beautiful, only slightly understated. The polished wood floors gleamed softly as I hung onto the knitted cap like it was a lifeline. Light from the tall windows beside the door would usually spill into the entryway, illuminating the staircase that curved gently upward. A rustic wooden console table stood against the wall, its drawers filled with woven baskets. The round mirror above it caught the golden glow of the lamp beside it—that was the only reason we could see at all.

Outside, past the door, the lake stretched out into the distance, though I couldn't see it now. Tall pines framed the shoreline, standing like silent sentinels that would keep tonight's secrets.

Julian motioned. "Come upstairs. Oh, and the house has an alarm system. We don't have the doormen, so we have the alarm. It'll call for help if we need it. Code is 1842. Come." I followed him up the stairs. There were doorways up and down a long hallway.

He opened the center one. "This one is yours."

Mine? I stepped inside.

The room was illuminated in the same soft glow as the rest of the house, the same lamp casting gentle light across the neutral-toned space. Two king- sized beds stood against the far wall; they had white linens and beige headboards. It was like an expensive hotel room. I had never been in one, but I watched a lot of television, and YouTube was full of them. Between the beds, a nightstand held the lamp and on the wall hung a framed painting that I would need to learn about if I was going to stay in this room.

The other side had dressers and a closet. But it was the far wall that caught my attention. Sliding glass doors. When it was daytime, I could open them and see outside to that lake that already seemed so serene.

"This okay?" Jules took my hand.

"Is it okay? Whose room is it?" It was hard for me to imagine any of them in this room. They weren't really white-curtained guys.

"Yours." He stared at me. "I just said that."

"Yes, but how?"

He held up five fingers. "Five bedrooms. We all have a different one. Hardly ever here, but it worked out that way. Anyway, it seemed like it was meant to be yours. The idea is that this is your room. We would all like to stay in it with you but this is where your stuff is. The door to the bathroom is there. You have to share it with Barrett. Only Jer's room has a solo. Not sure how that happened. Anyway, yeah, you can tell us no not tonight, leave me alone. It's your room. You aren't sharing it."

I blinked. "Thank you. But... I... I'm not sure what to say. I'm overwhelmed." It had never been permanently viable for me to live in Barrett's room in NYC, but that had left with it a certain impermanence that I understood. I was always being shuffled around. But this was mine? What was I supposed to do with that? No one had ever given me a room like this.

I walked over to the window and stared outside. I wanted to love it here, except I knew there was an element to this place that wasn't to be trusted, not for me, not the guys. Period. End of story.

Julian cleared his throat. "No pressure. I mean none, whatsoever, but can I stay with you tonight? Totally fine if you want some space."

"You can stay. I would really like that." I had missed it. Them with me. "All of you can stay tonight if you want. Why don't we assume I always want that, and I'll say no if I don't? Like the assumption is yes?"

I really didn't want them asking every night. That felt really awful, actually.

He nodded. "Okay. Listen, the rooms we're in are Barrett next to you. Jer next to him. I'm on your other side, but we don't share a bathroom, and Phoenix is next to me. Just in case you need to know that." He ran a hand through his hair. "It's been a long day."

I smiled. "Are there days that aren't long?"

"Yes, a lot of them. Days when I wish we had extra hours so we could be together. My birthday for example. I could have used six more hours in that day. Twelve. One hundred." He shook his head. "Your point, however, is taken. Are you hungry? You threw up all that terrible steak."

I laughed. He wasn't trying to be funny. Except he totally was without meaning to be, which somehow made it funnier. "No, I can't think about food right now. Sounds awful."

"Okay. Then why don't you take a bath. There's a big tub in that bathroom. Relax. I'll come in in a little bit. We aren't off the hook from work, so to speak. Given that we've all decided to take a break from school, we've been assigned jobs to do with the fathers so we can be productive. Well, except Phoenix." He smiled. "He's doing a different kind of work, the kind that keeps him clean. Although he is hacking tonight. So, anyway. I have to get my daily Stephen assignment done. My suggestion that I could simply be allowed to write did not fly. They support that dream but suggested I also had to support myself."

I shook my head. "You have a lot of money in a trust fund."

"Yes, but Lents work." He smiled. "We aren't sit-around trust fund people. I feel that in my bones. So I have to sell the play. Or get it made somehow by someone other than me. If I can do that, they'll back off because it will seem more career-y and less hobbyish."

I took a step toward him. "They can't have read the play.

Then they would know this is talent not a fictionalized dream."

"I love how you see me." He gave me a small smile. "I've missed your eyes on me so much. Go relax. I'm going to finish my spreadsheet, and then I can come lie with you in bed. I may not sleep much. I don't right now. But I want to be close. Save me a side if one of them finishes earlier?"

They had always been really good about giving Phoenix a side with me when he had been so needy. Right now, it felt like Jules was maybe the person needing that assigned space. Not that I considered sleeping with me to be such a privilege, but they did and that really was what mattered to them.

"It's yours."

He smiled. "So, obviously don't take a bath if you don't want to. I'm not trying to order you to do anything."

I grinned. "Go. It's fine. Yes, I want a bath. I haven't had a soak in a tub in a long time."

I closed the door behind him. One thing about this being my room—which blew me away—was that I could actually strip in it without worrying that I was going to interrupt whatever Barrett was doing. I didn't have to be locked in the bathroom. But for that second I just looked around, opening my closet and the drawers. They had really brought all of my stuff—which included basically my clothes and toiletries since I didn't really have anything else—here. The library book—*We Have Always Lived in the Castle*—that I had been reading before I had to go was here too. Wow. The fees were going to be huge. And my computer was on a small desk in the corner with their granny's journals.

I was home. I wiped at my eyes. I guessed home just meant wherever my stuff was, wherever they were, and wherever I was welcome right now.

I ended up undressing and sticking my stuff in the laundry basket by the bathroom. I placed my knit cap on the dresser,

I'd been holding it the whole time, and stepped into the bathroom. I shared it with Barrett so that meant that actually I had to be careful of privacy in here. Quickly, because I was already fully naked and not ready to deal with anything about that right then, I locked his door from the inside. I hoped he wasn't going to have to pee. Maybe I should have asked him if this was okay, first.

But then again this was Barrett. If I asked him, he'd say of course, stop what he was doing, and draw me a bath. I didn't want to be that level of needy. At least not right that second.

I'd start with just thinking it was okay to lock him out for a little bit. There were other bathrooms. He could use one of those.

I would do that for him if he needed a moment.

I put the water on and looked at my surroundings. It was a very nice bathroom. Big. At least compared to the one I'd been using in Manhattan, which had been small, but then everything was slightly downsized there for space issues, even in big apartments.

It was pitch-black outside, so I didn't bother to shut the curtains. Of course, not doing so might be a stupid way to pick up a stalker who liked to stare at beat-up girls with scars all over them. I shook my head. Catastrophizing wasn't going to help anything. The sound of the tub running helped bring me back to the now. I could shut the curtains if I was worried but decided instead to leave them. A small act of rebellion against my anxiety.

There was a white vanity to my left; it had a marble countertop that was clean and spotless. They must have a maid here too unless one of them had taken to cleaning. A simple mirror hung above it, and below it was the sink and soap dispenser and toothbrush holder. There were two toothbrushes in it. One was blue, one was pink. I was going to assume the pink one was mine. That had Barrett written all over it: he'd want to make sure I knew it was mine right off. I smiled at that touch. A towel rested on a ring beside the mirror.

I could see the renovation shows now if they came in here. They'd want two sinks, two vanities. It was fine by me to share. Intimate, sort of.

The water was high enough that I got into it and lay back, my head leaning against the frame of the tub. Yes, the hot water was awesome. It pushed my thoughts away and left me sort of in a state of nothingness. Maybe I should be worried about that except I would gladly take it over the mental gymnastics I'd been doing lately in my own head. Just quiet.

I breathed. I'd avoided the mirror when I got in the tub but after about ten minutes in the water, when the peace fled because there was only so long I could go without thinking— I was just built that way—I realized I should probably get a look at myself. I sighed. It had been nice for a few minutes. If there was a chance, I was going to buy some bath bombs to make the room smell perfumy. I had two hundred and fifty million dollars waiting for me. I could pay the guys back.

That thought made me sit up. Oh I liked that so much better. I hated being so constantly needy. I would pay them back. I smiled. Whatever happened, I would pay them back. There I went again, worrying about impermanence. The idea they'd be done with me and I would what—transfer them money? I got out of the tub. Yes, I wanted to pay my own way, but no I didn't want this to become transactional. Fuck. Why was I always so confused?

I opened the drain and got out of the tub, letting myself stare in the mirror this time. Okay . Let's see what I looked like. Four months in that place. What had they done to me? Jer had said I had lost a lot of weight and he might be right. I'd need to get on a scale to see how much. Maybe it was fashionable, but it didn't feel pretty on me. I had never seen my ribs before. Okay. My hair was gone. And it was ridiculous to get teary over it, except that I did. I ran a hand over my red fuzz. It would grow back. It would. But the scars on my body were evident. Lashes. Lifted skin. Red marks, some fading, some not. And some bruises that looked newer. They were green and purple.

All right, it was bad. I'd wanted to see how bad and here it was. I grabbed a towel from one of the drawers and wrapped myself in it. I would make looking in the mirror something I did as little as possible for a while. At least until my hair had filled in.

I could do this. I survived. It was what I did.

It was nice to be in my own pajamas. I'd been wearing them in the hospital, but this was nicer. Or maybe the sheets were nicer. One thing could be said about the Lents—actually many things could be said about the Lents— but one additional thing was that they never skimped on their sheets. They were always soft and cozy. The pillows were too. Was this Rosalind who did this? Or had they hired some kind of service?

I dug my face into the pillow. I'd turned off the lights, leaving the curtains open in the room, and the door cracked so they knew they could come in.

I heard it open slightly and then close again. On soft feet, Julian entered. "I managed to be first?" He closed the door to the bathroom. That was smart. If Barrett went in there to pee, we wouldn't hear him or even notice him closing the door.

Jules climbed into bed next to me. He was shirtless in sweatpants. I would bet they were the gray ones. Unless he'd gotten new ones in the last four months.

"Oh, the strawberry shorts and tank pajamas. They're a

favorite for me." He drew me to him, and I listened to his heartbeat.

"I didn't know you had favorites."

His laugh was small. "They're all favorites." He smelled clean. In addition to finishing his work, he had showered. "I'll close the curtain." When he would have moved, I put a hand on him to stop him. "I... I seem to want curtains open. Maybe it's an 'I don't want to feel closed in thing?'"

He settled back down. "That's fine. We have to get up anyway. You have an appointment at the clinic. I'll be awake. It won't matter that the sun will shine right in."

Maybe that would matter on a day that we could actually sleep in. Since he had sort of brought up the subject , I had to ask. "Why aren't you sleeping?"

"A lot on my mind." He kissed my head. I knew how shaved down it was now and internally I shuddered at the thought.

I ran my hand over his chest, feeling his muscles beneath my fingertips. They still jumped at my touch, even though I looked the way I did. "I love you, Julian." There, I had said it. Not drugged, not sick, not terrified. I'd just said it as though it was normal to do so and something to be sought after. It was a big step for me. "You can tell me what's on your mind."

"Oh, Alatheia, I love you, too." He moved until his head was on top of mine. I could feel him breathe on my skin. I didn't stop what I was doing. It was soothing to me and maybe he liked it too. Jules wasn't shy. He'd tell me if he didn't.

Finally, he spoke again. "They took my brother. The generic 'they,' because we still don't fucking know—even though whoever they are is sharing a zip code right now with us. He came back broken. He's trying to fix himself. It's new, and he's trying, but... they broke him. Whoever he would have been if it never happened is gone. Or buried so deep I don't know if he'll ever find it again.

"And then they—and this time I know who they are—took my girl. My Baby. And for four months, I've been terrified you'd be gone. That they would've broken you too. That you wouldn't want this crazy with me anymore. Because I know it's a lot. And you have to choose this—choose me—instead of some normal life. A life no one deserves more than you."

I heard him swallow, and then he spoke again. "And now your life is at risk. Or it always was only now we know. And..." His voice trailed off.

"And?" I knew he wasn't done.

"I kind of hate that I have to spend time doing spreadsheets for Stephen's businesses instead of writing. It's a small thing. But it bugs me."

I shook my head. "You are an artist. It's hard. Barrett is suffering from not helping make music. You two are the same that way. Trying to shove a square into a circle hurts. I get that." The other things were harder. "I'm probably broken. So broken I can't see it. But I still want you, want this. Even if I'm back to doubting because it's my default setting. The rest of it? I'm so sorry you have to keep living through this happening around you and feeling powerless to do anything about it."

He kissed me gently on the lips, which meant he had to move both of us onto our sides but that was more than fine, and I kissed him back. It was so lovely to be in the dark with Julian. Such a fucking gift. I stroked the back of his hair, and he did the same over the fuzz on the back of my head. We stared at each other in the dark, not speaking.

I saw it when his eyes started to close. He fought it. *Oh, Julian*, I wanted to whisper, *why are you fighting it?* But he eventually gave in. Maybe it was exhaustion, or maybe it was having me next to him that finally let him feel some semblance that things were righting themselves. Maybe both.

I knew he was really out when he rolled onto his back. Generally, that was how Jules slept. He dragged me up against his side. Yes, this was his "Julian was asleep" mode. The snoring I was used to from him started too. I smiled. I'd listened to nineteen other girls breathe in their sleep for four months. This was so much better. This was Julian. And it would be fine if Jeremy crawled in and started snoring too. I'd missed it so much.

The door opened and closed. I managed to lift my head to look. It was Barrett. He crawled in next to me on the other side, rolling onto his side to be tucked in right against my back. When he was settled, he kissed my shoulder.

I sighed. Yes, perfect. "He's out." He spoke in a low voice, almost a whisper.

I nodded. Yes, he was.

"Good." Barrett put his head on my shoulder and gave out an audible sigh before I felt his body vibrate. A second later he was quiet. Had he just conked right out?

I wished I could. I was with them. This was home. What was the matter with me?

Well... there was a proverbial price on my head. Two hundred fifty million dollars. What if I promised to give it to them? Would they leave me alone? I mean it made me sort of sick to think of them having that much money if they were doing bad things with it, yet I would happily turn it over and let the authorities get them. I could ask about that tomorrow.

Why hadn't my mother done that?

I wished I could ask her. The door opened again and this time it was Jeremy. He walked over, squeezed my foot, and then got in the other bed. Phoenix must still be doing whatever he was doing. He had jumped in to help as though it was the most perfectly normal thing to do. Was he okay?

"Go to sleep, Princess," Jeremy said loud enough for me to hear it but hopefully not so loud it woke his brothers. "Everything will either be the same in the morning or better."

I hoped that was true. I really did.

I let myself listen as he fell asleep, too. His own deep snores, different than Jules', sounded, and it helped. I wasn't alone. There was an alarm on. One Lent was actually awake, and three of them were piled in here with me. No one was getting through the door tonight. No one was going to lock me away where they would abuse me and eventually kill me.

Not only that, but they loved me. They had come for me. They kept showing it. I was safe. It was okay to sleep deeply. It was okay.

My own lids finally shut.

I hadn't been out very long when I woke back up, knowing I was hungry. I stared at the clock. It was two in the morning. Funny, Rosalind had completely predicted what time I would wake up hungry if I didn't eat. Well, I had eaten; I just hadn't gotten to digest my food.

Phoenix was in the room now. On his stomach, next to Jer with no covers on top of him. He was face down on the pillow while Jer was rolled to his side, facing us. They were all there. It was beautiful.

And I either needed to get up quietly and sneak downstairs to discover if we even had food, or I was going to have to wake one of them. I chewed on my lip. I hadn't seen the kitchen, but I wasn't stupid, I could find it. Still, it nagged in my brain that they had all made a big point of helping me and I didn't want to negate that by not asking for help when I could probably use it since I was a little bit dizzy.

Okay. Which one to wake? Jules snored, his eyes were moving beneath his lids. He was out, and he needed to stay that way. Phoenix needed to sleep. He'd conked out in the atrium lounge when we'd been looking at the lake and stayed that way after Barrett had come in. What he was going through probably required a lot of rest. Jeremy would want to be woken, but waking him might mean waking Phoenix since they were in the same bed. That left Barrett, who absolutely would help me and was right next to me. He was obviously deeply asleep, but I was either willing to wake one of them or I wasn't.

I smoothed his hair off his face. It was soft and familiar, like all of him was. Comforting. Barrett would always—right or wrong—shoulder my troubles if he could and never think anything of it. He needed care even though he would never ask for it.

"Barrett," I whispered in his ear. "Sorry to wake you."

His eyes fluttered open, and before they cleared, he smiled at me. It was adoring. Then he blinked awake. "What's up, Sweetheart?" He had the sense to whisper. "You okay?"

"I'm so sorry." I whispered back. "But I'm hungry. And a little bit dizzy because of it. I don't want to wander the house alone. Can you help me?"

His nod was fast. "Absolutely."

In an easy, swift move, he got off the bed and had me in his arms. I managed not to squeak. I hadn't meant he had to carry me. That was okay. I also didn't mind it. Like it was nothing, he quietly carried me from the room and down the stairs to the kitchen. He flipped on the light, all of it with me still in his arms.

Now that we were downstairs, I spoke at full volume. "I'm sorry."

"Are you kidding? Of course you should have woken me. You always should wake me." He set me on the counter. "I could try to make some eggs."

They didn't cook. I shook my head. "No, how about something just like some cereal?"

"Oatmeal. That'll be better. That I can microwave."

Sounded perfect. A thought dawned on me. Maybe it had been his carrying me right now that had made me remember what I'd forgotten. "You carried me out of the school."

He stuck the oatmeal in the bowl and filled it a little bit with water before he walked to the microwave. "Better to call it what you did on the YouTube comments. A prison. You were in an abusive prison. That was not a school."

"But it was you. You came in and got me. Thank you."

He met my gaze. "We were all there but, yeah, no one was carrying you out of there but me. I lost you. I was getting you back." The microwave dinged and he pulled the bowl out and then hissed, setting it down. "Sorry, a little hot."

"Don't hurt yourself."

He grinned at me sheepishly. "I should have gotten a potholder or something."

Or just given it a second. I wasn't going to argue with him. This time he grabbed a towel to hold it and brought it over to me. "Careful. It's hot. Oh. " He rushed to the drawer and came back with a spoon. "Here."

I kissed him on the lips, breathing him in, and he closed his eyes to sigh against me. "Thank you, Barrett."

I scooped some oatmeal and blew on the spoon before I took a bite. He was right. This was just what I needed. I took three more bites before I spoke again. "This is so good. Thank you. You didn't lose me."

"Felt, hell feels, like I did." He leaned against the counter watching me eat. "I had to get you back."

I smiled at him. "You weren't even there." I kept eating.

"That made it worse. I came out of class to hysterical texts from my brothers. Finally, one just said, come home. I was massively confused, got home as fast as I could. That's when it was finally explained. Phoenix was a mess. The twins were alternating between inconsolable and angry at the world. I just knew... you were gone. I knew it. Then it was confirmed. And everything was so quiet."

I shook my head. "There are four of you. No way was it quiet."

"It was silent. Phoenix left to come down here. We followed him in less than a day. No way were we leaving him. Still, silence. Just utter lost silence. We needed you. I need you." He kissed my shoulder. "So you wake me up when you're hungry. You wake me up if you have a bad dream. You wake me up if you can't sleep. You wake me up if the room is too hot or cold. Anything. Okay?"

I had been right. It was absolutely the right thing to wake Barrett tonight. "Okay."

"Good."

We were silent the rest of the time that I ate, and by the time I finished I wasn't dizzy anymore. Tiredness wafted through me. Barrett took the bowl out of my hand and placed it in the sink.

"I can walk." He didn't have to carry me around.

"I know. I still like carrying you." He picked me back up, and this time I let myself squeak. He patted my rear, and I laughed. He flipped off the light, and we went back upstairs. On quiet feet, he put us both back where we had been just half an hour earlier.

He crawled in next to me, and I wrapped my arms around him, bringing him closer. "Thank you, Barrett."

"Hush. No thanking me. I love you."

"I love you, too." I kissed his chin. Julian rolled over, wrapping his arms around me from behind. I really was tangled in both of them. And I loved it.

I took a deep breath. Okay. I was okay. I was all right. We were safe. "I'm sorry you'll be tired tomorrow."

"Worth it." He kissed my forehead.

I closed my eyes.

Time must have passed.

"Hey." Jer touched my foot, and I opened my eyes. "Princess, time to get up so you can eat something before therapy."

I rubbed my eyes and darted out of bed. "I'm so sorry. So sorry."

"Hey." Jer grabbed me. "You're okay. It's okay. Just time to get up. What are you sorry for?"

All four of them were staring at me when I finally connected what I had done. "I... I..." Fuck. "I thought I was in trouble. I couldn't oversleep. I don't know why I thought it was here. I just..."

"Woke up confused." Jeremy hugged me. He smelled familiar. "It's early days. Hasn't been a week. Don't get yourself worried about this."

I took a deep breath. "Well, I guess we can see why I need therapy. I'm off my rocker."

"Don't put yourself down to make us feel better. You don't have to joke. You were scared." It was Phoenix who spoke, putting his hand on my back. "We love you. We're all fucked up." He squeezed my shoulder, and I pulled back to look at him. "I got those numbers for you. Do you think it's safe and smart for you to be the one to call all these girls? I mean some of them are twelve years old, right? What are you going to say to them? Your parents want you dead in six years? I think... I think we need a different way. You contact your close friends. But the rest of them? I think we need Kit to get involved in this."

Okay. This was a lot for first thing in the morning but there was little time to waste. "Will he do it?"

"Yes. He will. He has people who will pretty much do

anything." Julian climbed out of the bed. "Hungry? I'll make you something."

I really wasn't. Not even a little bit. But I probably should eat something to try to get onto some form of a regular eating schedule. "Just something small. I ate in the middle of the night."

Three of them stared again. "You did?" It was Jer who asked.

"Yes, I made her oatmeal at two in the morning." Barrett yawned. "I took care of her. She was hungry."

Julian rubbed his eyes. "I slept through you leaving the bed?"

"You're exhausted. I was glad you did and I wasn't waking you."

Barrett stretched. "Come on. Let's get this done. I don't know what your day will be like, Alatheia, but when we're all back together, you can make your calls, and then we'll figure out something to do tonight that isn't too much but also fun."

"Sounds good."

Phoenix cleared his throat. "Hey, Barrett, can you come back for me? I know you're taking Alatheia, and I don't want to interfere in alone time. It's important for all of us. I think. But, I need a ride. I can ask Eric, but I'd rather not if you can take me. I need to go check in with my therapist but not for an hour."

"Yep. Got you." He smiled at his brother.

The morning was relatively familiar. We all ate breakfast together. Julian was more chipper than he had been, which I had to think was because he had slept through the night. He would probably say it was because he'd slept next to me. I smiled at the thought.

I turned to Phoenix before I left the kitchen. "I'm sorry I wasn't here with you when you were going through this."

He kissed the end of my nose. "Still going through it, Red. We're going to go through this next part together."

"Thanks for getting me that information. Really, thank you."

He kissed my cheek. "Wasn't hard, and I actually love being able to do something for you. I missed your middle-of-the-night meal. I was only asleep about half an hour."

I'd never been to a therapist before. I really had no idea how this was going to go. We stepped outside and I abruptly stopped. "I need my hat. The one that your mother made me. I need it." I turned and headed back in, taking the stairs two at a time. My head was going to be freezing otherwise. I put it on fast and ran back down.

Barrett side-eyed me. "Did you want that for the cold or because you are worried about what people might think about you? Because if anyone were to say or even think anything..."

I stopped him by squeezing his arm. "It's cold for me. I don't even have a coat."

"Hold here a second." This time it was his turn to return into the house, fast. A second later he had a hooded sweatshirt in his hand. It was his. "Raise your arms." I did as he said, and he put it onto me, almost taking off my hat in the process. It said Columbia on it. I'd seen him wear it a lot. "Jules is going to get you a coat today. This will help." He grinned. "Besides, you look adorable in my sweatshirt. I think it's yours now. Yep, it's definitely yours."

I smiled. "I should say no. It's yours. But I'm not going to. It's warm, fuzzy. And it smells like you. I want it to keep smelling like you, so you have to wear it in between me wearing it. Like back and forth."

"And when I'm wearing it, it'll smell like you." We got into his car together. "We'll have to wash it sometimes or it might get gross."

That was true. He turned us onto the small road to head toward the clinic. It was quiet. Houses every so often but mostly the big pine trees were visible everywhere. "Why did you guys build this here?"

"Eric thought it was essential we have some place to go where we could just be ourselves. There are enough doctors and nurses here to staff it. Our mother's births made them feel that way. Only Kit could be there when all of us were born. It would be weird, right, for his brothers to be in the room when his wife delivers. It's a high pressure situation. What if she slipped up?"

Those were all good points. "Makes sense."

"And like everything else, the Lents are forever wanting to show the people here that we aren't trash. That they can't mess with us." He frowned. "That they can't kidnap us."

I took his hand where it was between us on the center console. "What are you thinking when you say that? Your eyes... they went somewhere."

"I'm thinking"—he sighed—"that Phoenix was always the smartest of us all. He survived when the others that night were killed. He doesn't remember it. But he did. And I don't believe that now he's clean and focused that he is going to leave it alone. I think it's only a matter of time until he goes after them in some way." He met my gaze for a second. "And I'll be helping him because I'd never leave him to that."

I stared straight ahead. Yes, that was true. There was no way we would all be down here without that happening. "I will too."

"First, we help you too." We pulled into the clinic's parking lot.

The lake was huge, and the cloudy weather that had moved in overnight wasn't making it less gorgeous. The glass windows of the clinic gleamed from a reflection off the lake.

The beige facade blended harmoniously with the natural surroundings as I was sure it had been designed to do.

Once again, I was sure that the landscaping would be beautiful at other times. Right now, it looked like it had all gone to sleep for a while. It was cold and resting. Maybe there was something beautiful about that, but right then I couldn't see it.

"It looks dead," I said to Barrett. "Everything."

Barrett leaned against the side of the car. "It's not dead. It's taking a break from everything. We do that, too. Right? Sometimes we have to take a rest to start over."

He wasn't just talking about the grass. I smiled at him. "I don't suppose I could just ignore this and I'll suddenly be fixed? Like I won't have a freak out waking up. I won't freak out at the table. It'll just stop."

He winced. "Probably not. But I'll be here with coffee when you get out. Although truthfully the coffee is awful here."

Good to know.

❦ 7 ❧

"**H**ey, Sweetheart." Barrett stopped me when I would have entered the office on the third floor that was Dr. Trevor's. "You can tell him anything. I just want to reiterate that. He lives like we do, okay? And one of his kids... was with Phoenix. So, yeah, he really does know everything."

One of his kids was with Phoenix? It took me a moment to understand what Barret was saying. Then it hit me. So Dr. Trevor had lost a child the night that Phoenix couldn't remember. "Wow. Okay."

I didn't know if I felt better or worse about this situation knowing that. It did help to know that I wasn't going to have to hide something, which would have been really hard if I was actually going to make this work.

"Was this where they sent Phoenix after?" Because that had to be awful. His own son had died and Phoenix was here...

"No. " Barrett shook his head. "I've got to go pick Phoenix up actually. But no, where they sent him? That was really hard because he needed help so he went to a private clinic in New York City, but he absolutely had to lie—at ten —to the doctors about his life. This was still being built. But he comes here now, obviously. Saw Trevor initially, but I think they've moved him on because it's more of a check in thing and he does group stuff. He'll tell you about it." He kissed my cheek. "We may have to eat my mother's barbecue shrimp tonight."

I hoped I could keep it down. Puking with Eric, Kit, Daniel and Stephen Lent in the other room was going to rank among my most awful moments ever. Ugh. I walked into the office, leaving Barrett in the hallway.

There was a woman behind a window, and as I walked over, she opened it and smiled at me. She was older, gray-haired with piercing blue eyes. "Alatheia, hello and welcome, please have a seat."

Okay. So she knew me.

She had one of those voices that would have done very well on meditation apps. I'd tried one twice. It hadn't worked for me. Was this going to be a problem in therapy? That I couldn't do that. Clear your mind and picture the stress leaving your body...

I settled into one of the chairs, the quiet hum of the room that should have probably been calming only alarmed me more. What was I going to have to do behind the closed door to the doctor's office? Outside, trees stood in reflection against the water. This whole building had clearly been set up to make the lake the central view of everything. Actually, that seemed true of everything.

Dr. Trevor's sign above the door said he was the only doctor here in this office. Where did Phoenix go? The wooden tables sat between the chairs, their surfaces holding magazines and small décor, making the wait feel less clinical, more like an invitation to pause. Or I was sure that was what it would do for other people. Not me. No, I was starting to panic. It was a room made for waiting and I wanted to run out of it. Instead, I pulled my knees up and pressed my head into them. Yes, this was good.

The door opened, and I didn't look up. I was breathing. That was enough. A comforting hand touched my shoulder, and I looked up to see Dr. Trevor sitting there. Eric had called him Kirk. When he'd come around while I had been admitted, he had been nice, giving directions to the nurses but not much else right then. That time had been for detoxing. That was what they had said.

"It's okay." His smile was small. "I hate waiting rooms too. There's not a way to make them okay. I'm convinced. Just the very act of knowing you are going to have to sit and wait creates angst. If you can, come back with me."

Okay. I had to do this. There was no hiding the crazy now. He probably wouldn't like that word. But I could think it about myself if I wanted to.

I got to my feet. "It just feels better like that. It's a weird thing. I didn't used to do that."

"Not so weird. Trust me." He motioned toward his office, and I followed him down a hall lined with diplomas, every single one his. Wow. He'd been some places. Harvard. Yale. Stanford. We made a quick turn into an office, and he closed the door behind us before settling into a chair. With the same kind of gesture he'd used a moment ago, he indicated the couch across from him. Okay, this was happening.

The wooden coffee table between us in the center held a small potted plant and next to it an empty vase. There was a bookshelf against the far wall filled with books and carefully chosen decorative pieces, picture frames that showed his family, three men with a woman—I recognized her, she had been out front, the one with the great voice, and the gray hair and blue eyes—that was his wife—and two kids with them, two girls. There should have been a third but River, that was his name, had died. I swallowed at that thought. How awful.

I lifted my gaze to meet his. "Sorry. I look at details. I get lost in them." I used to do it with shoes but that was gone. What was the point? Almost everyone was awful. Their shoes didn't tell me how much anymore. I was back in my ratty sneakers. I didn't even mean to wear them but they were what I'd shoved on when I'd gotten dressed this morning. Actually, a lot of these clothes were Chicago clothes. The t-shirt under Barrett's sweatshirt was too. The jeans. My underwear was new.

"What did you notice when you came in here?"

I tilted my head. "Is that a test? Like you'll be able to tell things about me based on what I see here?"

"No, we're just talking today. At the end of this session I'll tell you my current plan for you. And that's adjustable."

Okay. He just wanted to talk? "Why do you want to talk?"

"Well, I'm hoping I can get you to trust me a little bit. That starts with talking. What details did you notice? I always wonder how my office comes across."

Trust him. Well, the Lents did. Clearly. I wasn't adverse to trusting him. "You have a potted plant and an empty vase next to it. There's a view of the lake in almost every room in this building. And you have a beautiful family. Your wife is your receptionist. She has beautiful eyes and a great voice. You went to Harvard, Yale and Stanford."

"In the opposite direction, Stanford, Yale and Harvard. That order. I should fix that in the hall. Didn't think about it. Yes, that's my wife. She is beautiful. I'll tell her you said that about her voice. Someone once told her she should read audiobooks for a living. Unless you don't want me to. Everything in here is private."

I shook my head. "Please go ahead about the voice. That's fine. I didn't mean it to be private."

He pointed to the vase. "Her name is Lily, and I keep lilies in this vase when they're in season. I won't put anything else in it so it's empty when they aren't. I don't buy them off season. Seems wrong they've been forced to grow when they're not supposed to."

"Barrett and I were just talking about the grass sleeping. Coming back. Must be in the ether or something today." I looked out his window. The lake wasn't sleeping, but I bet it would be cold if I touched it; I bet it would be almost too cold to stand it.

He nodded. "That happens. Like I have a topic with one person, seems random, and it comes up around me five more times that day. Like beets. Happened the last time with beets."

I scrunched up my nose. "I'm not food picky, but I don't like them."

"I actually love them. But I know a lot of people who don't."

Wow, he really did just want to talk to me. This might be one of the strangest experiences of my life. An adult wanted to talk who didn't want to show off, insult, instruct, or need something from me? That was... different.

He looked back at the vase. "Lillies need eight weeks to be unbothered. To rest. To not be asked to grow. Then they come back again. Eight weeks seems such a little time to leave them alone."

"Are you trying to be profound?" I almost couldn't believe I had said it as soon as I did.

"No, but it's interesting you think that." He rubbed his chin. "I am almost never profound."

I smiled. "Sorry, that was rude. I don't know why I did that. I am almost never rude."

"I told you we'd just be talking and you thought maybe I had lied and meant to make a point. You're wrecked right now. I wouldn't be surprised if it bothered you. So, here's the thing, Alatheia, and then I would like to talk about anything else you'd like to talk about. The way we do things here is a little non-traditional." He paused. "Maybe the reason for that is obvious." His accent reminded me of Rosalind's. "We don't live traditionally. There aren't that many of us here who do what I do. Three of us. And we're all well trained, but the thing is that there is little anonymity. We all know each other in the Life. I can pretend I don't know things, or I can tell you when I do. Which would you prefer?"

I hated making decisions. Or at least I did lately. "In one of those choices, you are lying and I know it. I don't think it can be helpful to do that. I think I'd rather you tell me the truth."

He nodded. "Okay. So you lived in Chicago before New York." Oh, he did know things. A lot of things. "It begs the question. Who makes the better pizza?"

Huh, wow.

⚜

I WALKED out with Dr. Trevor—who said it was fine to call him Kirk, though I wasn't sure I actually could. He was my doctor. Shouldn't he be Dr. Trevor?—and we stopped at the reception area, where his wife waited for us.

She smiled warmly. "I'm making oatmeal cookies for you and the boys. I'm going to bring it tomorrow when I visit with Rosalind. Been so nice having them all here, even if it's been awful, the reason why. One of our girls is just a little older than you."

That was right, because River would have been my age. He was Phoenix's friend. That would have made us the same age. "I'd love to meet her."

Maybe. I wasn't sure how I felt about new people right

now. I needed to go home and get my calls made. As Mrs. Trevor set up my next appointment for two days from then I asked her another question that had occurred to me but I hadn't been able to do anything about yet.

"Is there a gynecologist here?" I'd never been to one. It was the kind of thing that got arranged by someone's mother. Given my situation, that had obviously not happened. But I didn't think anything could progress with the guys if I didn't do that first. I didn't want much more right now. When that happened. Eventually.

Lily smiled. "Sure. Let me call up there and see if they can fit you in right now." Her smile was bright but behind her eyes there was sadness. I recognized it because I saw it in the mirror every day and frequently in the gazes of my loves.

I'd seen it in every girl who was in that horrible place with me.

"Maybe sometime you could explain to me how people send their teenagers to a place where they set them up to die."

He sighed. "I don't understand evil. Like you, I've stared it in the face. I can't say I get it better than you do." Dr. Trevor patted me on the back as his wife hung up the phone.

"Go on up."

Well... that was fast.

"Elevator." She motioned toward the door. "Fifth floor. Top floor. You'll see the nursery on your right. Keep walking. It's there. Dr. Kim."

Okay. I could do this. I had thought I might have a few days to get used to the idea but maybe better to just do it.

I needn't have worried about being alone. Standing outside the office waiting were Barrett and Jeremy. They both looked up from their phones and grinned like I was the best thing they had ever seen.

I wished I could roll around in how warm that made me feel.

Jeremy extended his arms, and I walked into them. "You okay?"

"Yes. You?" I was mostly okay. Just not *not* okay enough to bring it up right then.

He rocked me. "I'm good. Next time wake me when you're hungry. I can make you better food than oatmeal."

Barrett laughed. "That has been bugging you all morning, hasn't it?"

Jer pressed his nose to my hair. "Little bit."

"I can't leave yet. I'm going to the gynecologist." I stepped back. "I have to take the elevator up."

They looked at each other before they looked at me. Finally, Barrett nodded. "Jer will take you up since he's feeling so needy, and I'll wait here for Phoenix who is next door."

"I didn't get to cuddle all night and make oatmeal. Yes, I am feeling needy."

Dina had said to leave them alone when they were like this. They'd been brothers a lot longer than they had been mine. "You know I love both of you." I tried to wink. I might have looked deranged. I wasn't really a winker. I put my hand out to Jer. "Let's go."

He grinned at his older brother. "She loves us."

"And here we can be really obnoxious about it if we want to. Hear that, world?" he shouted. "Alatheia loves us."

The door to Dr. Trevor's office opened. Lily looked him up and down. "Barrett, please, don't shout."

"Sorry."

We pushed the elevator button to go up.

JERMEY TOOK MY HAND, and it was such a novelty to be able to do this in public without giving it another thought that I squeezed our fingers together. "I don't think I would have made it very long without calling you guys when I ran away in my hypothetical what to do when I'm eighteen. Before I knew I was going to die."

He brought our joined fingers together and kissed them, gently. A warm burst of pleasure surged up my spine. Jer held my gaze. "It kills me that you would have waited at all. Did you really think we were just done?"

It was hard for me to say things that would hurt him, but I did it anyway. "When you didn't come the first month I thought maybe you'd had enough or you'd been talked out of it."

He shook his head slowly. "No, Princess. I'm sorry we didn't come. I'd have battered down the door to get to you. Laid siege on the place."

I really wished we could be alone right now instead of about to get out of an elevator. "I'd really like to kiss you."

Jer backed me against the wall. We both breathed hard. I could feel his chest moving against my own. My head spun, anticipation rushing through me. Finally, he kissed me, hard. "Here? You can kiss me. It's one of the few things I like about this place. Anytime. Anywhere."

My heart beat fast. "Are you sure I'm not dreaming?"

"You're not, but I might be."

The very slow-moving elevator opened, and we stepped into the hallway. She had said to pass the nursery, and I headed that way, stopping abruptly when I saw two babies inside. A boy on one side of the room, a girl on the other.

I'd never seen a baby as young as those two. "They're brand new." I spoke aloud, as much to myself as Jeremy. "They're so small."

He kissed my neck. "They are. Beautiful." He was quiet

for a second. "Do you like babies? I mean hypothetically. We're too young for babies right now and everything is chaotic."

I wrapped his arms around me. "I'll be honest, Jer, before this very moment I have not given babies the least amount of thought. Remember, when we met, I was focused on getting through life long enough to be on my own and hoping to make a friend. Babies? Whole other universe."

"My mother was twenty when she had Barrett. I don't think I've ever stopped to consider how young that was."

I took a breath. "So twenty-one with you and Jules and twenty-two with Phoenix."

Rosalind was thirty-nine right now. She looked very young. When she was my age she had already been contemplating how to get out of her life. Now she was glamorous in New York and knitted hats in Louisiana.

"I have to make my appointment but will you remind me that I have to tell you something when I get out? Something that might take a moment so not now."

He nodded. "Sure."

I sighed, walking past the nursery. "I liked looking at those babies."

"Me too." He swung our hands together. "But our baby would be cuter."

I groaned and then stopped when I saw the sign for Dr. Kim outside of a door. Okay, I was doing this. Women did it all the time. I could do this. "This is the kind of thing that girls get taken to by their moms a lot. I mean not all girls, obviously. But some. I guess."

He nodded. "I hate that you have to go through so many things alone." He was quiet for a second. "Do you think she would have accepted this? You with us?"

Wow. That was a good question. I hadn't thought about that at all. The door was flung open and a beautiful Asian woman stood in the threshold. "There you are, Altheia." I didn't know her, but clearly she knew me. It was so weird that everyone here knew me already. "I'm Lynda Kim. Come on. I thought maybe you got lost, but now I see that you just found Jeremy. Stop making my patient late. I know it's your fault. Whatever you're doing. Don't tell me."

He nodded. "Yes, ma'am."

She pointed at him. "And come by this week and see Joel." I didn't know what that was either. With a nod, she turned to me. "Jeremy and Joel used to play together as kids. Back when Rosalind used to bring them here a lot. Come on, then. No one likes doing this. I know. But you're being very good getting it done." She closed the door on Jeremy. "Oh and because I'm going to go all doctor on you and forget to say this later, I wasn't born in the Life. You're new to it too. If I can help, let me know."

Everyone was so nice and helpful here. It would be so easy to just give in and love it. But Dina's words floated in my head. There was always the other side of the lake. They'd killed children and taken Phoenix. Their granny didn't trust it here. I would believe in Dr. Kim. But I was still reserving judgement on a person-by-person basis.

I LEFT in a little bit more pain than when I'd entered. After talking to me for an hour, she had determined that for multiple reasons I needed an IUD. And she had one to put in me right then. So that had sort of sucked but at least it was over.

No babies. Maybe it would sort out my period. She thought it would.

I was glad it was done. I came out to find all four Lents waiting for me. They looked up from their phones in unison.

"What were they doing to you in there?" Jules smiled. "I thought maybe I would need to call a rescue team."

Was there such a thing? "It took some time. I'm not going to get pregnant now and hopefully I'll have some kind of regular period. Hurts right now but that is supposed to stop soon."

Phoenix winced and they all sort of groaned and grimaced. Finally, the youngest spoke. "I'm sorry you're in any pain. Let's get you home."

I leaned into him. "I need to make those calls and then honestly I might be an old woman and nap until dinner."

"Sounds like a plan. I seem to fall asleep a little bit every day, like in the middle of the day, like I did yesterday here. I can't seem to help it right now."

"Well." Jeremy shook his head. "I'm not an expert but, low key, that might stop if you stopped staying up all night. Just sayin'."

His youngest brother shoved him gently. "Last night I was helping our girlfriend."

"And all the other nights you were playing video games."

Phoenix laughed. "Yes, I was. But last night I wasn't, and I'll go to bed tonight because I get to sleep next to Alatheia."

"Hold on," Julian called before I could step outside and he rushed to the car, coming back with a black coat. "Try this."

I caught my breath. "Thank you for this. I know Barrett said you would, but I'm sure you had better things to do this morning than coat shop for me."

I put it on and it fit, which earned me a Julian grin. "Never anything better than taking care of you."

"Oh, the cheese." Jeremy grinned. "He always wins at the cheese. Oh, wait, Princess, you had something you wanted to tell me. Do you want to talk alone?"

All four sets of eyes were on me right then. I swallowed. "No, it's probably better all together." I hadn't said anything about this yet. "Um, when they took me." I swallowed through the lump in my throat. "They ripped the pearls from my neck and demanded the sapphire earrings. Those were so thoughtful. My favorite things ever. Not that things matter. They're small. I know that quite well. But, I am so sorry. You gave them to me, and they're gone."

Phoenix hugged me before Jeremy could, he was closer. I closed my eyes for a second. "They took them at the school?"

"Yes." I breathed him in.

"I can't imagine how terrified you must have been. I don't give a shit about the jewelry. Just that you got hurt. There will be more jewelry. Better jewelry."

Jeremy took his turn to hug me. "So much jewelry. You looked beautiful in those pearls, but I can do better than that. You'll see."

The idea was terrifying. "No. Don't buy me any more jewelry. I'll never survive losing it. Okay? Something will happen and it'll just be gone. I can't."

And by that of course I didn't mean simply the jewelry. I couldn't lose them or anything else that represented them.

"I think I made the jewelry about you guys. You gave it to me, so it was mine because of you. When they took it, it was like..."

Julian finished for me. "Like you lost them. Jeremy and Phoenix. And eventually it was like you lost all of us."

I wasn't surprised he got it. Julian did tend to cue in on things super fast. "That's it."

"I'll wait to get you more jewelry." Jeremy smiled. "But I will not promise to never buy you any. I think you can count on that. And by wait, I mean only a little bit."

I sighed. It was no surprise he was determined on this.

"Come on." Phoenix took my hand. "Let's get you home."

8

We drove home together in the Jeep Barrett was tooling around in. I sat up front with Barrett, and Jeremy kept catching my eye in the rearview mirror and winking at me. It made me grin. Barrett drove in silence. Phoenix must have been thinking about something because he was quietly looking out the window, and Jules had his eyes closed. I was cramping a little bit and glad for the pad they'd given me before I left the doctor. Yeah... this was going to be painful for a few days. Worth it, but painful.

When we pulled into the driveway, he opened them.

I didn't guess you could make up a lot of lost sleep in one night.

"Gotta work." He groaned. "And then I'm going to write before we have to go eat shrimp. When was the last time my mother made this shrimp?"

Phoenix shook his head. "I know I ate it when I was young, but if she made it more recently I don't remember."

"It's been about three years."

Phoenix shrugged. "Guess I blocked it out or was too fucked up the last time I ate it to register."

We all climbed out, and Barrett leaned against the car. "Some people around here make incredible barbecue shrimp. Mom isn't one of them."

"Hey," a voice called to us, and we all turned around. It was a guy, about our age I would guess, who ran toward us. "How's it going? Phoenix, I was hoping to just have a minute."

"Yeah," Phoenix nodded at him. "Of course. Hang on, Alatheia." He put out his hand. "One second?"

"Sure." I walked over to him, taking his outstretched offering that linked us together.

"This is Sam. Sam this is Alatheia."

I stared at Sam for a second, still not sure exactly who he was. He stared back, not in an unfriendly way, but I became instantly aware of my hair. I touched the cap on my head. Thank goodness it was on.

"Don't worry about that." Phoenix caught my gaze and squeezed my fingers tightly. "You're beautiful. Perfect." That wasn't true. Even when I had hair on my head. "Sam is my partner in sobriety. It's part of the program here. He's been clean about a month longer than me. And we support each other."

Oh, wow. Okay. That made sense. "Like your sponsor?"

"No, not exactly. It's not the same program. We're both new to it, we couldn't be sponsoring anyone. And we have a mentor who has been clean for a decade, who works with both of us."

Sam made a waving motion. "Nice to finally meet you, Alatheia. I've heard so much about you that I feel like I know you. Sorry if I stared. I didn't mean to make you uncomfortable. I paint. I think I stare a moment too long at people like

I'm taking them and imagining recreating their faces. It's weird. Anyway, you have great bone structure."

Phoenix shook his head. "Don't hit on my girl, Sammy."

He held up his hands like he was surrendering. "I'm not. I wouldn't do that. Besides, she wouldn't care. She belongs to you guys. I can see it."

The other three brothers said some semblance of hello to Sam and headed into the house.

"Yeah, I won't keep Phoenix long. I could just use a minute. And, if you need anything, I live right there. The house next door to the left." He pointed.

Phoenix kissed my hand. "He lives there with his two brothers and three younger sisters."

"It's nice meeting you, Sam." I let go of Phoenix's hand so he could go off with Sam for however long they needed. Really, other than seeing Phoenix sober and knowing he had a therapy appointment today, almost no sign of what he was doing here had presented itself before now. Was it okay to ask? What was the protocol? Was it secret?

I just didn't know.

I quickly made my way inside to find that Julian was in the kitchen making a grilled cheese. He looked over his shoulder at me. "You caught me. I was going to surprise you with this."

"Thank you." I was hungry. I absolutely was. Also nauseous. Maybe the food would help. "I need to make calls, and I don't have a phone."

Jer scooted in next to me, appearing from the other room. "Here. Use mine. We'll go later or tomorrow and get you one. Not the same number. I want it to be kept away from your family. In fact, I think I'm going to get it for you under my mom's name. Like it's her second phone."

I chewed on my bottom lip. "Will that be a problem?"

"No," he answered me as Jules set the grilled cheese down in front of me.

He kissed my cheek. "Chew and call."

These were going to be the weirdest calls of my life. I took a deep breath. I had to tell my friends their families wanted them dead. Maybe it wouldn't be surprising; we'd all felt like that place was a waiting room for hell. I looked down at the paper that Phoenix had left me. It had the numbers.

I dialed Betsy's number first. It rang and a man picked up on the other end. It hadn't occurred to me that it wouldn't be the girls themselves. Of course it should have. None of us had cell phones anymore. This was her father's number.

"Hi, I'm hoping you can put me in contact with Betsy. Please."

There was a silent pause. "No." He hung up.

I stared at the twins as Barrett walked into the room. "He wouldn't let me talk to her. I don't know if she's alive or dead."

Barrett leaned against the counter. "Try the next one."

Okay. That was Sally. I dialed. This time it went straight to voicemail. I left one. "Hi, this is Alatheia, I'm looking for Sally. If she is there, could you give her this number and ask her to call me back? Thanks."

The food had helped. Thankfully, I didn't feel like I was going to puke. Hopefully that had just passed.

I hoped I sounded chipper. I tried three more times and was hung up on once and had to leave voicemails with the others.

I sat back. "I thought I would get through."

"We need Kit on this. Like maybe he could let the authorities know." Barrett gave me a small smile.

"He did." Jeremy took the phone back from me. "First thing this morning. I'll tell Kit that we need your friends contacted, too. Maybe we can get them your phone number once you have one tomorrow." Jeremy cupped my cheek. "I'm sorry, Princess."

I did love it when he called me that, and I leaned my head on his shoulder. "I'm so tired. Just bone achingly tired."

"Need a nap." Phoenix came into the room. "Sorry about that. Sam needed a second."

Julian frowned. "Such a good guy. He does seem to need more seconds than you do."

Phoenix sighed. "Who knows where I'll be a month from now and he doesn't have my whys." He walked over and took my hand, drawing me from Jeremy. "Take a nap with me. You haven't even been back a week. Hold on, what's going on?"

Julian quickly filled him in before he continued. "At some point Eric will want you to work for him."

"I know but not yet. Whenever that is, I'll do whatever he wants." He paused. "Hey, guys, I... I realized something in therapy today. And I wanted to tell you so since we're all here minus the parents whose opinion on this I don't want. I'll just get right to it." I felt him steady himself. "I'm glad it was me who was taken and not you. Let me finish," Phoenix said, quickly anticipating that they would all open their mouths, which they did. "First off, I still don't remember what happened. The magic bullet of sobriety didn't turn me around and make it all suddenly clear. I wish that it did. But it didn't. All I know is that River and Walt died and I didn't. Truth? I barely remember them. Like they have faded away too. But, I know they were real people who died and it haunts me. Why did I live? Also don't know. But I know that I did and I don't know if you would have. How can I know? If there was any possibility of you dying, it would kill me because you're my brothers. Also, I like who you are. I can't fathom you being different because you went through what I did. Even if you sometimes drive me crazy. Okay? You don't need to feel guilty, I feel grateful."

There was silence at his statement. It was finally Jeremy who spoke, it was barely a whisper. "Fuck, Phoenix."

"I know. It's big stuff. I think it's why I keep falling asleep. But, yeah, that's how I feel so please, if you're walking around harboring some idea that it should have been you and not me, don't." He ran a hand through his hair. "That's it. Come on, Alatheia."

Come on? I stared at his brothers as I left the room with Phoenix. They were stunned. Absolutely stunned silent. He had really dropped a bomb on them with his feelings. When we would have turned to my room, he went instead to his. I hadn't seen it yet. He closed the door behind and then the bathroom door that he shared with Julian.

"Little more private for me to breathe. I don't want them coming in to talk about anything right now. Later." He put his hands on his knees. "I didn't expect it to hit me so hard to tell them. Sorry."

I walked over and rubbed his back. "What are you sorry for?"

His room looked like mine. The maids had clearly been in that morning while we'd all been out. I never saw them, but the Lents didn't clean. Two beds. His room was gray instead of beige and there was a picture of him on a skateboard in the corner, framed in gold plated wood. Who put that in here? I doubted it was Phoenix himself. Otherwise it was pretty copy paste to my room.

I kept my rubs light circles on his back. When he didn't speak, I did again. "Being human?"

He laughed. "I am very human. The most human here. You're less than a week rescued and you're rubbing my back."

"Well... I'm one session in and haven't done anything but chit chat with Dr. Trevor because we're establishing trust despite the fact that he knows me and I don't know him, but maybe I have it easier thinking about someone else's pain rather than my own?"

He lifted his head. "That's a pretty big revelation for not having done any work yet." His smile was huge. "You're going to be better at therapy than me."

"Are we competing?"

He lifted me up, which surprised me, so I squeaked. "No. I want you better than me. I want everything better in the world for you. I have some deep questions to ask you but not now. I want to nap. If I open that door, neither of us are going to get any sleep." He grabbed his phone and set an alarm. "We should be up an hour before dinner or we'll both be groggy at the table and even though I can acknowledge they mean well, I like to be sharp with my family around. The parents are a mine-trap for me."

I kicked off my shoes and he did the same. He pulled off his pants and I did too, both of us now pantless. He stared at me for a second, tilting his head. Usually, I didn't do that. He knew it and so did I. When he pulled off his shirt, I did as well. My heart raced but I was sure of it.

"How about a little more skin-to-skin for this nap?" I swallowed through the lump in my throat. "Please don't misunderstand me. I'm in pain and kind of bleeding right now. I'm not suggesting we do anything different. Just do it with our skin touching each other. Or just sleep. Whatever.

He stared at me from where I was on the bed, and without speaking, covered us both in his heavy quilt. "I love that you want this. Come here. Closer. My chest against yours. I love your skin. Your pale, porcelain skin."

"Have you missed all the freckles?"

He laughed. "Some day when you're older I am going to have you naked, and you are going to let me count them."

Ooh. That was... exciting. "Is that really what you're going to want to do with me when you have me naked?"

"You like the idea." He grinned; his eyes were blazing with interest. "It'll be one of the things." He wrapped an arm over me, the other under his head and I did the same to him. With our foreheads pressed together, we were practically breathing the same air. I loved it and I didn't think I'd be able to close my eyes but when he did, I did.

He wasn't asleep yet because he moved his arm to stroke my back with his index finger. I shivered. I let myself stroke his abs. A peek told me we both still had our eyes closed. He took deep breaths, and because I was so close to him, I could absolutely feel what it did to him right then. In seconds, he was hard.

Phoenix had told me once he liked to be, because it told him what someday would be. I had been shoved into a place where they were going to kill me. Did I really want to count on someday? What if they had done that to me and I'd never ever had this moment?

It was enough to make me crazy, like the idea of his brothers dying in his stead did for him. No, I didn't want to think about that right now.

But I needed his consent. That meant I had to be brave. I opened my eyes. "Can I touch you?"

He lifted his own. "Unless I'm already dreaming or delirious, you already are." His smile was slow. "And I fucking love it."

"I know. I can feel that. I mean, can I touch you there? On your... dick?" I managed to get the word out. That was a win even if he said no. Alatheia successfully used the word dick and didn't call it something weird to cover up. Win for Alatheia. Oh boy. I was thinking about myself in the third person.

He lifted his eyebrows. "Alatheia, you practically choked saying that. You don't have to be obligated..."

I interrupted him. "Not obligated. More like... really

interested. Yes, I know I'm ridiculous with the word. Unless you don't want me to?"

He cleared his throat. "Oh, I want you to. I can't reciprocate right now. That's going to bother me."

"Bother you so much you're saying no?" I continued to stroke his chest.

"No. I'm not saying no. If you want to. As much or as little as you want or not at all. Feel free to stop anytime."

I smiled. "You are so careful with me. I don't break. At least not so far."

Phoenix kissed me. "Frankly it's shocking to me you want me at all after what happened. But, you seem to have held no anger for me. I love you. Yes, please, touch me, Red, as much as you want. I may come in your hand really quickly."

Well... that would really be something. What would that be like? I tugged at his boxer briefs, and he ended up helping me get them down. There he was. Hard, big, thick, and obviously very aware of me. I'd felt erections a lot now when they bumped into me but never actually seen a penis before. It was sort of... beautiful.

An actual physical response to show me how much he desired me.

I took him in my hand, starting at the bottom, and he hissed in his breath. Phoenix seemed to shake for a second before he kissed me hard, his hands coming around my back to hold onto me tightly. I kissed him back but concentrated on running my hand over his skin, finally getting to the top.

He stopped kissing me to moan, his eyes closing. Okay. So he liked that. I did the whole thing again. "Am I doing it how you like it?"

"Anything your sweet hand does to me there, Alatheia, I like."

Okay, but that didn't tell me anything. "How do you like it?"

He took my hand in his. "You can grip me harder." He put our joined hands on his cock—easier to think that word than say it. "And when you get to the top, cup me there for just a few seconds. If you want to, you can also play with my balls. Or don't do any of it because I think I might be delirious in a second and there is nothing you can do I won't like. I promise."

People put their mouths on it. This much I knew. I didn't think I was ready. I would need to be braver. It wasn't about them; it was about me.

I did as he instructed, up and down the way he wanted, increasing the pressure each time. When I could, I squeezed his balls. He kissed and kissed me. His sighs and moans would come right into my mouth, like I got to taste them.

Inside, I got heated. No, I couldn't do anything right now, but boy did I want to. I squirmed, and he pulled me closer, running his hands on my stomach now, coming close to my waist but not under it. My breasts ached, my nipples were hard against my bra, which we hadn't taken off.

I smiled against his lips. "I love this, and I love you."

As I spoke, he jerked, a sigh releasing from his mouth that almost sounded like an ache. He came in my hand. Oh wow. It was warm, a little bit sticky, and it went on longer than I would have imagined it would.

He closed his eyes tightly, our foreheads pressed together. I didn't stop my strokes, and he moaned toward the end. "Thank you. I love you so fucking much."

"I love you, too."

He kissed me, once, twice, a third time. "When you're feeling better, if you're ready, I am going to make you feel how you just made me feel. Over and over again."

I smiled at him. "This made me feel good, too. Giving you pleasure?"

"You're like an angel I imagined." Phoenix pulled away

from me, getting up to go into his bathroom. He came back, wiping himself with one towel and handed me another. I cleaned up my hand and he took both towels and put them in the laundry. "Come on. Let's nap in the other bed." He yawned. "I may think I dreamed this."

He put his underwear back on.

Oh, yes that made sense. We'd kind of made a mess in this bed. I grinned. Things I'd never thought about when I pictured this kind of thing. I got up and he scooped me up, putting me in the other bed.

I giggled, which he must have liked because he kissed my lips over and over. "You never cease to be a miracle. I kept saying that when you were gone. That I had lost my miracle. The doctors didn't argue. Everyone here has a miracle in their lives, but none are as amazing as you."

I wasn't even sure what to say to that. A miracle? I really didn't feel that way. I still had my cap on that I'd shoved on outside. I hadn't even thought about it, but Phoenix took it off my head. "Wasn't going to bring that up earlier but unless you're cold, keep it off. You don't need to walk around like you have something to hide."

He put it between us. "Pretty sure I'm going to disagree with you and wear it a lot."

"Okay. You're right, of course. I just hate that you think that you have to." He winced. "Getting bossy?"

We were wrapped back up with each other, and I was too tired to care that he had gotten that way. "You're forgiven."

"Thank you." Our foreheads touched the way that they had been before. This time when our eyes closed, I drifted off easily. I was comfortable, warm, and able to ignore the cramping that was happening. I was just happy to care. That had just happened.

I woke to the alarm which I rolled over to turn off but Phoenix didn't. He was silent and out cold. I ran my hand through his hair. It was soft and a little bit longer than I remembered it from before I was taken.

His eyes opened a little bit into slits. "Are you okay?"

"Yes, time for us to get up."

He sat up with a groan. "Sorry, I didn't hear it. You knocked me right out, hard. I slept like it was night." He rolled me under him and kissed me all over my face. "I love you."

"I love you, too." He had said he wanted to have a hard conversation. Did he want to do that now?

It didn't seem he did because he got busy kissing me for a long moment.

A knock sounded. "Hey, I heard talking. You two up?" It was Barrett.

Phoenix lifted his head. "I think I've taken my max of Alatheia alone time for the day." He rolled off of me and grabbed my shirt which he handed to me. I hadn't even thought about it.

"Just a second, Barrett," he answered, putting his pants back on. Okay. We were covered. I didn't mind Barrett seeing me that way, but it was nice of Phoenix to think of it. Barrett came in and sat on the end of the bed.

"Is this a precedent? We nap in our individual rooms?" He smiled at us. "It's a good idea, actually."

Phoenix yawned. "Thanks."

"What's the matter?" There was a heaviness to Barrett that I hadn't seen earlier.

He held out his phone so Barrett and I could see. It was an unknown number. I didn't even recognize the area code. A text was visible. *She's better now. Take her home and leave. Before something bad happens to your family. Again.*

I gasped, but Phoenix didn't. He stared at it, hard, and then looked up at his brother. "You got this an hour ago?"

"We thought it best not to wake you until you were up.

Both of you are recovering. Dads know. Eric wants to load us all up and leave. Like maybe leave the country. But Kit says that's a bad idea. We can't be run out of town by some text message. Except of course because of what happened to you, Brother."

Phoenix shook his head. "We don't even know that it's the same person. It might very well be someone just pressing on a sensitive spot they know we have. But give it to me. I can try to track it. Maybe I can. Tell the parents I'm skipping dinner to do that."

"No." I usually just let them make decisions. But I didn't like that. "Come with us. This is bigger than you're making it, and I want you with us tonight. So you remember that we love you and you're not alone."

Phoenix stared at me. "I love you. Okay. I'll do that."

Later he could find this person. Later tonight.

9

D inner was subdued, and all of the beautiful endorphins I'd gotten from my moments with Phoenix and my nap were gone. One thing that was particularly obvious was that their fathers and mother were fighting. Oh not that they were fighting with Rosalind. She actually seemed to be the only one not fighting, but their fathers were fighting and Rosalind was sometimes joining in and sometimes keeping her back to everyone, singing to herself in the kitchen.

Eric slammed down his soda onto the table as we ate the pretty good barbecue shrimp. I'd never had it before, and I particularly liked the buttery taste that I hadn't expected. Not that I was particularly interested in food right that second.

He glared at Kit. "We need to go. End of story. Safety comes before anything else. We're rich. Very, very rich. What more do we need in this life? I need Rosalind and the kids to be fine. That's what I need. What do you need? More wins in court?"

Kit slammed his hand down. "Fuck you for saying that to

me. Fine. You want to leave here? We'll leave. We'll go back to New York and put guards on them. Like we should have done years ago."

My guys were tense but clearly not afraid because Julian looked up. "Alatheia can't go back to New York. Not until her family is dealt with."

I shook my head. "It doesn't follow that I have to be the reason for anything happening or not happening."

"It does." Phoenix shook his head. "It absolutely does."

Rosalind sighed. "We're not going anywhere. The kids need the doctors here. Frankly, after this, I might too. We're staying."

All of them stared at her. Wow. She had just... told them how it was going to be. Eric stood and walked from the room, Rosalind's gaze chasing him, but she made no moves to follow him.

The front door opened, and we all turned to look. For a second I couldn't believe what I saw. Being wheeled inside in a wheelchair was Dina. I wasn't alone in jumping to my feet. The woman who pushed her was new to me; she was an older woman with brown hair and brown eyes. She gave the room a kind smile.

Dina waved her very frail looking arm. "Hello, darlings."

"Mom." Stephen walked around the table. "We weren't expecting you until tomorrow. We would have met you at the airport."

She smiled at him when she took his hand. "Why waste a day when what I want is to be here?"

"Granny." Jules rushed to her side. "What's going on? Why are you in this wheelchair?"

We were all around her then, but I hung back. They were her family. Dina sighed loudly. I looked around. Eric came back into the room.

"How was the flight, Mom?" He kissed her on the cheek. "You must be exhausted. Come in. Are you hungry?

It was clear to me what had to be clear to my guys—their parents were not as surprised by how Dina looked as they were. But the "how long had they known she wasn't okay" discussion could happen another time. The Lents did like their secrets.

"I know, my darlings. This is a shock, but I asked them not to tell you while Alatheia was missing unless there was no other choice. Oh, there you are, Alatheia, come here."

I didn't hesitate, taking her hand. "Are you okay?"

"No, I'm obviously not. But don't feel sad or sorry. I won't have any of that. I am here to be with my family for as long as I can be and that's all there is to it."

Jeremy stood with his hands crossed over his chest. "What's wrong with you, Granny? What's happening?"

"I'm dying, my darling."

He turned around and stared at Eric. "How could you allow this?"

Eric blinked rapidly. "How could I allow it?"

Shock hit each of my guys at once. Jeremy almost seemed to vibrate.

He was shouting now. "We live in New York City. Most of the time. We're very wealthy. You're a doctor. Don't you know people who can fix this?"

"Oh, Jeremy." Rosalind took two steps toward him and stopped. She visibly swallowed.

Dina squeezed Jer's arm. "I know it's a shock. Yes, Eric did everything he could. This started a few years ago. I battled it then. It stopped. There was no need for you or your brothers to know about. Now the cancer is back. And I'm afraid there's little to nothing to do about it now."

Jeremy took a couple of audible breaths before he did what

his father had done and tore out of the room. I wanted to talk to Dina, but Jeremy needed me right then. I chased after him into the backyard where he stood with his head down.

I didn't think I'd ever seen Jer cry before. Without a word I wrapped my arms around him, and he put his head on my shoulder. He was silent in his sobs, and it was heartbreaking. I wanted to cry too, but I wouldn't. Not then. This wasn't about me. This was about Jeremy and his brothers.

He squeezed me tightly. "She has always been there for us. Always. When they vanished because they were having their own freakouts about life, she never did. Even before that, we were perfect to her instead of these pale substitutes for our fathers."

I ran my hand through his blond hair. "You are not pale substitutes for your fathers. No one would think that ever. Not ever. But, yes, she is incredible. Just gives and gives. This is absolutely awful. I don't have words. I love you." The words came out in a flood of emotion.

And I loved her. Even after so little time with her, I loved her. Maybe the first person to ever be nice to me who had no reason to be. She picked me up before she met me, and it was because of her that I was even here right now.

He shook some more and then eventually lifted his head, wiping his eyes. "Well, I think we're not leaving."

I laughed. "I guess not." I put out my hand. "Come on. Let's go back in. I guarantee she's worrying about you."

He nodded and wiped his eyes. "I am going to hate that you saw me like this."

"Maybe not. Maybe you'll realize that I love you, and you're a human who just found his beloved granny is dying."

He touched my cheek. "She brought you to us."

"She was the first person." I caught my breath and stopped talking.

Jer raised his eyebrows. "Princess?"

"She was the first person to be nice to me for no reason at all. There was absolutely no reason Dina Lent had to take me on, give me journals, and introduce me to her family. She started all of this before she even met me. When she heard how my aunt was speaking about me she just went ahead and did this." By the time I finished speaking, one tear had dropped from my eye. "Anyway, she's not dead so let's not act like she is."

I wrapped my arm around his waist, and we walked in together. Inside, Dina was no longer in the hallway and everyone had dispersed except Phoenix. Maybe they had gone with Dina wherever she was staying.

"Hey, I just wanted to tell you I'm meeting up with Sam and then I'm going to Group because I feel a little shaky. I'm sure it's normal to feel this way with this news, but it's making me nervous as hell."

I hugged him. "Okay. See you later?"

"Yeah, I'm going to work on getting more phone numbers when I get home, so I might be late to bed, but I'll be there."

Jer nodded toward the end of the hall. "Her room is down here."

At least they didn't need to worry about getting her up and down stairs.

"Hold on." Eric stood in the shadows of the hallway and strode toward us. Jeremy braced himself. I saw it in the way he held his shoulders. He had hollered at Eric; he wasn't expecting this to go well. Next to me, Phoenix stiffened too. Eric wasn't coming for him, but he was ready for it as though it was happening to him.

But when he reached Jeremy, Eric didn't yell, he hugged him. Tightly. Jeremy was so stiff in his embrace that it was actually awkward to see. But after a second he hugged Eric back.

"I would do anything to save her. She was through with

her cancer treatments the last time she had it before she even told me about it. I don't understand it either but it's the way my mother is. You know your granny. She's stubborn. This time it was too late for much and she wouldn't even let me do what I could." He kissed Jer's cheek. "And I love you for the fact that you can express yourself. I know I let you down a lot. But I've loved you every day of your life, since I knew you were coming." He stopped. "This is going to be the worst thing. Just the worst. When my fathers died..." Whatever Eric was going to say he didn't finish. "You're going to be okay."

Jeremy didn't speak for a second. "Thank you."

"Go see her. Bring Alatheia. She is worried about both of you." He stepped back. "Come on, Phoenix. I'll drive you." He wiped at his eyes as he walked toward Phoenix and smiled at me. "Have I told you how proud of you I am?" Eric put his arm around Phoenix. They were biologically father and son. I could see it right then so clearly. The shape of their faces, the slope of their noses.

"Wow. You're all kinds of mushy." Phoenix laughed as they walked out.

Jer put out his hand in the way that he did when he wanted me to take it, so I did. I stared at him. "You okay?"

"No. Are you?"

I shook my head. "Let's go see your granny."

Slightly down the hallway was her bedroom. It had red painted walls. I smiled at the sight. Everywhere she went she painted her walls red. It was like her signature. I loved it. They had medical machines in the room ready for her. I didn't know what all of them were, but it was a bit of a makeshift hospital situation. They did have the clinic nearby, but I guessed she wasn't going to it.

She lay in bed, the woman who had brought her in fussing over her while her grandsons and sons sat around the bed.

Julian had her hand. Rosalind sat next to Kit and smiled at me when I came in. I smiled back. She was really trying with me. I took off my knitted cap.

"Phoenix went to a Group meeting," Jeremy told everyone.

Stephen nodded. "Thanks for telling us.

Dina grinned at us from where she sat upright on pillows on the bed. "Now don't worry, I will be more upright tomorrow. The trip? It took a lot. You missed introductions. This is Lucy. She knows what our lives are like because hers used to be too. She lost her husbands last year and now she is taking care of me. Lucy, this is Alatheia and Jeremy."

"Hello." She had the slightest accent, but I couldn't identify from where. "I'm going to give y'all a minute."

With her eyes on the floor, she left the room. Instantly, I knew she had a story but somehow that couldn't be surprising. Everyone here had a story. Even if they were raised in the Life, it didn't seem to lend itself to a simple, easy time. You did have to want it.

Jeremy cleared his throat. "I'm sorry for my outburst."

"Don't be silly. We're all outbursting all the time. That's just what we do." Julian rose and gave Jermey his chair before walking over to me. He squeezed my arm and then pulled me against him.

Dina stared at me. "Well, I can't say it's your best haircut. I mean I wouldn't recommend the stylist."

I burst out laughing and then covered my mouth. Oh wow. I had just cracked up in a sick room. That was probably really impolite, but Dina must have loved it because her face lit up in glee. "I need to hear all your stories, if you're telling them. Otherwise, I will just say I am glad you are back. So, so glad. I won't get to give them the journals, but you'll do that for me. I know you will."

The tears I kept holding back fell out of my eyes. "I will.

The first set would be done if I hadn't been... taken away for a while."

There it was again: the hand-wave I'd always associate with Dina. "Kidnapped. Your family is such trash. I can say that because I'm dying. I can say as I wish now." She hadn't been before? What more did she want to say? The thought at least made me stop crying. Barrett rose and walked to my other side. "But I hear you are a Monk. Come see me tomorrow. You won't get to the Monks until the second set of journals, which will take a long time. I know Daisy Monk. She is frightening. Even for me. And it drives me a little crazy that she is going to outlive me. But perhaps she sold her soul or is really a vampire. Anyway, she won't get her claws in you because you are too strong for that. Don't be a Monk. Be a Lent. It's safer even if it's a little bit crazy."

"She will be. In three years. If I can convince her." Jeremy sighed. "I mean she will be in three years. That's happening. I just need her to believe it."

Barrett choked. "You told her that?"

"I did. Why not all be on the same page?" Jeremy shrugged.

Rosalind widened her eyes. "Three years?"

Daniel laughed. "Same age you were."

"Older than me." Dina met my eyes. I might be the only person in the room who knew the whole story. Not for the first time, I loved that she had decided to trust me.

Our house was quiet that night. They all seemed to be dealing in different ways. Phoenix came back from Group, kissed me, and went straight to his room to try to find the owner of that phone number. I hoped he could. Was he still working on his video game? I needed to ask.

Julian went to his room, took off his clothes, and went and got in bed in my room, in the spot that would be next to me, and proceeded to fall asleep. Almost instantly. He was a bit of a zombie, sort of mumbled some semblance of goodnight and closed his eyes before he was out. I had been brushing my hair. A little bit worried, I set down my brush and walked over to him, smoothing out his hair. How did he always keep it so soft? He breathed deeply, which quickly changed to snores. Wow. He was just instantly out.

Was Barrett okay? Jeremy? I found both of them on their computers. Barrett was reading about end of life care while Jer was doing his work for Kit. They both looked up from their computers when I walked into the living room.

"Jules just pretty much passed out." I thought they might want to know.

"He usually does in stress. Just not when they took you." Jeremy stopped typing. "Then it was the opposite. It's actually better if he is. It's early, but we can go to bed if you want to."

I shook my head. "No. I have something to do."

⚬⚬⚬

FEBRUARY 1ST 1967

SOMETHING HAS TO CHANGE. I love my husbands more and more every day. Truly I do. But seeing them in the morning with a goodbye kiss and seeing them again in the evening, sometimes very late before, ah, evening activities is no way to spend my day. I have decorated as much as I possibly can. They didn't like the red walls. I could tell, but I haven't changed them. Okay, I am being immature, but they can tell me they don't like them or they can learn to live with them.

It isn't their fault I am so... uninterested in life right now. I am not pregnant. I really hoped maybe I would be.

I have discovered a new show called Star Trek and it amused me for a few minutes. The vision of the future. Of course, they are still battling things and for that matter there is always the possibility that one of them could be drafted to Vietnam. No, I am not going to write about that. Some things are too much to think about.

I have decided to go to work with them. I can be helpful. I know that I can. I just can't tell them that I am going to do this. I will show up tomorrow after they have arrived. They won't tell me to leave once I am there. If I try to go with them, they will come up with reasons I shouldn't. Really, some of their old-fashioned upbringing can be a lot to deal with. So I will handle this in my way and get what I want in the end.

In the meantime, I am going to cook a dinner that I will eat alone because they are bound to be very late tonight.

DL

FEBRUARY 15ᵀᴴ 1967

MEN ARE BURNING *their draft cards. I saw it first hand in Union Square today when I went down to meet the wife of my husbands' business contact. They need a better deal on men's ties. They're going to get it. Turns out I am charming. I am just discovering this, too. She said I was adorable, and I did try to look really put together today.*

I wore my camel-colored wool suit—the one with the perfectly tailored jacket and those lovely flap pockets, each secured with a neat little button. The sleeves hit right at my wrists, making it just right. The matching skirt fell a little above my knees, prim but smart, giving me that effortless, polished look I always aim for.

I paired it with my brown leather pumps, the ones that click perfectly on the pavement, making me feel purposeful. And of course, I finished the outfit with my cream-colored hat, a subtle but elegant touch. The whole ensemble made me feel sharp and sophisticated—

just the way I like it. Not the most expensive outfit. We have money but so much is going into Lent's Department Store that I am not going to overspend. Besides, it was a good idea for her to know she was above me in wealth and power.

I lowered my eyes a lot, thanked her for opinions, and acted the right amount of grateful. Some day I won't have to do that anymore. But for now, I do. I am simply grateful I can help. I went back to the store after seeing those men burn their cards and realized as I watched them and the women cheering them on how completely different my life is from others my age.

I didn't feel sad about it. They're still searching for their futures. I found mine. But still, I stopped and watched. Then I went back and folded skirts. The guys were never going to get it right, and we couldn't hire new employees without making sure they understood exactly how it needed to be done.

DL

❦

I CLOSED THE BOOK. Reading her always made my head spin. I looked over at Barrett and Jeremy where they typed. Phoenix was involved upstairs, and besides, I sort of preferred him not coming along to do what I needed to do. Or even hearing it.

"Guys, can we take a walk?"

They both looked at me. Barrett rubbed his eyes. "It's midnight." Jeremy finished with, "It's cold."

Was it? I hadn't even noticed on the walk home, and it might have been midnight, but I was wide awake.

I rose. "I'm taking a walk. I have something I need to do. You can stay. I'll be fine."

There was no way they were letting me do this alone. I

knew that. I wasn't usually manipulative, but I really would do what I said I would do and go alone if they didn't come. I just knew they would come.

Both of them jumped up. When I went to the coat closet, so did they. It was Barrett who spoke again. "What are we doing? "

"We'll talk about it outside." I put on my coat and my knitted hat. It wasn't as cold here as it would be in New York, and I had taken the train in Chicago in the winter. I needed to toughen back up. Or maybe I just had to relax and be gentle with myself. If only the world wasn't trying to kill all of us.

I couldn't heal when I was battling. I didn't think. Dina was dying and she had battled in her way her whole life. She would do this, and I wouldn't do less, even if it was in my own way.

I stepped outside, triggering motion sensors. The guys hurried out after me.

"Is this something we should drive to do?" Barrett asked, and I shook my head no.

"I want to walk. But put the alarm on. Phoenix is distracted and Julian is out cold. I don't want to leave him unprotected."

Jer pulled out his keys and hit a button. "Armed. I hope Phoenix doesn't accidently open a window. It'll scare the shit out of Jules."

"Send him a text telling him to not open a window." That seemed sort of obvious.

Jeremy shook his head. "That'll tell him we left, and he'll want to come. You clearly don't want him to."

He was always sharp as nails. They followed me down to the lake where I turned and headed a distance more.

This was the only place I could sort through these thoughts. The only place I needed to be. "Your granny said to me once that there was always the other side of the lake. I have read a lot about it in her journals. I am thinking there will be more to read. I'm not going to spoil her keepsake for you by saying too much, but I will say that she has never been comfortable with this place."

Truthfully, it was probably the last place she wanted to die. Although her family was here so maybe she didn't care.

"Go on." Jeremy nodded. "We know that our mother's family is a problem and most likely had something to do with Phoenix's kidnapping and the death of the kids. They probably sent that text."

I nodded. "Sure. They were involved, but they didn't plan it, and they didn't do it. There is a social hierarchy. I learn it again and again. Everywhere I go." And Dina knew it was important when dealing with people. "Rosalind's family is not powerful anymore. They don't have the resources to kidnap a Lent. To make you sick, Barrett. To terrify you, Jeremy. You were little, but I bet already you were not easily scared."

Barrett winced. "That's true."

"I'm sure Rosalind's family played a role, but they didn't do this and they don't have access to phones with hidden numbers. Maybe they're smart enough, but money talks. Someone on this side of the lake is involved. You know all of them, but you don't really know them. They invite you to visit because they hardly see you. They know us. We have to know them. Phoenix is still trying to figure out how to survive this, and ultimately, he has to be able to do what he needs to do to make peace with what he can't remember. That doesn't mean it's his battle to fight alone. I'm here. You're here." I touched my chest. "Jules is here when he wakes up. They know us. We need to know them. When we look hard enough, we'll know. Your parents think it's her family. Again, I'm sure they play a part, but they can't see the forest for the trees because this side of the lake are their friends. But they weren't Dina's friends. They're not."

Jeremy touched my cheek. "You're just back a week. What you're saying makes sense. But maybe we wait to do it until you are feeling better."

I wasn't going to be left in the house when I knew I could help. "I'll tell you if I can't do it."

I already knew that I could.

❧ 10 ❧

Barrett leaned over and kissed me. He wasn't wrong, it was cold out, but the way it made his lips feel cold, even frost kissed, was perfect. When he was finished, Jeremy did the same. It was like we were sealing the deal among us. We were going to get some answers. I was sick of being victimized and that had to mean that they were well and truly done with it.

Jeremy cupped my cheeks. "We love you so much. I wish this didn't have to be your battle, too."

"My battles have become yours, why shouldn't yours be mine?"

Barrett stroked my hair. "That is really beautiful. Sounds almost like a marriage vow. Since Jer apparently introduced that topic."

"Months and months ago." I grinned.

Barrett groaned. "You have no game."

"I don't need it with my Princess."

I wasn't quite done with what we had to talk about. "We aren't going to hide this from Phoenix. We're not lying to each other." I cleared my throat. "Ever."

Barrett nodded. "Okay. There's another vow. He's going to hate it."

"We're going to start with Sam's family. Who is this dude hearing all his secrets? Low key, if he turns out to be part of this, I am going to be so disappointed in life."

Well... maybe more disappointed.

※

MARCH 1ST 1967

WE OPENED. *And we had a crowd. What a day it was. Actually, what a week it has been. If I thought we'd get into a routine and be settled after it opened, I was wrong. I've never been so busy. I am in charge of all of the female salespeople. They call me Mrs. Lent and think that I am just Nathaniel's wife. Some of them make passes at Robert, Ed and Victor. Right in front of me.*

It's hard. I never considered the subject of other women and their interest in who they think are eligible men. I suppose I will get used to it. Robert thinks it's funny that it makes me worried.

"I only have eyes for you, Dina. I only ever will. The Lents love once."

My father only had eyes for my mother, I think.

I am not pregnant, and it is bothering me more and more.

DL

※

"HEY," Phoenix said with a small smile, catching my attention. "It's two in the morning."

Was it? I glanced around. Barrett and Jeremy had plopped

down beside me after our walk, which had stretched on for some time after they agreed to my plan. I wanted to read just a little bit more. Now they were both asleep on the couch. Jeremy wasn't snoring. Perhaps that was why I didn't notice.

I rubbed my eyes. "Find the owner of that phone?"

"No, it's well hidden."

That was not surprising. I'd talk to him about it in the morning. I touched Jeremy's face and he roused quickly. "What's going on?"

"Bed. Upstairs."

He nodded before he rose and hugged Phoenix. I wasn't sure I'd ever seen Phoenix so surprised, but still half-asleep, Jeremy stumbled away and up the stairs, presumably to make his way to my bedroom. Barrett was so great about always waking me up gently or carrying me around. Unfortunately, I couldn't do the same for him.

I kissed his cheek. "Let's go sleep upstairs."

He sort of nodded but didn't move. Phoenix grinned. "Am I this hard to wake?"

"Yes." I grinned back. "Come on, Barrett. Up. We'll go to warm beds."

Finally, he sat up and without really saying anything walked upstairs. Phoenix chased after him. "I don't want him to fall."

That was probably smart. I turned off the light in the living room and set the alarm by the door. We were about to potentially poke a bear. I didn't want it catching us unaware.

By the time I got to the room, they had all taken their spots. Jeremy was on the bed with Julian while Barrett and Phoenix were on the other one. It was quiet. Dark. This was my happy place. The way that they breathed. The way that room felt full with them in it.

I stood in the door and stared at them. Dina loved her husbands. She worked with them. Obviously at some point she had gotten pregnant and had a family with them. And she had lived for two decades without them.

The thought almost brought me to my knees. I'd lived four months and I didn't want to go a day more.

None of them were awake. Even Phoenix had seemed to go right to bed. I stepped into the room and stopped. In the back of my mind, I could feel the way the air had felt sticky in the place where I had been held.

My first nights I had been in solitary. Drugged. Sick. Crying. Oh wow. I took some deep breaths. I wasn't there now. I was here. But... that was still there. I wiped at the tears silently leaving my eyes.

I was going to die there, and I'd had no idea because I was a big fucking dumbass.

I sank to the floor, my back to one of the dressers and pressed my face to my knees. This was my safe place, but my stomach was cramping. It hurt. But that was okay because everything hurt. No that wasn't true. I tried to breathe again. Why was it so hard sometimes just to do that? Dina was dying. Tears rushed, silent. At least I wouldn't wake them with my freakout. My mother had died and now Dina was going to. My father before any of them. I couldn't remember him. The girls were all going to die. They were so alive. Maybe some of them were dead.

My mind raced and my chest hurt. I just stayed like that. Why wouldn't it stop?

"Alatheia." Jules' voice reached me, and I lifted my head. "What are you doing down here, Baby?" He wasn't whispering but he was quiet. "Was I keeping you up?"

I put my head in my hands. "Didn't make it to bed. Can't make my head stop."

"Oh, I see."

There was light from the window. Early morning light but it was there. I had never been to bed. How much time had passed? He took off my shoes and laid me next to him on the bed between him and the still-sleeping Jeremy.

He pulled me against his chest. "I don't know if this will help or not, but if you're going through it, then I am going through it with you."

That was really sweet. His heartbeat was steady. Actually, it did help. I tried to match my breath to his as he ran his hands through my hair. I didn't know if he was going to want to talk. But, I was just done. Listening to his heartbeat, I finally managed to shut off my mind as the day ended.

"Shit." Phoenix's voice woke me. His voice sounded rough. "Guys, it's two in the afternoon. I slept like twelve hours."

"You did." Julian squeezed me. "But she was still up at six having a panic attack. I would have been okay with her sleeping all day."

He might have been, but I wasn't.

"Really?" Jeremy rubbed my back. "Why?"

I lifted my head and forced my eyes open. "You know, life."

He laughed, kissing the back of my neck. "Sure."

I put my head back down. It was too hard. I was basically sprawled on top of Julian. He rubbed his hand in a circle. This couldn't be comfortable for him. Had he been awake the whole time I had been like this?

"Are you okay?" I asked him.

"Never better. It's usually Jer or Barrett who get to comfort you. I got to do it. Feel lucky."

How sad was it that there was a running list of who got to talk me through being not okay?

Phoenix got off the bed. "Tell Dr. Trevor tomorrow. It's not surprising. We're going through a lot. That being said, I am sorry that happened. You can wake me, too. I know I haven't traditionally been the person to comfort you, but I can be."

Okay. I had to move, if for no other reason than to pee and change my pad. When I finally did move, I saw that Barrett was watching me with hooded eyes. He was worried. I didn't blame him. In his shoes I'd worry about me too. I had to pull it together. Their grandmother was dying.

"Um, listen, Phoenix and Julian, last night I kind of had an idea and came up with a plan. We went for a walk and talked about it."

Phoenix looked at Julian. "While I was working and he was snoring?"

"Yes."

Julian groaned. "I can go see if I can get it stopped."

I put my hand on his arm. "Don't worry about that. Really. Unless it's because something is wrong."

"What's the plan?"

I held up my hand. "Barrett can you tell them? I have to pee."

"Go." He nodded. "Sure."

I hurried into the bathroom and closed the door. As quickly as I could I made my way through some kind of cleaning routine. I would need to shower that night. I changed the pad and was glad that the amount of blood was minimal. Maybe it would be over soon. I wasn't cramping right then at all.

I needed to change my clothes for whatever we were doing next.

I came out and they all turned to me.

"Did something about Sam give you the impression he's not to be trusted?"

Phoenix met my gaze. He wasn't happy. That much I could understand entirely. I held up my hand. "No. I don't trust anyone, except the four of you, really. And Dina." There

I had said it. "But I get that you trust him. So, let's get to know him and then we can cross him and his family off the list of the co-conspirators." I frowned. "I mean it's either this or we go to the other side of the lake and try there. The thing is no one is inviting us to dinner there."

He groaned. "Okay. We'll clear Sam today. Then maybe we can enlist his help. He knows even more people than we do." Phoenix ran a hand through his hair. "Everyone shower. Then we're getting Altheia a phone. By then my friend will be home from school. The right time to drop in for a visit."

That was right. It was absolutely normal for most people to be in school right now. Well, people my age. I had completely blanked on real life.

That was so... strange and not okay.

Barrett kissed my forehead. "It's a good plan. Who's after Sam's family?"

I blinked. "Dr. Trevor. I mean arguably that's insane. His son died. But, my family tried to have me killed and I was surrounded by people who had the same fate. It would be kind of sick if he was basically taking our confessions in his office and plotting at home."

Phoenix laughed. "No wonder you're a writer. Yes, it would be. Okay. This is going to work out where we get to clear people right away. After that may be more complicated. Start compiling who has invited you places." A thought dawned on me. "The nurse. The one who was really mean to Phoenix and shitty to me. Where does she come from?"

Jeremy frowned. "I hate her. The other side."

"Then there is our in. Later."

Julian pointed at me. "No more plotting while I'm asleep."

If this was my normal, I was incredibly grateful for it. Well, everything except the panic attack or whatever that was.

"We need to see Dina, too."

They all nodded. Okay. A shower. That was first.

◈

AFTER EATING, we all piled into Barrett's car. This time I was in the back between the twins. "Where did you get this car?"

"Stephen bought it for him when we first got down here. We actually considered shipping his car from the Hamptons down here. That didn't seem to make a lot of sense on these roads and with this weather." Julian smiled at me. He was bright-eyed despite the fact that he'd had to spend the night uncomfortably because of me. Or rather the morning.

"Is that what happened?" Phoenix laughed. "I didn't remember."

I hadn't been in the town yet. After a long drive down a two-way highway, we arrived. Barrett parked the car, and we got out. Jeremy nodded left. "This way. The store is over there."

Given that this whole area was basically a hiding place for families who lived the way the Lents did, it was crazy how this small town was so normal looking. Hair salon. A drug store. A place to get cell phones. A bakery. A grocery store. A place for kids to take karate and ballet. Even something that was called The Shack and smelled like barbecue and spices.

"Is that good?" I asked them, and Phoenix nodded.

"It's great. Let's go there soon. When we're not having to investigate our neighbors."

We walked toward the store with the cell phones, and I tried to take all of this in. "It's like we're on a different planet from Manhattan."

The brick storefronts stood charmingly along the side-walk. The bakery had a maroon awning, the scent of freshly baked bread. Next to it, the pharmacy's green awning stretched over the entrance, followed by the grocery store just beyond—another green awning marking the way in. "The Shack" stood beside them, its black awning giving it a slightly understated presence that seemed to illustrate it was a restaurant, not a shop.

Further ahead, I noticed a building with a sign reading "Coalition," its clean, simple lettering standing out against the brick. What was in there? Parked cars lined the curb. A single streetlamp stood near the bakery. Barrett had parked us in a lot down the way. A small place out of time in some ways.

Phoenix turned around to walk backward, staring at me. "Hey, guess what? I forgot to tell you."

I blinked. "What?"

"You are making a lot of money. I opened you a bank account. First thing I did when I got out of the clinic. Anyway, you're earning. Sending you the link and your login. You can get the app on your phone. So... you don't have to wait for your inheritance."

My mouth fell open. "Phoenix, you did. How did you?"

"Anything is possible. I promise you that." His smile was huge.

That reminded me. "Which one of you did *The Poor Relation*?" I hadn't thought about it at all. Not in the days I'd been back. I wasn't even sure how I would get it started again. I needed to feel Gretchen and right then whatever let me do that was just a blank. Nothing.

"Phoenix and I did it together." Julian smiled. "What did you think?"

"I only saw the one episode, and I was sort of shocked to see it. I don't remember thinking anything except being stunned. I had... well, you know I had sort of given up on us and then I couldn't really understand why you'd do it. But I commented because it just felt like I absolutely had to."

Barrett nudged me with his shoulder. "You won't have reason to give up again. We'll always be where you can reach us. On that note, when my father says that we have to go back to New York and we tell him no that doesn't work for you right now, don't say you don't have to be part of the decision making. You have to be part of the decision making. Okay?"

I sighed. I'd totally forgotten I'd done that. "I think I must be broken."

"We all are." He smiled at me. "But we're putting ourselves together, all of us together. We'll crack here and there but not shatter. Okay?"

I loved that. "Okay."

We reached the outside of the store and Phoenix took my hand, pulling me to the side. "Give us one second and we'll be right in."

"Sure." Jer smiled. "Just don't abscond with her. Okay?"

"Oooh." Phoenix laughed. "SAT word."

His blond-haired brother gave him the finger, and they all walked into the store.

I turned to Phoenix. "What's up?"

He cupped my cheeks. "I just wanted to tell you what yesterday meant to me. I... I know the whole day took a turn because of the horror of what is happening with Granny, but I want you to know that I never expected that and I love you. I just love you.'

I kissed him. He caught his breath like he was surprised before he kissed me back. I really had to do more to initiate physical contact since clearly my doing so was startling.

Finally, I pulled back. "It meant a ton to me, too. So much. I love you."

He nodded. "Just had to say that. Come on, Jeremy probably has your phone set up already."

In the two minutes we had been outside? I did love how quickly the Lents were able to accomplish things.

"You know I wouldn't do this for other people but your

people are from here." An older woman spoke to Jerem y with her eyebrows raised. "And we would like you back. So, if I do this will you move back?"

Jeremy smiled at her. It was his most charming smile. I'd seen it whenever he meant to get what he wanted from strangers. It wasn't his real smile, and I was glad he had never used it on me. When we'd been strangers he had mostly scowled.

"I can't promise that. You know it's not just about me. The whole family has to decide. And besides, I don't know if my girl likes it here enough to stay."

This landed her attention on me. I swallowed. Yep, Jer had just done that on purpose. I stepped toward him. "Hello. Everything okay with the phone?"

"Sure. Ms. Mabel isn't sure she wants to give me the extra line on the account." He smiled again. "But she does. I know she does."

She waved her finger at Jeremy. "Oh you. Yes, I will. I was trying to convince him to move back here with you. You're Alatheia. Everyone is all abuzz with you. Thinking after all those generations the Lents might come home. We have long memories here. It's easier to be us here than anywhere else you could go. You don't have to hide here."

"I know that's true." This was an opportunity. The woman started to type, and I decided to pretend I could do what Dina did with people sometimes. I could get her to tell me something I wanted to know. "I'm just not sure I would fit in. Are people friendly here?"

Jer shot me a look. He really had no idea what I was doing. That was fine. If he didn't want to play along, no problem, he just couldn't get in my way of doing it.

Mabel lifted her head. "Oh absolutely. So friendly here. Lots of girls your age."

My knit cap itched, but I wasn't going to take it off right

then. Maybe I was overwearing it. "Have you known all the families here long?"

"Oh yes. I've known the Lents and their friends for a long time."

I turned to Jeremy and then back to her. "How many groups of friends are there?"

"Oh well, there are the Lents. The Trevors, of course. Their neighbors, the Walters. The Reeds. The Cardeauxs." She shook her head. "I don't need to tell you about all of that. They come up for visits every year."

Sure. The visits that were supposed to set the boys up. Ding. Ding. Ding. Like a bell going off in my head.

She handed me my phone in a box and rattled off instructions. Barrett came over and squeezed my hand. He'd followed that. He knew just what I was thinking. Who had been there who hadn't lost children? Had any of the families not gone?

I smiled at her. "Thanks."

We exited and Jeremy shook his head. "What was that about?"

"She just made a connection we should have made. About who was there that night when Phoenix was taken. The families that were there. Only two of them lost children. Would have been three if Phoenix hadn't survived."

"Look, I think it's possible someone could set their own kid up to die. I'd never have thought that until recently, but it's possible."

Barrett nodded. "Let's assume it's not them. I mean, maybe last resort? The Trevors were destroyed, from what I remember. So were the Reeds. But the Reeds didn't make it. They broke up. They're not here anymore. That's very, very unusual, Alatheia. Divorce is almost non-existent in this community."

I was going to take the Reeds off the list then. They didn't plot a kidnapping and then break up. "Did they ever ask for ransom?"

Phoenix sighed. "No. So they took us to torture us and torture our families. And kill us. Punishment. Hatred. I don't know." He rocked on his feet. This was making him uncomfortable. "We wouldn't have to play detective if I could just remember."

"Banging your head against that is pointless." Barrett touched his arm. "Trauma does what trauma does. You've already made huge strides this year."

"Thanks for that." He rubbed his eyes. "Thing is... the last two nights I'm wondering if I do actually remember something. It's just a sense, more like a scent."

Why hadn't he said anything? "Phoenix?"

"Bourbon. It's the scent of bourbon. Drenched in it. I never could... stand alcohol. With everything I do to myself? I don't drink. I think... I think that whoever had us, they were drenched in it."

We stared at him like he'd dropped a bomb. That was huge. I remembered when we first all got together the guys had said that Phoenix didn't drink. I'd never thought to ask why. He did all kinds of drugs. Why not alcohol?

Well... maybe there was a reason that hadn't been on his list of poisons.

Jer's phone rang and he physically jolted. He blinked. "An actual call? What kind of spam this time?" He grabbed it. "Huh. Might be a real number. Not an area code I know, but it doesn't say potential spam." He frowned.

"Pick up the call or don't." Julian rolled his eyes. "Don't make a thing."

Jeremy answered it and then widened his eyes. "Can I tell her who's calling?" He was quiet for a moment before he motioned for me to take the phone. "It's Sally."

Sally? I grabbed the phone.

❧ 11 ❧

"Sally?" I spoke into the phone. Could it be possible? I'd left a message, but no one had gotten back to me anywhere I'd called yet.

"Alatheia," she squeaked. "It is you. My father, he mumbled something and gave me a number. I wasn't sure the name he gave, it was close but not right. How are you?" She sounded almost frantic.

It was ridiculously good to hear her voice. "I'm okay. How are you?"

"I've been so worried about you. The way your boyfriend carried you out." Barrett. Okay. It made sense that she thought it was my boyfriend. "And he had his brothers and all those men. You had a whole hoard of people come get you. They were yelling. Demanding doors opened, and the head-mistress did it. She was actually doing it. Then we got cleared out and sent home. I felt so sick. So sick."

Right. She'd had to go through withdrawal too. Everyone did. Maybe not as much as I did because I had the drugs in solitary. But, we'd all been dosed every week. I'd had so much help. It sounded like Sally had none.

"Me too, but I... Sally, listen, I have to talk to you, and it's serious. I heard that no one really left that place. Not ever. They didn't get to go when they turned eighteen. They were killed. I know my family wants to kill me. Is there... is there any reason your family might want to kill you?"

She was going to holler or hang up. That's what any rational person would do. But she was silent. Then when she spoke again she whispered. "Yes. Wow. I thought I might be crazy."

"You're not. Why? I mean for me it's money." I couldn't expect her to share if I didn't.

"My grandmother left me money. A lot. I mean we're not rich, but she was. I get it when I'm eighteen." Her voice shook. "Oh. What the fuck? What the everloving fuck? They were going to kill me. Oh my god. I have to get out of here. This is my number. Text or call me. I don't know where I'll be, and at some point I'll have to ditch this phone."

"Sally." I tried to stop her, but she was already gone.

I stared at the phone before I looked up at the guys. "Well, she wasn't... um surprised. She's running."

"She's running?" Julian stared at me wide-eyed. "Where?"

"I don't know. Honestly." I swallowed through the lump in my throat. "All the care you guys have given me, all the help in the hospital, and the therapy and the love, she hasn't had any of that. She's alone." I pulled at my knitted cap. "With her head shaved." That was a small thing, but for me it had come to represent a lot. "Running for her life now." I stared at them. "Is everything always about money?"

Barrett nodded. "Ninety percent of the time everything in life is about money. Ten percent of the time it's something else."

"I can't do anything for her. I don't even know where she's going."

Phoenix drew me to him. It was cold out and after my

phone call I was feeling it more acutely. He was warm. "She'll call back and then we'll see if we can help her. Text her from your phone when we get home with your number in case you aren't with Jeremy when she gets in touch."

"I don't know if I could have survived it without you guys. How did she?"

With his warm lips, Phoenix kissed my head. "You could have. You're so strong."

I wasn't. I kept trying to be, but inside... I was just a wreck.

WE SAT with Dina while she slept. Eventually, each of the guys had something they had to go do. They all had jobs for their fathers, and Phoenix wanted to go skate to clear his head. But I sat with her, which gave her companion a break. Technically, I was supposed to be that, but I was pretty sure at this point that had all been a ruse to just get me to do her journals. The lovely woman had just wanted to save me from a fate I wasn't sure I could really be saved from.

So, I read them. That was the least I could do. The very least.

APRIL 1ST 1967

THE WEATHER IS BEAUTIFUL TODAY. Mild. In the 70s. My father would have loved this weather. My mom liked it hotter. Funny, I can think about them in little bursts now without wanting to weep or crawl into bed. I think they would be proud of me, for getting away from my uncle, for doing things with myself day in and day out. They were busy, smart, studious—yes, that's a funny word but that is what they were, future me, in case you've forgotten—and they would like that I was being that way. Even if they'd thought I would have a more studious life than I am actually having and they'd be sort of shocked that I am eighteen and married.

I wondered while I folded shirts this week what they would make of my life. Of my being in the Life. I will capitalize it because it seems the thing to do. My father was a very open-minded person. He would have found it fascinating that this has existed in plain sight for so long. That people, even people who left the Life, seem happy to protect it. He might not be thrilled I was living a life where I had to lie to everyone.

Last night, as I cuddled with Victor and he did that thing I love so much where he played with my hair, he asked me if I was unhappy, if I wanted to go back to Louisiana where we could just be without worry about what others might think or say. I told him no. I didn't want to go back there. It was scary to me. The longer I'm away from the place the more I'm glad that I left it. I don't think a single person there tells the truth ever. They lie to themselves. I can't say that to my Lents. They don't hate it like that. They want their kids to spend summers there and to visit for holidays, to sometimes have some of those people here in our home—our safe home that I have painted red.

Oh how I am going on tonight.

Kids. I am once again not pregnant.

The store is booming and that is something, especially since my husbands have all started to notice that they can't do it without me. I'm so good at handling the floor that Nathaniel doesn't have to come out anymore at all and can concern himself with things in the back office, which he prefers greatly.

I watch the women who come in, the young wealthy women who shop at our place. I'm grateful for their business, but I can't imagine being them. It's not like they went and participated in the Be In Central Park last week. Maybe it was more than just last week, maybe it was two weeks? I'm losing time.

I need to go to bed. Our days start very early.
DL

૭౫ఄ

I ROSE FROM MY CHAIR, listening to the whoosh of the IV in her arm that was delivering whatever medicine kept her comfortable. How had this happened so fast? Four months ago she seemed fine. Maybe the key word was seemed.

On quiet feet I walked over to where someone had placed her framed pictures. They were close enough she could see them if she looked in that direction. I'd never seen them before so they must have been in her bedroom in Manhattan, her private sanctum I had never visited because it hadn't seemed inappropriate.

There she was as a young woman standing in front of Lents. She wore a suit that showed her legs, and her hair was cutely fashioned with a clip. She had one hand on her hip, and she smiled brightly. I'd never seen the department store she spoke of in her journals. But there it was. On the frame was written 1967 so it wasn't far off from where I'd been reading. That was amazing.

I looked at the other photos that stood there. She held a baby in one but looked a great deal older. She smiled at the camera. The frame had been labeled. Dina and Stephen. 1985. He was the third oldest. They'd all been a year apart. That had made her thirty-six. She kept mentioning not being pregnant. That wasn't going to happen for her for some time. She'd said twenty years one time when we spoke, but it wasn't quite that. Maybe she rounded up.

She held a blond-haired little boy and pointed at the sky in another picture. Dina and Kit. 1989. He looked to be about six or seven. The next one was Dina kissing a toddler. There was no label to indicate the year, but it said Dina and Eric.

He had curly hair. The last one was a young man holding up a ribbon, and she had her arm around him. Dina and Daniel. What had he won? She had obviously been very proud.

The next row was different. The first one read Store 2, Dina and the Boys. It was Dina with who had to be her husbands. All four of them smiling at the camera. 1969. So they had really moved fast. Maybe that was because Nathaniel had been allowed to just work the back office thanks to her help. The second one had Rosalind in a wedding dress. She was twenty years old. Blonde and gorgeous. Dina had her arm around her, she wore dark blue and they were both grinning. And the last one had her with my Lents—to steal a phrase from her journal. They were babies. Or at least Phoenix was. He had chubby cheeks and a big smile. Jeremy and Julian wore matching outfits on both her sides, a blue sailor kind of a look and Barrett stood grinning next to her. It read, My Precious Loves.

Okay. The tears started, and I wiped them away. She and I would never have a photo together, and it was stupid to even think about that. She'd only have known me for seven months or so when all was said and done. I wasn't that important in her story. Even if she was going to be huge in mine.

A hand touched my arm, and I managed not to gasp. It was Rosalind. She smiled at me. In a low voice, she spoke, "I used to love to go into her room and see all her photos. I'm not surprised she picked these to bring. She has shelves full of them in her room at home. These are all so early. Except the boys." She lifted up that frame and stared at her sons. What did she remember when she looked at that? It would be ten years before her life would blow up and change to almost unrecognizable. Rosalind set it down. "She used to keep them so we could have date nights. It was such a gift. I don't know if I appreciated it enough at the time. I think I was selfish and thought it was just what grandmothers should do or something. My own mother—well, may be best left unsaid. Anyway, when I look back I should have been dropping to my knees in thanks to Dina."

"Well that would have been awkward." Dina's voice made us both jump and then Rosalind laughed.

"Leave it to you to hear that." She took her mother-in-law's hand. "Did I say thank you enough?"

Dina waved her hand. Even like this, she was still Dina. "More than." Rosalind laughed as we both turned around. From her bed, Dina spoke again. "You have always been lovely to me. Always."

She shook her head. "Let's face it, I haven't been much of a mother. Thank god the boys had you." Rosalind adjusted herself next to the bed. As I had done so many times in my life, I observed from the outside. "It's too late now for me to mother them. I wish I had let myself fall apart earlier. If that had happened, maybe I could have been able to handle things better. Without you? Honestly there isn't a day that goes by that I'm not grateful."

She smiled and sat up a bit. "I thought I would be stronger today. Listen to me, the boys may not need you to mother them anymore, but that doesn't mean that there isn't somebody who could use a little mothering."

They stared at each other for a second. Who did she mean? I wasn't usually dense, but I absolutely had no idea.

Rosalind turned in her chair. "Come sit, Alatheia. I interrupted your time. Join us. Please."

On leaden feet—the kind that only came from wondering if I wasn't really welcome—I sat by Dina's bedside.

She met my gaze. "Is that my journal?"

"Yes, I'm trying to read them more quickly. I'll type it tonight."

Dina lifted her brows. "You know what I would love? Can

you read me some of it? What I wrote? Can you? Maybe that would make me feel like they were here?"

My heart sank. "I would love to more than anything. You may not know this but one of the things about me is that I'm very dyslexic. I can't read aloud. Not unless I practice a lot beforehand. I really won't be able to."

Rosalind let go of Dina's hand to squeeze mine. "That must be so stressful. In school, I mean. And you had that awful teacher, Ms. Collins. She's gone now. I heard that in the school's parent group. Let go permanently."

"Was that your doing? Or one of you?" It seemed kind of random to have happened otherwise.

"I wish it were us. I think Barrett had Daniel working on it. But I think it was the Monks. I think... I think they are taking some ownership of you before you even get there. That's something you'll want to think about. If I can help you navigate that, let me know. Dina would be better. I am here. Dina helped me navigate everything."

I stared at our joined hands. Rosalind had cursed in what sounded like Cajun the day she had thrown me out of the Hamptons. Out of everyone, she seemed to want me around the least.

"You called me a charity case," I managed to say. This was probably not the time and place. I couldn't seem to control myself. "In the Hamptons. I... I have been pretty sure you don't really like me."

Dina sat up further. "Oh how awful."

Tears shone in Rosalind's eyes. "I am so sorry, Alatheia. I do like you. I should not have said that, and it's terrible that you had to hear it. I apologize. Dina was so much more welcoming to me than I have been to you. I am constantly so afraid, so worried about strangers coming to hurt us. That's part of what I have been attempting to deal with. I have no excuse. Please accept my apology."

I supposed I could understand that. Given everything she'd lived through. How could she not be wary? "I don't... I don't want anything from your sons except their love. I'm after nothing."

"I know that." Her voice was low. "I am so sorry."

"I forgive you." I answered her. It was enough already. "Maybe you could read Dina's journal to her."

She looked at her mother-in-law. "Would that be okay with you?"

"Yes." She smiled at both of us but winced.

"Are you in pain?" I could get someone for her.

"Always a little bit and then it gets worse. Now is fine. I may fall asleep. You'll forgive me?"

Rosalind squeezed my hand tighter which was the only sign that she wasn't okay. "Rest when you need to."

I handed her the journal, and she opened it up to the page I indicated.

After a second, Rosalind nodded. "March 16th 1968."

"Wait." I stopped her. "That's a jump of a year. It was just April 1967."

Dina did her wave. "I started and stopped a lot. You know how it is? Days pass and you think maybe none of what you're doing is very interesting. Then I would come back to it again for a while. Can you imagine if I wrote every day since 1966?"

I would have loved that. Every day of her thoughts although I supposed that made sense from a real-life perspective. Who would want to read my thoughts? I didn't even want to think them most of the time.

Rosalind started again. "March 16th 1968. Well, I have decided to write again. Truthfully I haven't had any reason to put my thoughts down lately." In Rosalind's southern drawl, Dina's journals sounded much more sophisticated than my own voice in my head. "The store is doing well. So well that Nathaniel and Ed think we can open a second store in a year.

They have been looking at property. Oh, and Robert has grown a mustache. I hate it. But I don't dare tell him. He is so proud of that mustache. The other thing about us all doing so well financially is that we are taking a vacation. Well, their version of a vacation. I might like to see the Grand Canyon."

Dina laughed. "Still haven't."

Rosalind returned her grin and then kept reading. "But we are instead going to Louisiana to see their mother. I am not kind, but I don't like their mother, and I doubt I ever will." Her daughter-in-law lifted her head. "Oof." That was obviously not part of the journal. Dina would never say oof.

"I wish I could say I was hard on her, but I wasn't. I may have been too kind."

I loved how Dina sounded like herself when she said that.

Rosalind went back to reading. "Her initial support of my husbands' absence has waned. She wants them home. She doesn't care what we're doing here in New York, and she basically blames me for their not returning. Of course they left before they ever knew me but that is neither here nor there to her. They aren't where she wants them. She will not come and visit. She has no real idea of the store that we are devoting ourselves to and does not wish to know anything about it. She simply knows that I have not had a baby, something that she feels I should have done by now. I have seen a doctor. No one knows why I'm not pregnant. It breaks my heart. Not that I intend to discuss that with her. If I did, she would just wish harder they had married someone else."

Rosalind leaned forward. "Little did you know how many kids you were going to have in such a short period of time. Boom. Boom. Boom. We share that experience."

"We do."

Rosalind turned to me. "Don't ever feel pressure to reproduce from me, Alatheia. That is none of my business."

"I can't imagine kids. I'm barely functioning."

They both laughed like I'd said something funny. I was being dead serious but that was okay. Maybe I'd been unexpectedly funny. A noise caught my attention and Phoenix came in. After leaning his skateboard against the wall, he walked over to us and sat on the floor next to me, putting his head in my lap. Dina smiled at him, and he gave her one back.

After a second, Rosalind started reading, and I gently petted Phoenix's soft brown hair. He hadn't said anything. Maybe he just wanted to listen.

"But we are going. Maybe my good breeding keeps me from really telling them how much I hate their mother. Frankly I'm not sure what they would do. At least they have no intention of moving back. I'm not sure I could tolerate it. Sure, we all pretend to be fine when we're down there, but we really aren't. That other side of the lake. They hate us. I knew it when we visited, but I said nothing. Not even in here. They hate us. They are as much in the Life as the rest of us, and that isn't going away. I think distance is all that can keep us safe. That kind of hate? It always needs an outlet. Of that I am sure. But I had better finish up here. There is an actual war waging in this world not just the one in my head. D.L."

Rosalind looked up, and I followed her gaze. Dina had fallen asleep. In a quick moment, the boys' mother wiped at her eyes. "She was right. So right." With a sad smile she handed me back the book. "I love that you have them. I know you're typing them up. But hold on to the journals, too, okay? If you don't want to, I will keep them. They are a treasure."

They really were. Phoenix rose quietly and kissed his granny's cheek. "If you're still up for it and want to go to Sam's, we should do that now."

I was. Yes, that sounded like a good idea. "Rosalind, I would love any help you can give with the Monks."

She seemed to brighten with that. "How about lunch tomorrow? We never did have lunch."

"Tomorrow is therapy. Next day?"

She nodded, fast. "Next day."

Phoenix grabbed his skateboard and led me from the house. I still held onto her journal. "I need to take this back to the house." I wouldn't risk anything happening to it, ever.

We walked together. The wind, having picked up when I was inside, blew at my head, and I put the knit cap back on. It was cold but beautiful. Jeremy had given me my phone, and I had it in my jacket pocket. I pulled it out. He'd stored everyone's numbers in it. His entire family. And one additional—Sally's. He had that from when she called him back.

I quickly typed out a text. *Wherever you are, I hope it is beautiful.* I then took a picture of the lake. It really was pretty. Serene, even in this cold weather.

I went back inside and set down the journal on the table by the door. Upstairs, I could hear the maids working. That was maybe the first time in the course of my time with the Lents that I had ever heard them.

It took just a few seconds and then I met Phoenix back outside. He held up a helmet he must have pulled from somewhere, and he put it on my head. I grinned. "Well, that is one way to cover my hair."

"Not funny." He kissed my lips firmly. "No, this is to keep you safe. Jump on the back." Phoenix indicated his skateboard. We'd done this several times now.

I noticed he wasn't wearing a helmet. "You need a helmet."

"I have exactly one. I need to buy one. For now, your brain is more important than mine. Hold on."

I would have argued with that, but when I stepped onto his board, he took off almost instantly. The driveway was a little bit of a hill. And we flew down it, the wind hitting us like we were flying. I shrieked.

S am lived just next door but Phoenix took the long route, winding us in and out of the roads, never quite getting to the house. I held on tight and eventually, down the driveway to where I presumed we were going because Barrett's Jeep was on the driveway, we stopped. I was frozen but so happy. Almost exhilarated.

"Did you pick me because you felt you had to. I mean, I know you love me now. I know you do. And you know how I love you. I am not in doubt of it. But at first? Did you take me because you thought you had to because you had fallen for my brothers?"

I stared at him, his words not registering for a second. Then they did. He had wanted to have a serious conversation. This was it. "No, of course not. I fell for you the second you threatened that PI. And then more so when you fell asleep and put your head on my lap. You snored. Oh my gosh, did you snore. You don't now. Very quiet. But you hadn't slept in who knew when and you did right there on my lap in the limo. Snored. Like you had just been waiting for my lap to sleep on forever." I couldn't close my mouth and stop talking.

It was probably too much. But Phoenix had asked. "And you have always been this mix of strong and vulnerable. So tough sometimes. So capable and then so soft inside, at least with me. Like maybe you need me too. And, Phoenix, even when you were out of it all of the time, you are so smart. Like you know so many things. I am in awe of you. Did I choose you by default? No. Absolutely not. Even if I had met you all by yourself, I would have chosen you. I'd have had a huge crush on you and never spoken to you because that is what I was doing."

"Fuck." He kissed me. Again and again and again. He had really been worried on this topic. I held on and let him. It was almost like a reclaiming, like he could do that now that he was able to let go of this worry he had that plagued him.

"Hey, I know it's easy to get lost in her lips but we're all inside visiting and it's a little weird without you." Jeremy called down the driveway and Phoenix stopped, breathing hard.

He rubbed his thumb over my cheek. "I have an addictive personality. That will not come as a surprise to you. And I need your love more than I have ever needed anything. I don't care if my level of obsession for you is unhealthy. Okay? I just do." He whispered in my ear. "I am soft inside. Love you."

We walked up the driveway together, Phoenix holding his board under his arm. When we reached Jeremy, he kissed me, quickly. "I mean, I can't blame him for taking the chance to make out with you. I would have done the same."

There were two homes up the driveway, like the Lents had. Was that normal for around the lake? I supposed I was going to find out. Samuel's family's homes stood with a kind of elegance against the soft afternoon light. I hated to think it because it felt disloyal, but they were nicer than the Lents' houses. I'd just think it. I would never, ever say it.

The first house had a broad front porch, its white railings framed the doors. The shutters were neatly aligned beside each window, painted a deep green that contrasted beautifully with the light brick exterior.

The bigger house was slightly taller, its windows reflecting the golden glow of the sun on the lake. The trees lining the street swayed slightly in the breeze, their branches casting long shadows over the sidewalk in the winter light.

Maybe it wasn't that it was prettier than the Lents' homes. Maybe it was just more readily lived in. There was a sort of coldness to the Lents' house here that hadn't been true in the Hamptons and was certainly not true in New York City. Or maybe I was projecting. I was good at that.

"Hey, Jer? " I asked him before we stepped inside of the bigger of the two houses. "Do you miss Manhattan?"

He really was a city boy. I didn't know how long he was going to hold out here. He blinked. "Yes. But I missed you more, so I'm good."

"Really? What if I can never go back?"

He kissed my temple. Wow. He smelled really good. Like sandalwood. I breathed him in. He seemed like he was doing the same to me. "You're going to be eighteen in less than a year. You can go back then for sure if we can't figure out something before."

It wasn't just me who couldn't go back right then. Phoenix was doing really well here. Did he ever want to go back? Should he?

I looked at his strong profile. Had he really thought I'd just settled for him?

He turned to me. "Alatheia." Oh, it was serious if he wasn't calling me Red. "In that scenario you gave me where you had a crush but wouldn't speak to me? Yeah, I'd never have let you not speak to me. Why do you think I stole your wallet?"

We stepped inside, my head whirling. Wow. Okay. I was going to have to mull over that. But now we were inside of Sam's house. His very big house with a big gaping chandelier. But it was the only fancy thing I could see because otherwise it looked like chaos. Happy chaos. I smiled. This was once what I had imagined having a family looked like.

Three little girls—I didn't know how old they were— ran through the house shouting, one of them holding a doll in the air like it was a prize she was protecting. The other two shrieked. In the corner, Jules and Barrett spoke to two guys I didn't know—they were probably Sam's brothers. I didn't see Sam anywhere until I spotted him across the house standing on the porch by himself.

There were three older men mi lling about— one of them seemed to be picking up toys— and I heard a woman's voice from the kitchen talking about orange juice.

Phoenix nodded toward the porch. "Be right back."

He walked quickly toward Sam, and I dropped my gaze. Whatever went on between them wasn't my business unless he proved to be some kind of liar who was involved in what had happened. But seeing this house? I doubted it. This was a happy family.

"Hey." One of the guys raised his hand to us. "Jeremy. You found her."

He put his arm around me. "I'll always find her." He looked down at me. "Even if it takes four months. I'm sorry that took so long."

"Jeremy, it's okay. I know you were doing everything you could do. It's okay to let that go."

"Maybe someday but not yet."

We walked together toward the crowd, and as we reached them, I took off my hat. It was hot inside. Just better to take it off. The whole town knew what I looked like by now or had heard.

Barrett took my hand. "Alatheia, these are Sam's older brothers. This is Jadon and Carl." He motioned to both of them. They looked a lot like Sam, same smile, same facial structure.

"Oh my gosh, what happened to your hair?" A little girl behind me shouted. It was partially a question, partially a shock.

Carl's eyes widened. "Kelly, you can't talk like that. It's not polite."

"No, it's okay." I didn't have to look at my guys; I could feel how stiff they had gotten. I needed to fix this if we were going to progress. I got down on her level. "I had it shaved. It's pretty funny looking, right?"

I wasn't going to tell this eight-year-old—at least I was pretty sure she was eight, maybe nine—what happened to my head.

She grinned and had two dimples. "Yes."

"Right. So, it's fuzzy. Want to feel it?"

Her smile broadened when she did. "Do you like it like that?"

"No but it'll grow back. That's what hair does."

That must have satisfied her because she ran back up. I stood up straight. "Hi, I'm Alatheia."

Jadon opened and closed his mouth. "Do girls like this just fall from the sky in Manhattan? Like for real? How did you manage this woman?"

"No," all three of them answered together. Julian must not have liked that because he pulled me against his side. I was happy to be there. It was a comfortable place.

"Here we are. Orange juice." A brightly smiling woman who had gray hair and kind brown eyes exited the kitchen. "Sorry this took so long. Anyone want some juice?"

The girls rushed over, and Carl shook his head. "Thanks, Mom. I think we're okay over here."

She walked over to us. "I couldn't find the juice. It was all the way in the back of the house. I swear when Seth unpacks the groceries he puts them in the most random places. Oh, I'm sorry. I am Kate, you must be Alatheia. It's so nice to meet you. Usually we come up for the summer but I guess it was canceled this year?"

Barrett nodded. "That's right. Sorry about that."

Had they canceled it? I guess maybe because we hadn't been there. They couldn't have all the kids from here there if their own weren't going to show up.

She kept talking. "I am so glad y'all finally stopped by. We look at your houses all the time and just wish you were here more. Oh, look there is Phoenix with Sam. What a blessing he has been." She met my gaze. "I mean really, I don't know what would happen to Sam now without Phoenix. It wasn't going well until he showed up."

That was interesting. Sam had been in the rehab program a month longer than Phoenix. I stared out at the porch just as Sam laughed at something Phoenix said.

"Those two. Always thick as thieves." She sighed. "When they could see each other. Why, I sometimes wonder, what would have happened if we'd been there that summer..."

"Mom," Jadon interrupted her, his cheeks turning a little pink. "Not appropriate."

Jeremy held up his hand. "It's okay. We shouldn't hide from it like it didn't happen." As I knew that was a very un-Jeremy phrase; he had to be playing along on this. "Why weren't you there? Remind me. I don't remember. Most of that time is a blur."

She grabbed his arm. "Of course it is. My mother had been very sick for a year. And she died that week. We were with her."

As they couldn't have faked that, I took a deep breath. I mean if I wanted to really go down a conspiracy hole I could say that they had used that as a way to not be there, but that was just getting out of hand. This woman wasn't a mastermind of Phoenix's kidnapping and the death of children. Her husbands, who I hadn't met, were running about cleaning, and everyone laughed.

I didn't know what had happened with Sam. That wasn't my business unless he shared. But, they weren't it.

She caught her breath. "And you all stopped coming."

Yes they had. They'd wanted Phoenix and Walter and River dead. Or at least three kids that were there and those were the ones who ended up getting taken. Why? Who had it out for those families? Not this one for sure.

Carl cleared his throat. "So seriously where do we go to find our Alatheia, because I just can't with the women we know here."

"There's no one like Alatheia. " Julian kissed my head. "Yours will show up. Assuming they want to put up with you."

That made everyone laugh. I didn't have an answer, but it was a nice visit. And at least I knew Sam was safe for Phoenix. As much as anyone was for anyone else.

※

I LAY in bed listening to the guys breathe. I couldn't sleep. Barrett breathed deeply. He was actually closer to the window when he usually slept on the other side. Phoenix was out cold where Barrett would usually be. His face was scrunched up. I couldn't sleep and he was having a nightmare.

I ran my hands through his soft locks. "It's just a dream. You're safe."

"They're going to take me to the dark place." He shook his head.

I hated this nightmare. He had it a lot. I blinked. They were going to take him to the dark place? Why hadn't I focused on it before? Well, because usually it was about someone trying to take me to the dark place. And it was just about trying to comfort Phoenix. But what was this dark place?

I didn't want him to get stuck in this dream. But was the dark place... the play? It wasn't like I could coax him to tell me. It was just something to think about. I moved to face him. "Hey Phoenix, just a dream. It's over. That time is over. You're here with me."

His eyes opened to slits before immediately closing again, but he didn't look like he was in pain. That was good. How often did that happen when I didn't know? He worried about so many things. Did the others?

This time I turned to Barrett. He wasn't having trouble sleeping. You would think after the night I'd had the night before not sleeping that tonight I could. I flopped onto my stomach. This just fucking sucked. Was this going to be a thing now?

I had therapy first thing in the morning. My pillow was hot. I flipped it over to the cooler side. Barrett tugged me to him, not awake. My flopping was probably bothering him. I scooted out of the bed and walked into the bathroom. Quickly, I used it, making note that my spotting had stopped. Most of the cramping had too.

I didn't want to wake anyone. It wasn't like I needed help. They couldn't turn off my brain. I walked through the house, touching things as I went. I still hadn't seen Barrett, Julian, or Jeremy's rooms. I wasn't going to go in and just enter without their permission. They'd tell me it was fine, only it wasn't. It was kind of rude.

When I got downstairs, I flipped on the light in the living room and grabbed the journal from where I had left it.

MAY 1ˢᵗ 1968

WELL, we are at the Lake. Maybe that is a good thing. It feels like the world has exploded. Since the last time I wrote, Martin Luther King has been assassinated. Is everything going to blow up? I have to write it here because I find that if I start to get too low, my husbands get very concerned. If it's possible to over care about someone's mood, they do when it comes to me. But oh how I love them. I love them enough to come to this place and be insulted by their mother every other minute.

I wish that was an exaggeration.

Nathaniel has noticed and started to stop her. He keeps trying to talk to me about it but there are some things it's just better to keep inside. At least for me. Lately when I sleep I am dreaming about my uncle. I haven't seen him since I ran away. It's doubtful I would run into him, so I would love to know why I am thinking about him at all.

Ed took me rowing on the lake. It is beautiful here. Even though I hate it. We ran into another group of boaters. One woman took one look at Ed and me and started weeping. I didn't understand it, and it wasn't until later that he sheepishly confessed that she had wanted to marry them. They'd known her their whole lives and maybe at some point one or the other of them had liked her but never for very long and promises had never been made. At least not by them. Their mothers might be a different matter.

It had to be really hard when you were expected to live this life to have what you thought would happen be ripped away from you.

When I'd asked Ed if he had liked her, he adamantly told me he never had. Maybe he's lying. I'm going to let him get away with it.

That seems like a box even Pandora doesn't want to open.

I am letting my mother-in-law think that I'm taking birth control. I'm not. But I'm not pregnant. No reason. No explanation.

Just no baby. Perhaps I'm not meant to be a mother. I don't know if I'd be a very good one.

DL

❦

I CLOSED the book as my eyes drifted closed. The couch wasn't that comfortable, but I didn't care.

❦

"HEY. " Phoenix smoothed the hair off my head. "Why did you sleep down here?"

I smiled at him. Early morning sun came through the window. "Came down to read, and I guess I drifted off."

He hugged me to him, and I breathed in the essence that was Phoenix. "Good morning."

"Good morning," he whispered in my ear. "The others aren't up yet. But it's time. You aren't sleeping well. You should tell Kirk that. He might be able to help you. In any case, he should know."

PHOENIX OBVIOUSLY DID NOT HAVE the problem I did with using Dr. Trevor's first name. He was right nonetheless. "I'll get up."

"I'll make coffee. We can have a minute like we used to at home."

That was right. Before school it was all just Phoenix and me after Barrett left. Except the one time that Julian had stayed home and Phoenix had not been happy.

"What are we going to do about school? I mean... when

they arrested me, my family had turned my whole life into proof I was a bad person. Do you think they could do that because I'm currently not in school?"

He shook his head. "They don't get a say if you're in school. That's Monk business now, and as far as I can tell, Daisy Monk is leaving it be for the moment. But we should probably just be in school because education is important. Do you want to enroll in an online school? We could do it together. Sit next to each other and not have to put up with people like Collins and crazy classmates."

I hadn't thought about my friendships from Pullman. "How are the people there that I left? Any idea?"

"No. But Jeremy might. I'm totally checked out of there right now in my mind. Pretty sure Jules is too since he is also done, and Barrett graduated. So, yeah, ask Jeremy. He just knows things."

He brewed coffee, and I sat listening to the grinding sound as the aroma filled the room.

"Hey, you two." Barrett came in rubbing his eyes. "How did I miss both of you getting up?"

"She didn't sleep with us. Found her on the couch this morning." Phoenix yawned.

I winced. "Can't sleep. I'm going to tell the doctor this morning."

Barrett drew me into a hug. "You know what I'm going to say, right?"

"Yes. Wake you. But my insomnia need not be your insomnia."

He laughed. "You sounded just like Gretchen then. Time to start the *Poor Relation* back up?"

I caught my breath. I really had. "Maybe."

The idea had been inconceivable yesterday, but maybe today... yes, maybe I would put something together later.

"The Real Deal has been aching for her. She could come home." Phoenix smiled as he handed me a coffee.

"She doesn't have a home. Not really." I sipped my coffee. That tasted good. Phoenix did know how I liked my coffee.

This was such an easy, happy moment. Barrett shrugged. "Then maybe it's time to give her one. You have one."

"She was never entirely me." I had always held that belief.

"No, she wasn't, but she was kind of you." Phoenix drank his coffee and handed one to Barrett. "She can still be the Poor Relation. She's what happens next to her."

That was something to think about for sure. There was no movement upstairs that I could hear. "The twins are really out of it."

"They are."

So out of it they continued to snore when I dressed and left the room. Barrett was waiting for me, and Phoenix sat by the window looking out, holding his coffee. "See you in a bit."

It felt weird not to say good morning or goodbye to the twins, so I shot them good morning and goodbye over texts and jumped in the car with Barrett. We got to the clinic, and he leaned over to kiss me.

When his lips met my own, I knew it wasn't going to be an easy, fast peck. No, and not because of Barrett, but because I really wanted to kiss him. I wrapped my arms around his neck and held on. Barrett quickly got the idea and caressed my mouth with his own. He sighed against me before he slipped his tongue into my mouth. It was like our tongues danced together. Barrett moaned. I loved that sound. I knew a little bit more what exactly that meant, and I loved that he felt that way.

Finally, he pulled back and sank into his seat, panting. My own heart raced. "Fuck. I mean. Thank you. I am going to be... really excited all day now." He ran his thumb down my cheek. "I love you. But if you don't get out of the car, I'm going to keep you here kissing you all day and you have to go to therapy. It's important."

I tilted my head. "Kissing you might be better therapy."

He groaned. "Go."

I bit my lip. "Soon, Barrett. Okay?"

He would know what I meant, and the intake of his breath told me he did. I meant it too, which was amazing.

The cool air bit me as I left the car, and I realized I hadn't brought my knit hat. Well, my forgetfulness was going to mean that my head was cold most of the day. I hoped Dr. Trevor could be trusted. Sam had proven to be fine. But what happened now?

And why did I think I could suddenly become Detective Alatheia? I could barely pass school.

I went inside to his office. This time I knew where I was going and didn't have to be walked. Lily had the window open and waved to me when I entered. I quickly took a seat. Was this supposed to feel this stressful? Shouldn't I be glad for therapy? What the fuck was wrong with me?

The door opened and Dr. Trevor walked in. "Alatheia, right on time. I love that. Or is that Barrett's doing? He definitely has Kit's sense of punctuality."

I smiled. "I think I'd have been early if Barrett had his way today." I'd waylaid us in the car. "But I was up on time to be here on time."

He motioned for me to come and I did. We were back in his office, and I sat down. Everything was the same. That was kind of nice.

"Today " —he sat down— " I'd like to talk to you about an idea I have for how we can progress."

Uh-oh.

❧ 13 ❧

I managed not to pull my knees up and lay my head on them. Instead, I stayed very still. "Like what?"

"You sound terrified." He didn't move. "Are you?"

I nodded. "Yes. All of this is just so scary for me. I don't know why. But I have to remember to tell you that I'm not sleeping. I had a panic attack almost all night two nights ago, and last night I just couldn't sleep. Finally read myself to sleep on the couch."

He leaned back in his chair. "That's not surprising to me. Not at all. Don't forget among other things that you have been through you are going through a drug withdrawal. Now I haven't seen any signs of you missing the injections they were giving you. Are you? You can tell me if you are."

Missing them? "I've never been so relieved to not have something in my whole life."

"Right, but for example, a drug addict might be relieved when they finally get through detox but inevitably also miss it. There are reasons for this. If you're not, it could be because what was happening to you wasn't so much an addiction as a medical trauma."

I supposed that made sense in some ways. "I'll for sure tell you if I want to use something. What I'd really like to be able to do is go to sleep."

"I'm going to suggest some things for that. But I also want to talk to you about something called EMDR. It can help people deal with trauma. I think it would be a good fit for you."

I took a deep breath. "So like dealing with the way that they took me?"

"Sure. That will come into play, but I think, don't you, that isn't the start of your trauma? Where do you think it started?"

I just wasn't sure. "There have been a lot of things I guess we could call trauma. I mean my teacher was awful to me. A girl drugged me."

He looked at me with kind eyes. "Further back. What started all of this?"

What started it? My hands started to shake. It was getting harder and harder not to do the knee thing. "Um, my mother died. I was eleven. My mother died. My dad died too, but I can't really remember. I'm blocked or something."

"That's right. We'll start with what you do know. Your mother died. And I think maybe it's time for your brain to come to terms with that."

I looked down. "I knew I was going to hate this."

"For a while, probably."

⚜

NO ONE WAS WAITING to pick me up when I came out. That was so strange. I looked at my phone and there weren't any messages. I quickly texted the group but didn't hear anything. Okay. Well... as I looked around the parking lot I realized I didn't have a lot of choices. I was going to have to walk.

It was several miles, but I'd walked longer. At least it was pretty. About a minute into my trek I really wished I had my hat. But I put my head down, grateful I had the coat Julian had gotten me. Even though it wasn't icy, the ground felt cold even through my sneakers. I should probably get some boots.

Cars passed me but none of them were Barrett in his Jeep. What bothered me more than walking—it was a good idea to get some exercise particularly after feeling like I had been trapped in the room with Dr. Trevor—was that something was wrong. No one answering their phone?

Was it Dina? It had to be Dina.

A van pulled up next to me. It was white. I gasped. What was happening? I had a very bad feeling about this. I didn't have a great history with vans. The door slid open from the inside and two hooded people rushed toward me.

Oh fuck. I was right. This was a kidnapping. Or something else bad. They rushed toward me, and I tried to run, but one of them got a hold of my arm. Okay. No, I dragged my feet. I'd never learned to fight. That was obviously a big fucking problem. I lifted my leg and kicked whoever it was right in the shin. They fought back and a second person grabbed me. No, I wasn't going easily. I wasn't. If this was related to Phoenix, or fuck, my own family, I didn't care. I wasn't. No. No. No.

I fought as hard as I could until a second set of screeching tires arrived. I didn't look up. If this was my doom, I was too busy trying to prevent it to look it in the eye.

"Hey," came the shouts. It was Barrett. Jeremy. I couldn't see. Someone grabbed me by the waist and my kicking wasn't going to help.

There were shouts and yells. Bodies in the way of the people trying to take me. Finally I was loose and the van skidded away so fast the tires screamed on the pavement.

I would have hit the ground if Jeremy hadn't caught me. "Princess. Oh my god. I've got you. Shit."

Barrett touched my cheek. "You're okay. I can't believe..."

I didn't hear what he said. I'd never been a fainter, and I had fought as hard as I could, but it was too much. I collapsed right there in Jeremy's arms. The world just went black.

I walked with my mother. She held my hand and we stared at the lake. "I would have liked it here. I wish I knew places like this existed."

This was a dream. She was long dead. Unless... I was dead? "Am I dead? I knew I would see you when I died."

She met my gaze, her green eyes so similar to mine. I must have gotten them from her. I'd never thought about it. Tricia's were the same. But they looked different.

"Do you think you're dead?"

I thought about it. No, I really didn't. "I'm dreaming."

"Okay. Sounds good." We walked again, but she stopped. "Alatheia, I ran from two of the most powerful families in Manhattan. I hid you from the world. I survived and didn't touch millions of dollars to keep you safe. I adapted and tried and tried and tried. Do you think I did all of that to overdose on drugs? Does that sound right to you?"

It really didn't. The wind picked up, blowing my hair off my face. "Is this happening because Dr. Trevor told me I haven't processed your death?"

"I don't know. You tell me."

I sat up, gasping for breath. "Hey, easy. Easy." It was Jeremy. I was still in his arms on the street.

Okay. I'd fainted. But not for very long. Barrett knelt down in front of me. He was pale and his gaze was strained, angry. At me?

"Thank fuck we got here." He looked at Jeremy. "Are you okay?"

"Are you... mad at me?"

He blinked. "What? No. I'm mad at whoever that was. And I'm terrified about what could have happened to you. We were late because we were with Granny and had our phones in our pockets and on silent. We didn't mean to be late. I am so sorry."

"This is not your fault." A thought dawned on me, and I tried to sit up. "I'm... I might be in shock, but I'm okay. But, you know what?"

Jer kept smoothing his hand over my forehead. "What? I... I can't think right now, I'm sorry. I just almost lost you."

"The second one who came out to grab me just as you got here, he stank. Like bourbon."

They both stared at me and Barrett finally spoke in a low voice. "Anyone think that's a coincidence?"

"No," Jeremy and I answered together.

He looked up at his older brother. "We have to get out of here. They told us to leave. I can't have Alatheia taken. I can't. I just can't."

"You think I can?" Barrett looked at the street. "We're always in twos. That's how this is going to go. We can't leave. The doctors are here. Granny can't be moved. She really took a turn today, Sweetheart. Afterward, we'll talk about leaving."

I shook my head. "They came for Phoenix in the Hamptons. You think that there is anywhere we could go we wouldn't be looking over our shoulders? We stay." I was the one who had just almost been taken. I had to say this. "We must be making them very nervous by simply existing here."

Barrett picked up his phone. "I'm calling Kit. Then I'm taking you two home and going back for Phoenix who is still at the clinic. None of us are walking anywhere."

Jeremy nodded and closed his eyes, leaning his head against mine. It seemed like he was taking a lot of deep breaths. Finally, he opened his eyes. "Barrett, teach me to drive this car."

"You don't have a license." We all rose as Barrett spoke, heading toward his Jeep. That was when I noticed Jeremy's hand. It was bleeding.

I took it in my hand. "You hurt yourself."

"Yeah, I guess I did. I punched one of them. I don't care that I don't have a license. Teach me, and I'll get a license later. I need to be able to get to her in a car if you're not available."

Barrett nodded. "Sure."

"Good." Jer looked me up and down. "I saw you kicking them hard. Good job. Really proud of you."

Something they said finally hit me. Dina had taken a turn. "How bad is she?"

"It's soon. That's what the nurse told us. Soon. She was pretty much asleep the whole time we were with her." Kit must have picked up because Barrett stopped talking to us and spoke to the phone. "Someone just tried to grab Alatheia off the street. No, I'm not kidding. Why would I be kidding?"

I leaned on Jeremy as he walked me to the Jeep. "You just saved my life."

"I can't think about it. I can't even believe this just happened. We're in this god-forsaken place so you can heal, so Phoenix can get support, and we're supposed to be safe here. Safe from discovery. That's what they always say." He was shouting by the end. "You could be in this kind of trouble at home."

Barrett jumped in the driver's seat. "Come on. We're going."

I leaned against the back of the seat. My head started to pound. "I really don't feel well. It's been a long day."

"It's ten in the morning." Barrett winced. I could see it in the rearview mirror from where I sat in the back with Jeremy. He hadn't let go of me.

"Fuck," Jer said again, banging his head into the back of the seat so hard it vibrated.

I looked over at him. "Don't do that. You'll hurt yourself."

He met my gaze, there was so much unexpressed rage in his stare I wasn't sure how he didn't explode. "You are covered in dirt and scraped up. Can you even feel it yet?"

I looked down at myself. Oh, I sure was. "I have fingernail marks on me." They were going to hurt. "That's gross."

His phone rang which at least broke the tension in that moment. He grabbed it. "Jules? No, it's real. What Kit is saying. Yes, almost home. I know." He closed his eyes. "I know. Fuck. I know."

He hung up. I touched the side of his face, and he finally lifted his lids. "What do you know?"

"That if we can't keep you safe, we're failing you. It's fundamentally my job before I do anything else or think about anything else."

I shook my head. "I love you. We keep each other safe. I'm not some precious jewel you have to keep locked in a safe."

"You are. You are the most precious jewel. The most expensive, rare diamond in the world. More than that. That is what you are to me. To all of us. And I am failing. I have never failed at anything in my life, but I am failing at keeping you safe and happy. Did you see how Carl and Jadon reacted to you last night? You are a gift from the heavens, and I am..."

I shook my head, which seemed to stop him. "I love you. I'll say it as many times as I need to. I love you."

When we pulled into the driveway, all of the Lents, minus Dina and Phoenix stood there. I got out of the car and was instantly in Julian's arms.

He didn't say anything—maybe because his parents were

right there too—but I could feel his body vibrate against my own. I didn't try to pull back or say anything.

Barrett took off back down the driveway. Obviously Phoenix could not be left on his own. Although I sort of imagined he'd do a better job of defending himself than I had done. If they had been the least bit ready for me I would have been screwed.

I breathed Julian in. Soap. That was what I smelled on him. He had taken a shower recently.

Finally, I pulled back to stare into his blue eyes. "I can never get over your eyes." I whispered to him. Maybe it was ridiculous to say that right now. Yet, it seemed important and what, really, was there left to say about any of this?

He cupped my cheeks. "You're okay."

"I am." I nodded and pulled back. "I... I obviously didn't plan this, but I do apologize that I am taking attention from Dina where it should be. So we can talk about this later. Okay?" I looked at Kit. "I don't know cars. I'm sorry. Makes. Models. No idea. White. Van."

He nodded. "Okay. I'm getting security. My family won't be threatened. You are my family by the way, Alatheia. So that includes you. You'll all have people watching you from now on. Just know that. For now anyway."

Truth was, between therapy making me wildly nervous and now this, I needed a shower and a nap. I squeezed Julian's hands. "I need to go clean up and lie down. You should go be with your granny."

He nodded but looked at the ground. "I love you. Maybe we should leave the country."

"Not today." Wherever they went I would go. I was sure of that.

"Would one of you tell Phoenix that he smelled like bourbon? Would you make sure he hears that?" Now that I could think again I knew Phoenix was going to lose it over this. He might need a meeting or however he was coping right now. Plus, if his granny had taken a turn today it was only going to be worse.

He nodded.

"What does that mean?" Rosalind called out. It was the first time she'd spoken, and I could swear that she had paled since then. Or maybe not. I hadn't focused on her.

I swallowed. "I guess maybe Phoenix hasn't said anything yet and I... I mean, it's not my story to tell but..."

Julian interrupted me. "He remembered that one of the people who held him smelled like bourbon. Really badly. Drenched in it. Might explain why he can't stand alcohol, never could even when he was on the drugs. Drug user but also a teetotaler. And Alatheia is saying that one of her attempted kidnappers was the same. Should we call the police?"

Rosalind rocked back on her feet. "No. No don't do that." She walked into the house and returned a moment later holding a gun.

Everyone gasped except Daniel who ran a hand through his hair. "Roses, that is a really bad idea."

"I'm going to do it. They can arrest me. I don't care." She stormed toward the garage, which was separate from the house. "He isn't touching anyone else who belongs to me."

Jer looked between us. "He? You know who that is?"

"Yes. Yes, I do." She kept walking. "I always wondered, you know? I really did. And now I know. I'm sure of it."

Kit seemed frozen, which was remarkable considering that his wife was about to go shoot some unknown person who she was now sure was the perpetrator of all of this. But Stephen chased after her.

"Roz, listen, I know who it is now too. But we should talk about what to do. How best to handle this. He can be made to suffer without you going to jail. Okay? I know you want to kill him, so do I. Maybe we do that. Okay? Not tonight."

She stopped walking and turned around, slowly. "You promise? You promise we can kill him if that's what we want? You won't... decide to listen to reason. Yes, I know that is what Kit is about to say."

He held up his hands. "I wasn't, actually."

"Mo vé le mort." She spat out. I had heard her do that once before, speak a foreign language when she was upset. Right before she had thrown me out of the Hamptons.

"Who the fuck is it?" Jeremy finally shouted. "What are we talking about? And if Mom is reverting to Cajun then all shit is about to hit the fan. Someone start talking because maybe I'll go kill him."

Rosalind shook her head wildly. "No way, my darling. You will do no such thing. No one is fucking with my children anymore. It's my brother. It's Cade. The one right below me. He stinks so badly of bourbon I can barely sit in the room with him. There's no question in my mind. We wondered if it was my family, and it was."

"Sure." I nodded. It was clearly time to talk to them. "But it can't only be your family. Look what they tried to do. They tried to shove me in a van. They failed. It was the middle of the day on a street Barrett drives up and down constantly. Anyone could see. Lazy and poorly thought out. What happened to Phoenix? That was constructed and well done. Otherwise you would know by now who it was. How did they get to you? How did they have the ability to send a text we cannot trace? They are being funded by someone with resources."

Everyone stared at me in silence. I could practically feel my own heart beat, it was so wild.

Finally, it was Eric who spoke. "That's smart. We never thought about it like that. You're so smart."

"She is." Julian squeezed my hand. "We have been pseudo investigating the families you're friends with. The ones who would have reason to have been there that day. To not be accidently discovered. We know Sam's family is fine. I think next up is the Trevors."

That was right.

Kit crossed his arms over his chest. "They lost River. There is no way they would have placed that child in danger knowingly. None. They have never been the same. No way."

"None," Eric nodded. "But it's a good thought. I get why you would think that."

"One of our friends." All the fight seemed to be gone from Rosalind. When she would have dropped the gun, Stephen took it from her.

It was like Kit had his voice back. "Stop your investigation. You're already at risk. No one is hurting any member of my family. I'll do it. Clearly I should have done it five years ago. I'm blind to this. I can see it now."

I pointed at the house. "I'm going to shower. Maybe take a nap. I might not be able to. And if it wouldn't be too intrusive, could I please stop by and see Dina for a minute after?"

Daniel nodded fast. "It's not intrusive. You're ours. Hers. We'd love you to visit."

I would. When I could see straight again.

I STARED at myself in the bathroom mirror. My eyes were haunted, but that wasn't new. My hair was fuzz on top of my head. I was still beat up looking and scarred. Maybe I should ask Eric if there was something I could do about that. I didn't want all of these scars for the rest of my life. Maybe the new ones wouldn't scar, but it seemed lately everything did.

Jeremy was in my room. I chewed on my lip. I wanted to

be brave. I wanted to be alive. I wanted to be somewhere other than where I was today. I wanted to be with him. I grabbed what was probably Barrett's bathrobe and put it on. I had heard Barrett and Phoenix pull into the driveway. They hadn't come storming in, so they were probably visiting with Dina. Maybe Julian had told them I was showering and sleeping, to leave me alone. Jeremy hadn't stayed away and that was fine by me.

I stepped out in the bathrobe to find him staring at the ceiling. He leaned back on his elbows, a tilt to his head. "Something wrong?"

"No." I shook my head. "Wondering if I could shower in your bathroom."

He blinked. "Sure. Don't like yours?"

"I do. A lot. I just want to shower in your bathroom and maybe take a nap in there, too. What do you think? Fine to tell me no."

Jeremy got to his feet, slowly. He walked over to me, tugging me by the belt of the bathrobe toward him. "What are you saying? Be clear with me. My head is befuddled."

I smiled, stealing a phrase for Phoenix. "Oh, look, SAT word."

"Princess?" He was dead serious right now. Not the time to joke with him.

"I thought we could get in your shower together and make out in your bed. Maybe... maybe move things along a little bit if you want to. If you don't, I understand. That's fine, too."

He bent over to whisper in my ear. "Yes. I want to. So much you can't believe it."

I probably could. "I just had the IUD put in, I feel pretty good, but we could stop short of actual... penetration." I was getting good at saying these things. "We could, ah, touch each other."

I had to be red in the face. Completely and totally red.

But I'd done it. Jeremy didn't make it any easier because he seemed to be determined to hold my eye contact the entire time. He simply, through the force of his own gaze, wouldn't let me look down.

He nodded. "Have you, ah, ever done that before?"

"I have... touched someone but never been touched myself. Oh forget it. If you don't want to then..."

Jeremy kissed me, gently, silencing my response. "I want to. I'm simply trying to ascertain whether or not you know what you're asking for. I want to follow instructions and boundaries. I want to make you happy. Come with me." He took my hand, and we practically ran into the hall, stopping in his bedroom. He was the one who had his bathroom. The only one. He locked the door to his room.

Then he kissed me again. And again. And again. Finally, he lifted his head. "Shower. Come."

Were we down to one word at a time? I let him bring me into the bathroom. His room was exactly like Phoenix's had been, with one framed photo of him and Julian in the corner. Someone had set frames in these rooms. They were identical. Jeremy turned on the shower. I wanted to be brave. That had been on the list. So I had to be brave.

I dropped the robe. I had never been entirely naked in front of anyone for very long. He caught his breath.

"I know I'm pretty beat up right now."

"Hush, Princess. You're beautiful. So beautiful you take my breath away."

❧ 14 ❧

"**Y**ou really must love me."

He shook his head. "I do, but I'm not lying."

Like I had dropped the robe, Jeremy pulled off his clothes. We were completely naked in front of each other. Well, this had been my idea. Jeremy was beautiful. I knew he would be. And it occurred to me what I looked like right then.

I swallowed. "Pretty beat up."

"Beautiful." He took my hand and brought it to his mouth to kiss me. "You're stunningly beautiful. But we can stop right now if that's what you want."

I shook my head. "No, I want this. I just got nervous. I guess both things are possible."

"Very possible. Because that's just how I'm feeling, too."

He was? This was Jeremy. He was something of a legend at Pullman for how much he hooked up. I couldn't imagine he was actually nervous. "Sweet of you to say that."

"You think it's not true?" He kissed both my cheeks before he placed his hand over his heart. "Feel that?"

It was racing. I smiled at him. "So I guess you're telling the truth."

He nodded. "I don't lie to you."

Jeremy drew me to him, our skin touching. We stepped into the shower together. It was a little bit warmer than I usually had it when I wasn't freaking out, but it was good enough.

He looked at the floor for a second. "I've never done this before." He held up his hand. "Showered. With someone else. Unless maybe when I was little. And this is different, obviously. I'm rambling."

Jeremy totally was. It was so not like him. I kissed him and he kissed me back, hard. Yes, this was so much more Jeremy. I wrapped my arms around his neck and the water covered our bodies. Soon, we were both soaked. And he was hard. But he made no moves to do anything but kiss me. I was warm and it wasn't because of the water.

I pulled back to grab the soap and poured some from the bottle onto my hand. I smelled it. "I wasn't thinking, but I'm going to get to smell like you for the rest of the day." This was where he got the sandalwood scent that was always on him.

He blinked rapidly. "You like the way I smell?"

"Yes I do." I kissed him as I soaped him up. He grabbed the bottle and then did the same to me.

We were quiet about it. There was almost a reverence to this moment. Maybe he understood what was dawning on me —we'd only have a first time doing this once. After this, it would be fun when we did it again, something to look forward to with anticipation, but there was only one first time for this. Every move I made would be repeated someday but not discovered like it was right now.

There was every possibility I was overthinking it.

"Okay if I touch you?" I whispered in his ear, keeping it reverent.

He nodded, kissing my neck. "Sure. Assume consent with me, okay? The answer is yes to whatever you're wanting to do. But I'm not going to touch you until I have you on the bed. That's where I'm going to make you feel so good, Princess."

Actually, that sounded better than right here under the water. There was something sort of sacred about being wrapped up in the bed together. Here, it was like we could feel each other, but the water was slick and might actually make me anxious.

He kissed my shoulder as I took him in my hand. He moaned, a long sound. "Fuck. I knew it would be intense, but even I didn't imagine what having you touch me there would do to me."

I wasn't sure what to say, so I said nothing at all. This was Jeremy. As I was always being reminded, he had plenty of experience with this. I ran my hand over his cock like I had learned to do and squeezed him. "You'll tell me if the pressure isn't right."

In response he put his forehead on my shoulder. His breathing was shallow, and he didn't answer me. Pressed against me, I could feel how his whole body was tense. He was beautiful like this. Who was I kidding? Jer was always gorgeous but right in this second he was only mine to see, and the effect was stunning.

I kissed his cheek, breathing him in while he lengthened in my hand. His moans almost sounded pained, and his hold on me tightened. We stayed like that for a while, me stroking him as he breathed in my ear, letting out sounds that I knew would always be personal between us.

Finally, I whispered in his ear. "I love you."

His whole body jerked, and he came hard in my hand. He didn't move except to hold me tighter and shake against me.

Finally, he lifted his head as I put my hand under the water to wash it off. "I fucking love you, too."

He kissed me. Again. And Again. Usually I could keep up. Not this time. My head spun and he picked me up in his arms, wrapping us both in a towel before he carried us over to his bed.

His mouth claimed mine again. Finally, he lifted his head, still breathing rapidly. "I've never come that hard. I mean never." He kissed the end of my nose. "My turn."

I swallowed. "Just got a little bit nervous."

"This is your show. Always. But there is no reason to be nervous. I'm going to take such good care of you."

That made sense. I nodded. "Okay."

Jeremy unwrapped the towel around us like he was unwrapping a present. He grinned at me. "I love everything about your body. I want to memorize it. You're just giving me a new way to learn you tonight."

I supposed that made sense. I had just learned things about him I hadn't known, like what it sounded like when he came.

"There isn't pressure," he whispered in my ear. "Just let me love on you for a little while."

He kissed down my body, starting with my mouth and then traveled lower to my neck. I shivered at his attention. I did love to be kissed there. It made me warm inside. I guessed I had a spot. As he did this, he grabbed my knee, gently, and pulled it up just a little bit so that I wrapped my leg around his ass. It was a different position, but considering how heated his kisses were making me I couldn't complain. I actually really liked it.

With my leg where he wanted it, he took to running his hands up and down the side of my body. This time I trembled. He really wasn't doing anything but kissing and touching me. I was really, really turned on. Or maybe I just wanted these moments more than I could have imagined.

He traveled down my body again, stopping at my breasts.

This time he lifted his gaze to meet my own. "Have I ever told you how much I love your breasts?"

I shook my head. "Not specifically, I don't think."

"I do, Princess. I do love them so much."

I swallowed. "Have I ever told you how much I love it when you call me that?"

"You're my princess. What else would I call you?"

I loved the glint in his eyes.

He took my nipple in his mouth, and I cried out. The pinch of pain startled me, and somehow I loved it too. Jeremy sighed, a long sound.

I was so distracted by his ministrations that I didn't notice when he pressed a finger inside of me. But there it was, Jeremy Lent was right where I had wanted him to go and where I had been terrified he would.

He sucked harder, still stroking my side with one hand and pressing his finger against the spot that sometimes throbbed for a second when I was pressed close to them or they kissed me a lot. I knew what it meant and so did Jeremy because he started to stroke it. Slowly and then he picked up the pace.

I caught my breath. The heat that had been there had turned into pressure. I closed my eyes, understanding now why Jer had pushed his head into my shoulder. I did the same to him. It was almost too much to handle if I wasn't right up against him. I needed his skin on my lips, to smell his scent.

I almost told him to stop. What was I supposed to do with this? How was it going to end in any way that could actually happen? I wasn't even making sense in my own mind. I just knew that I needed... something.

Finally, I just exploded. Right there on his fingers while he made love to my breasts with his mouth. I cried out and he lifted his head but only to kiss me, again and again, on my mouth while I gave into what he had done.

My heart raced and my body arched off the bed, bumping into his. We were tangled up in each other when he stopped stroking me.

"Beautiful." He kissed me again. "You're so fucking perfect."

I didn't know about that. I just knew that tears leaked from my eyes, and he kissed them away, not seeming to be freaked out or concerned by them. Instead, he slowed down, our embraces getting longer and more languid as the minutes ticked on.

I'd had no idea it would feel like that. I held him to me. My head didn't quite want to turn back on. But the sadness that was always with me these days seeped in, despite my wishing it wouldn't.

"We... we almost didn't get to do this together. If you hadn't found me. I'd never have known."

He smoothed a hand over my forehead. "I know. It was always going to be everything when we did this kind of thing together. But it's even more so. It's everything. Made even more sacred because I almost lost you."

How did Jeremy always know the right thing to say?

That was the last thing I thought before the day just turned off for me for a while.

A knock on the door roused me sometime later. The sun must be setting. I could see the light through the window had changed color. Jeremy lifted his head and then kissed my cheek, pulling the sheet up over me that we must have kicked off. I so rarely needed blankets. The Lents were heated enough.

"Sorry," he whispered. "Stay right there."

I rubbed my eyes. "No. I should get up. We're sleeping the whole day away."

"I think we both need it." He grabbed his underwear from the bathroom, calling toward the door. "Just a second."

"Sorry." It was Phoenix on the other end. "I've tried to be patient, but she was attacked and I haven't gotten to see her. I really... I really need to see that Alatheia is okay."

Jeremy nodded, not that Phoenix could see that, and swung open the door.

"Hey." Phoenix stared at me from the doorway. "I'm sorry. I know you were sleeping. It's important. But, yeah, I needed to see you. They came at you with a van and tried to kidnap you while I was in session."

Jeremy patted him on the back. "Not going to lie, it took years off my life. But she's okay, and we got to her. That's why it's good we're a team. You rescued her in the City from the PI. We take turns."

I groaned. "I would love not to need rescuing."

"For real." Phoenix walked in and kissed me, gently. "You should probably come see Granny soon."

We really did need to. I sat up. Getting nearly kidnapped and then what Jeremy and I had done had distracted me. I had needed the nap, but it was time to go see her.

"Thanks for getting us up." Jeremy headed toward the bathroom. "I might have been playing denial. Needed a little time. But, yeah, we should get moving."

He was absolutely right.

⚜

IT WAS quiet in the house. Their granny was asleep. Everyone sat around quietly. Rosalind was knitting. She looked up when we came in and smiled but didn't comment. Eric walked over and hugged Phoenix. I didn't know who was more surprised by it, Eric or Phoenix himself. He stood stunned for a second before he gently hugged his bio-dad back.

"You okay?" he asked in a low voice. "I wasn't gone very long."

Eric shook his head. "No. I'm not. Neither are you. But I'm so proud of you, and I just wanted to say that."

Barrett patted the seat next to him, and I sat down in it. He and Julian seemed to be playing a game on their phones. It was some kind of card game, and they were doing it silently. I'd never thought a second about what went on in the room when people were passing. But if they were sitting there all day, then it wasn't surprising that they were actually doing quiet activities while they sat with their loved ones.

I rubbed my arms; goosebumps had broken out on them. This was their granny and their mother and mother-in-law. I loved her, but I had known her so brief a time. It was a little bit like I was an intruder, even though I knew they wouldn't say that.

I let myself look at them for a second each. Obviously, their parents had known of her illness way before the boys had known. I could see the strain on their faces. Kit stared out the window, not looking at her right now. He had a lot on his plate all the time, which now included me. It really would have been easier on them if the guys had fallen for someone easier than me.

I chewed on my bottom lip. Of course I would want to kill her because they were mine. Even if that made no sense. It didn't have to.

Eric stood by his mom's bed, his gaze alternating between staring at her and then back at the monitors in the corner that showed her vitals. I didn't know what any of it meant, but Eric did. He frowned and I looked away. I wasn't staring, just trying to take them all in.

Stephen was staring at his phone. I didn't know what he was reading or if he was just blankly staring while Daniel had his head down on the table in front of him, resting his head on his arms.

Jeremy plopped down next to me. He had a coffee cup in

his hand, which he sipped. Phoenix walked past us to stand next to Kit by the window. They stared out together.

"She hates it here," Kit said, which made Daniel lift his head. He had clearly not been sleeping.

He nodded. "Hates it. With a passion. Like she loved our fathers and wanted them and their life, but not this part of their life." He looked over at me. "You've been reading her journals. Any sense of why?"

"I... I've only read her first impressions and now she is visiting here again on vacation. Your grandmother didn't like her. And a lot of the locals treated her badly because she took your grandfathers. There was a presumption that they would marry another woman. I think it was devastating."

Rosalind shook her head. "There is always that presumption here. Everyone thinks they know. They count on things that are none of their business. Or, I should say they behave that way on the other side of the lake. Our neighbors aren't doing that." She sighed. "They might have kidnapped our son and killed two other kids. But sure they don't assume where their kids will get married."

Kit rocked back on his feet. "And she is here, where she hated it." He shook his head. "I'm sorry, Mom. We have to be here right now. We all have to be. But I hate it for you, and I am sorry."

I didn't see any sign that Dina heard him. But Rosalind did. She rose and crossed to him, putting her arms around him. "She just wanted to be where we all were. No way is Dina upset about being here right now."

Phoenix walked over to me. "I think... I think you need to come outside right now, Red. Guys, come on. We have something to do outside."

I blinked. "We do?"

Kit looked over his shoulder. "Something we need to be concerned with?"

"Not this. No." He shook his head. "Stay here."

I really had absolutely no idea where we were going. None whatsoever. What could require us to go outside?

Without a word, I followed him outside. My guys were with me, and it wasn't until we got outside that I realized what had happened. Although it took me a second too long because the gust of cold that slammed into my face and naked head, stealing my breath for a second. But then I saw it. Sam stood in the driveway with his two brothers, and in the center of them was Sally.

I caught my breath. "Sally?" I practically shouted. She rushed to me, putting her arms around me.

"I saw the picture you sent me, and I put it in the search engine. It said you were here. So I dumped the phone, I bought a ticket, and I walked." We were twins with our shaved heads. She held onto me like I was a lifeline. "And I was walking. I really had no idea how to find you. This place is huge but they saw me and stopped. Maybe I was stupid, but I got in their car."

It was kind of stupid to do that, but that was okay... they were nice. "They're safe."

"Right. They stopped to see if I was okay. They were the second car to do that. The first one kind of creeped me out. They stared at me like I was a sandwich, and I told them to fuck off. But these guys were polite. They said they knew you, that you lived next door to them, and I took a chance." Her voice hitched. "I am so fucked Alatheia. I have nowhere and no one."

That was not true. She had me. But damn the timing for this really, really sucked. "I'm here. You're safe."

"Thank you." She closed her eyes. "I'd give him the money to leave me alone."

I knew she would. I had the same thoughts myself. More than once.

"Alatheia," Jeremy spoke my name. "It's cold. Let's go inside the house."

He was right. I took her arm and led her into the smaller house. What was I going to do with Sally right now? Granny might die any moment—which made my chest tight to even think about—and I had almost been kidnapped earlier in the day. We were living in a private place that I had exposed by sending one picture, and yet I couldn't regret that if it made her safe. I really had no idea what to do. None.

We stepped inside and she looked around. "This is beautiful."

Sam, Carl and Jadon all followed us inside. Sam and Phoenix spoke by the door, the former nodding his head a lot.

"Can I stay? I mean, will your boyfriend mind?" She looked at Barrett. Interesting. Why did she think it was him? "I saw you carry her out. You're her boyfriend, right? "

He cleared his throat. "Yes. I am."

"It's not a good time here, " Jadon said to her. "I didn't realize, but their grandmother is dying next door in the big house. Sally is welcome to stay with us. We have a guest house." Their smaller house that appeared vacant. "She would be welcome. Right next door. Can see you anytime."

Her face fell. "I didn't realize that someone was dying. I am so sorry. My timing always sucks."

"It doesn't. You're a ballerina. Your timing is near perfection."

She laughed, and that made me smile. I had never seen Sally so low. Once again I was reminded she had gone through everything I had but had no one to help her except the person who had done this to her in the first place.

I turned to Jadon. "She's very important to me." I said that to him for her benefit as much as anything else.

He nodded. "We'll take good care of her. Won't let anything happen to her."

The kidnapping attempt. Phoenix must have told them. Or maybe it was just public knowledge in the way that things seemed to be in small communities. I looked back at my sad looking friend. "Would you be okay with that?"

I didn't know how Sam's family was going to keep their secret, but Jadon had offered. He must think it possible.

She nodded. "I'd be grateful. I could work somewhere or whatever."

"Don't worry about that." Carl took a step toward us. "You'd be our guest. Our mother loves guests. She'll fuss over you, and we have three little sisters. They're going to decide you are their personal friend, there specifically for them to love on you. Please. Come stay with us. If you don't like it, we can figure something out for you. The point is you're safe and whatever is happening to you—that I think is similar to what is happening to Alatheia?—we can help. I promise."

After a second, she nodded and cleared her throat. "If you're sure I won't be trouble."

"No trouble at all." Sam nodded. "Come on. Let's go. I think it's not going well here right now. We can let them get back to their family."

She stepped toward him. "Lots of big families here."

"Yes, we're very... family oriented around this lake." Sam patted Phoenix on the shoulder.

It wasn't until I heard the door click behind them that I let out a breath. "I didn't mean to get her here. I didn't mean to potentially expose everyone."

Jeremy hugged me. His familiar smell, particularly after what we had done earlier, surrounded me like a blanket. "Of course you didn't. This will be fine. It's not like people from the outside don't come here. I mean, we didn't grow up here and haven't been here in years, but yeah, I know they do. They'll take care of this. Maybe she can be trusted with it. I don't know. You're fine. No one is upset with you though."

"I'm glad she's safe." Phoenix ran a hand through my hair. "That was weighing on you. I know they're all weighing on you."

Clean and sober Phoenix was maybe the most empathetic person that I'd ever known. He told me once he worried about everything all the time. I could see it now. He really felt things in a big way and did worry. His granny was going to leave us soon and he was thinking about how I felt about Sally and the others.

Julian patted Barrett on the arm. "Looks like you won the role of public boyfriend."

"One of us was always going to have to. How do you think it ended up Kit?" He shrugged. "Tends to be the oldest."

Jeremy shook his head, letting me go. "I'm not accepting it's automatically you. Just so you know. For this, fine. We'll see how it goes going forward."

Phoenix sighed. "I think we can shelve this for today. We have a million big problems. This can wait."

He was right. But Sally's arrival was both a gift and a curse at the moment. Only time would tell how it ended up.

❧ 15 ❧

Dina's voice startled me out of the near daze I had been in for hours.

"No, my darling, I'm not arguing. He does look just like you did at that age."

Who was she talking to? I looked around. She stared at the wall but not at any of us. What was happening?

Eric sighed, rubbing his eyes. "This is normal." His voice was low. "Sometimes people, toward the end, they see their departed loved ones."

"Really?" Phoenix widened his eyes from where he sat across from me. "Why?"

"Well, we don't know why." Eric sunk into a chair. "Maybe it's something happening in her brain or maybe she is, indeed, seeing the people she loved who have moved on. I am not really in a position to say."

Dina's helper, who I'd discovered was a hospice nurse among other things, fussed with her blanket before leaving her and slipping out of the room.

Everyone was seated now, and Kit shook his leg, looking left and right. Daniel put his arm around his older brother, which stopped the movement. I had never seen Kit when he didn't seem like he was in control of the room. This had to be throwing him for a loop. Or at least I imagined it was. I had found my mother dead.

I really never thought about that. My father had died—and I didn't know the circumstances surrounding it—and my mother I had found dead. I blinked. This was absolutely not the first time I had been around death. I just never let myself think about that aspect of it. The before and the after, that was how I existed. Only I had a before, and an after, and an actual moment where the two existences had collided. Right that fucking second. Why did I never think about that?

Dr. Trevor was right. I really didn't deal with my trauma. Ever. And I certainly wasn't going to deal with it now.

"No, I am so glad to see you." She laughed gently at something. "When there were four of them, I knew you guys were with me then. Four boys. That had to be your doing. Your personal wink that you had never really left me."

I turned toward Barrett who I sat right next to and took his hand in mine. He was silent. I wasn't sure he was even seeing his grandmother in that moment. It was like he was present with us but not really present. He squeezed my fingers, bringing our joined hands to his mouth so he could kiss my palm. It was a relief when he did that. I wasn't sure where he had gone, but it couldn't have been any place good. Barrett carried the emotional burdens of his entire family, mostly silently. He and Phoenix were bookends to the twins, each one shouldering things in the ways that they could manage.

"Oh, hello. " She smiled. "No, I would know you two anywhere even though we never met."

The twins looked at each other. Yes, it was a little bit strange that she would be speaking to people she didn't know? Wasn't it?

"Your love was all over her. I could feel it. So perfectly meant to be with the children. Why yes, it's the red hair."

Rosalind jolted and met my gaze. Who was she talking to? Did she think—or was she seeing?—my parents?

Barrett squeezed my hand tighter. "It's okay. It really is," he whispered. "Whatever is happening... it's a good thing. I mean, I'd rather have people around me as this happened than not, even if it's only in my head."

That was true.

Dina had known loneliness when her parents died, for a little while. She had known it again when some of the people she was seeing now had perished in a car accident. But she was a Lent and they always turned up for one another, particularly when it mattered.

My first tear slipped out of my eyes, and I batted it away. This wasn't about me. This was about Dina who had adopted me into her life last June and changed everything.

If I lived past my eighteenth birthday, it was quite literally because of her. If I got to love the four Lent brothers for the rest of my life, it was because of her. I had her diaries. I would do what she had asked me to do. It was the least I could do.

❧

THERE WAS silence in the kitchen except for the sounds of water dripping. Eventually someone—maybe Daniel—got up and messed with the faucet to make it stop.

"Someone has to write an obituary." Kit looked at Rosalind and then over toward where I sat with my guys. "Julian, could you do that?"

He rapidly blinked. "What?"

"It's four in the morning." Rosalind touched Kit's arm.

"Let's do this a little later today. Okay? Noon. Ask Jules at noon or later."

He nodded. "Sure."

There turned out to be a lot of things that had to happen after someone died. My father didn't have an obituary, not really. A statement—two lines—of death in a local Colorado newspaper where we hadn't been mentioned. That was because he wasn't real, had been hiding who he was. My mother had one. Her family had done it. But it had been vague. If Julian wrote Dina's obituary, it was going to be beautiful.

"Sure, I'll do it, Kit." He nodded. "I may need to ask you for some details. Dates. Things like that."

"Yep."

We walked in silence back to our house. It was raining, a cool drip, and for once I didn't mind it. My body was numb, and I could at least feel the coolness on my head.

"Anyone hungry?" I looked around, not really expecting a yes, and the shakes of their head confirmed it.

When we climbed into bed, I was between Phoenix and Barrett. Minutes passed and no one had spoken or fallen asleep. There was just oppressive silence in the room.

"I don't think she expected this to happen so fast," Julian whispered. "When she arrived she thought she'd have time. A little bit of it anyway but maybe it's better."

Maybe it was.

The night—or was it the day—ticked on.

❦

I MUST HAVE FALLEN ASLEEP. We all did because I woke up and they were all still asleep. The clock read noon. The familiar sounds of the Lents sleeping were all around me. Phoenix's hand was tangled in my hair, but he looked like he slept peacefully. Barrett had his legs over mine, essentially pinning me to the bed. He murmured in his sleep, which was probably what woke me. Sometimes he did that, and usually I slept through it but not this afternoon.

The twins snored on opposite sides of the other bed. They were really out. I stared at the ceiling. I could lie here, or I could get up and do what she asked me to do. I could read her journals.

Somehow I managed to get out from under Barrett and untangled myself from Phoenix without waking them. I went to the bathroom, cleaned up, and brewed coffee before I sat down to read. All of it felt mechanical, like I couldn't think of anything except the actual movement I needed to do those things. I was a robot—I could perform tasks.

But I opened the journal and caught my breath. Could I actually do this? I hadn't considered I might not be able to read her at all. She was gone. Okay. I was doing this. I just had to pull it together. That was all. I didn't do grief well, and I was going to bet the Lents didn't either. We were all kind of a mess on a good day. So I had to do this because the nicest woman I had ever known asked me to.

Of course she had been big on me not stressing myself out. Telling me not to read it during the summer when she wanted me to have fun. She might not insist on the day of her death that I open the journals and do this.

I steeled my shoulders. I could be a turtle, or I could take the world by the horns the way she would have. She'd learned to make it move for her. She was going to teach me how, and even though that hadn't happened in person maybe she still could.

Okay. I was just going to do this.

I opened it up and I thumbed to the last page I had read.

JUNE 1ST, 1968

THEY HAVE DEMOLISHED Radio City to build it. The glass building my uncle was going to make the glass for. But he is dead. I saw it in the newspaper, a small mention that he had died. Alone. In his apartment. A neighbor eventually found him. The article didn't say how. I could imagine some horrible ways.

Vic had been right. I never had to see my uncle again. I might have even missed the article if I hadn't been lazy and reading the paper when I should have gone to work. He will not live to see the glass in those buildings. Someone else will do it. That feels... right somehow.

I'M NOT PREGNANT, and I am going to stop thinking I might ever be. Birth and death and everything in between.

I DON'T EVEN KNOW why I'm writing today. I am sad. I am happy most of the time but today I'm sad. I think that Robert just noticed.

DL

Fuck. That was apropos. I closed my eyes. I needed to keep going.

JUNE 1ST 1968

I'M WRITING a second time today. I picked a fight. With all four of them. I have no idea why. I picked a fight. A big one. They've all left the house, and I can't blame them. Maybe forever. I don't even know. I'm a terrible wife. Maybe a worse person. It's debatable.

DL

SHE PICKED A FIGHT. It was hard to imagine.

"You don't have to do that right now." Julian sort of fell into the room, finally sitting down next to me at the counter. "You really don't."

I rose and went to get him some coffee. If he was going to be awake, he was going to need some caffeine. I poured it and put some cream in it. When we went to coffee houses, he got more complicated things, but at home this was how he drank it.

I slid it over to him, and he smiled at me. "Thanks, Baby."

"How are you?"

He shook his head. "I don't know."

Well, that was a true answer. I didn't know either.

❧

I HAD a black dress because Dina had bought me one, and I was wearing it, standing in the living room watching people talk. It was funny because none of them really knew Dina. These had not been her people, and from all accounts she had never really dove into knowing them very well or trusting them at all.

There was always the other side of the lake... that was what she had said to me. I had the smallest headache forming behind my eyes. As for my guys, they were holding up really well. Even Phoenix was chatting with people around him. Sally was in the corner with Sam's family. She had come by to hug me and then whispered in my ear that she had figured things out. So, that secret hadn't lasted very long.

We needed to talk about it, but I was more comfortable not talking today. It had been my default response for years. Maybe it was my trauma response to death. I didn't care right then. I sipped my water as Barrett eyed me from the corner.

The door opened and closed, more people entering our open house to visit with the Lents. For all the years they hadn't come down, they still had friends here. I watched all of them. It felt like Dina whispered in my ear that I shouldn't trust anyone. It didn't matter. I had thought maybe I would play detective, but the energy for that had fled with the kidnapping attempt and death.

I could barely get through reading and typing up the journals. My head itched, and I hoped that it was because my hair was growing.

It was Dr. Trevor and his family that came through the door. I'd not met his children, but I recognized them from the photos in his office. There was a man with him, too. It must be one of the other husbands. The door opened and closed again, and a third man came in. It was his co-husbands. Joint husbands? I smiled. I would need to ask how they referred to themselves.

It was hard to stand at Dina's funeral when I was currently reading how unhappy she was. It wasn't just once that she had picked a fight. The guys were pretty unhappy with her right now.

Phoenix walked over, scratching the back of his neck. "I am... I'm not sure."

Sam was in the corner. "Do you need to talk to Sam?"

He shook his head. "No, it's not that kind of thing. I don't know. Just off."

I leaned against him. This was his Granny's funeral. If he was feeling off then, it was probably to be expected. I imagined we were all feeling off. Rosalind had never looked paler than she did right then.

He squeezed my shoulder. "You're quiet."

"You know that sometimes I'm quiet. This isn't about me. I promise. Don't worry about me."

He frowned. "I'm always going to worry about you if there is something to worry about." He side-eyed me. "I miss her, too, but I don't think that's all that's bothering you. Am I right?"

I stared at his handsome profile. "I love you so much. You know that, right?"

"She answers a question with a question. I do know it." He touched my chin until I looked at him. "What is it, Red?"

"I don't know." That was the truth. I was just... off.

From his place in the corner, Dr. Trevor watched us for a second before he walked over. Standing so close, I could smell his cologne; it was dark, a little musky. He didn't wear it in the office. "Are you two okay? For obvious reasons I want to check in."

One of his two whatever we were calling them walked over and handed him a soda. He took it with a nod. "You two know my brother Kal, right?"

I shook my head. "I don't think we've met."

Phoenix grabbed his head, and all thoughts of Kal fled my mind. "What's wrong?" I held onto his arm.

"I don't know." He bent over, grabbing onto his knees. Was he going to get sick?

He lifted his head, staring at Kal, breathing hard. We'd gotten a lot of attention. Everyone was around us now, including Eric who had a hand on his back. "Son?"

I'd never heard Eric call him son before. We were all a little bit off. It didn't matter since we were here.

"I know you." Phoenix stared at Kal.

The other man paled. "You don't. Or you haven't for years. I used to come to your house for summers before River died."

'No, I know you." He stood up straight now. With my hand on him, I could feel his body vibrate.

Jeremy was to my left, his arms crossed over his chest. "Sounds like you don't like him."

"Phoenix?" It was Daniel who spoke. "What's going on?"

With his gaze fixed on the ever paling man, Phoenix poked him in the shoulder. "You were there."

The room fell silent. I didn't think anyone could be confused about what he meant. I caught my breath. River was this man's kid. Had he killed River and Walt? Tried to kill Phoenix?

"I... I..."

Phoenix shook his head. "Don't deny it. I know you were. Not just you. The other man too. The one who stunk like bourbon. But you were there. Two others. You were in charge. It was blurry because you kept us drugged." Phoenix was slightly taller than this man, but he was a teenager, and we were in a room full of adults. Still, no one moved except Phoenix who stepped into this man's space like he had every right to be there. "You were there."

Kal's chin began to wobble. "It was a terrible mistake."

"What was? Taking us? Killing them? Trying to kill me? Doing something to me in the hospital—you were there too —so I wouldn't talk. What was it that you did?" He was shouting now. "It was such a dark place where you kept us."

Jeremy grabbed onto the man's shirt. "You hurt my brother?"

"I..." When Kal spoke this time it was to his pale wife and brothers. "It wasn't supposed to go like that. No one was supposed to get hurt. No one. I took the kids. River wasn't afraid because obviously it was me. Made it easier. They just came with me. Then I returned to the party. Yes, they were drugged. And everything would have been fine if they hadn't fucked it up. They overdosed the kids. It was supposed to be so easy. I don't know what happened. He didn't need to do anything to them at all. They were sedated. That was it. An easy sleep. But he messed with the dose. And Phoenix got away. There was a struggle. You wouldn't let them dose you again. You ran. And yes..."

"Why would you do this?" His wife shouted now. Dr. Trevor took two steps back like he couldn't be near his brother. His other brother had his arms in front of him like he was trying to warn off the world. "You killed our baby."

I couldn't breathe just imagining this, but Phoenix looked strong. "You're right. I got away. I ran for help, but I couldn't find home because I was so confused. The one who smelled like bourbon, he hit me in the face. I was drugged and scared. I ran. And ran."

"Why?" she shouted again.

"Because the Lents spoil everything. All of our development here? The things we dreamed about? The hotels? They've taken all that land. They own it and they do nothing with it. They live up there in their fancy New York life, and we are stuck here, and they won't even let us develop our own land." He was shouting now. "And her family hates them. Hates them because they blame them for all kinds of shit. I just wanted them to feel threatened. To shut down so they would stop what they were doing and concentrate on home. That's what I wanted. I took the kids so it would seem like it wasn't us. Since River got taken too it was supposed to be obvious it wasn't us." He was shouting at Phoenix now. "I hate being a doctor. I hate it. You never remembered. Just a little scopolamine."

He shook his head. "Maybe it was the drugs, but you told me that if I said anything, then you would kill my family like you killed the kids and I just... forgot."

Well, he hadn't really. He'd repressed it. That had to be worse. I threw my arms around him just as Kit pushed Jeremy aside and struck Kal right in the face. Hard. The other man went down and the room erupted. Crying and screaming.

Phoenix backed up, and I held onto him. He turned and ran from the room, puking over the side of the balcony when we got outside. My guys were around us. Everyone was talking, but I couldn't hear any of them.

Their mother came outside. She carried a shot gun. "Phoenix. I am going to kill your uncles. My brothers won't get away with this."

As though she hadn't said she was about to commit murder, Rosalind stormed from the house. "Your fathers will kill him if his own brothers and wife don't. This will all be done by the end of day."

How could she look so calm?

"Mom," Barrett practically choked. "Even here there are laws. You can't kill them. I want to, too. What if they kill you?"

She shook her head. "They won't."

Stephen tore through the door, staring at us before his wife. "Go to the house. Your house. Now. Lock yourselves in."

Rosalind turned left, heading for the garage, and Stephen —who had once told me that he was the calm one—chased after her but apparently not to stop her as much as to help her. Or join her. My heart raced.

"No." Phoenix shook his head. "I want to see them. Like I saw him. I want to see them. I need to see them. Barrett?"

His older brother nodded. "Come on."

We had agreed when the time came we would help him, and even Julian seemed on board. These people had destroyed Phoenix's life. Broken him, as Jules had said to me once. He would never be who he should have been. I loved who he was now but that wasn't the point. He'd been vulnera-ble, and friends and family had betrayed him.

Something shattered inside. We piled into the Jeep, Barrett keeping up behind his mother's car. They wouldn't get to stop us.

It turned out they didn't try. I was finally on the other side of the lake. The houses were smaller, as Dina had described them, some of them looking like they were going to fall down any second. But the one we stopped at—it was upright. Old but standing just fine.

A man sat on the porch drinking a beer in a chair. When Rosalind jumped out of the car, he leapt up.

"Roz?" he shouted.

She cocked her shot gun right at him. "Where is he, Daryl?"

He paled. "What are you doing with that?"

We were all out of the car next to Stephen in a second. He looked at Phoenix. "Was he there?"

Once again I watched a grown man pale. "I wasn't." He held up his hands. "I never want trouble. Just to be left alone. You live your life up there. It is none of my business."

Phoenix shook his head. "I don't know him."

"Where. Is. He?" Rosalind shouted. "I won't ask again. He hurt my son. His kin. I deserve this and you know it. All these years forgetting I grew up here too. I know and remember the same lessons you learned. Where is he?"

He cleared his throat. "He ran with Miles when they fucked up the kidnapping. He's gone as far as I know."

Phoenix took a deep breath. "Fuck."

"Language," his mother said; it almost seemed more like a reflex, and she didn't turn to look at him. "You tell him if you hear from him that his days are numbered. I'm not scared of you anymore. Any of you. I was scared too long. But maybe I finally found Dina's backbone. They're dead."

I couldn't help but think Dina would love this. She believed in revenge, and it turned out, so did I.

❧ 16 ❧

We turned toward the cars when another one screeched to a stop and Eric and Daniel rushed out of it. Eric grabbed his wife. "Did you kill them?"

She shook her head. "They're not here. They've gone missing."

He pulled her to him and then after a second Daniel took her from Eric to give her a hug, too.

"I thought maybe I was coming to bury a body." Eric laughed. "But okay. I'll go home and ice Kit's hand."

She visibly swallowed. "I can't believe he hit him. I've never seen Kit fight outside of a courtroom."

"I wish I had gotten some swings in. His brother actually killed him. So, they are dealing with hiding the body now. They do like to keep the law unto themselves here. I mean, were you listening to the crap he was spewing?"

I stopped listening to them. Hiding bodies went above my paygrade. I was glad he was dead. He had killed children—including one of his own—and hurt my love. All my loves. He had gotten to live too long unscathed.

Eric touched the side of Phoenix's cheek. "We failed you. We let that man into your life. I'm sorry."

Phoenix caught his breath. "You know, Eric, I ah... I'm not sure what to say exactly. A lot of things went wrong. I can't... I can't seem to really focus on them right now. I'm just trying to breathe."

His bio dad nodded at him. "Okay. Just know that's how I feel. How we all feel. In case you ever wondered if Kit loved you—I know you guys think he's hard—you should know he was absolutely going to kill him."

Barrett cleared his throat. "We know you guys love us. It's just... not always easy."

"No, it's not and that's our fault." Stephen spoke fast. "Not yours. Never yours. And our fathers would be ashamed of us because they were wonderful. We've always been so concerned with hiding that we haven't... been enough out there with how we feel."

Rosalind covered her eyes with her hand. "That's my fault. I've always been terrified. I wanted a life away from here, but I didn't have the first idea how to do it. Dina tried to tell me, but I was really consumed with trying to do it myself."

"Maybe we should continue this conversation elsewhere and at a later time." Daniel kissed her head. "Let's go home."

I wrapped my arm around Phoenix's waist. I wanted to ask him if he was okay, but time and place was an issue here too. I didn't know how much he wanted to say in front of his parents.

"Hey, you four." Stephen stepped back toward the car. "I love my brothers tremendously. I would do anything for them. But I have never seen anything like the way the four of you are and always have been with each other. I just want you to know that."

He turned his back on us, walking toward Rosalind and the car that Daniel and Eric had arrived in. Like a zombie, I walked toward the other car. We all climbed in together. Barrett didn't turn it on. We just sat there in the driveway silently. Julian was up front with Barrett, and I was in the back between Jeremy and Phoenix. He put his head down in my lap, breathing hard. I put my hands in his hair.

This had been an insane day. But as much as I was reeling, his entire life had just been upended. His memory had just come back. His hair was soft, and I petted it slowly. His eyes were squeezed shut. No way did he want to talk right then. In the rearview mirror, I met Barrett's gaze. He was worried, and I couldn't blame him. I was too.

As abruptly as he'd put his head in my lap, Phoenix sat up. "Anyone find it really fucking bizarre to see our mother holding a shot gun? I mean, did you know that she could do that?"

Jeremy snorted before he threw his head back and laughed. "Totally bizarre."

Julian shook his head and some of the wariness in Barrett's gaze lessened in its worry just a tad. With my hands in my lap now I stared straight forward. It hadn't shocked me to see her with a shot gun. First, it wasn't her first time with a gun in front of me. She'd done it when she thought she was going to get her brother the first time. Also, she had a whole background that no one discussed where she grew up here. They'd tried to marry her off to old men and she had traveled the country alone to escape them. Yes, she was a woman who could take care of herself.

But, I was glad they were laughing. I wasn't ready yet. I might never be again.

I RUBBED my eyes and stared in the mirror. It was two in the morning, and no one was sleeping. I could hear the television on in my room playing at a low volume. The guys were all up doing things quietly around the house.

He had kidnapped Phoenix for the land? Because they wanted what the Lents had? And Rosalind's family had helped—probably murdering the children—because they were jealous? Things were not very different here than they had been in Manhattan. Was there anywhere where people didn't do this? Or was life really a constant war between those who had things and those who wanted the things others had?

Yeah... I was dark in my own head right then. Maybe I should call my psychiatrist. Oh that was right. I couldn't do that. His brother had almost gotten Phoenix killed and had messed him up pretty badly for the rest of his life.

The door to the bathroom opened, and Phoenix walked in. I met his gaze in the mirror. He wrapped his arms around me from behind.

Finally, he spoke. "I would go through it again. I would choose to. If I had known that eventually I'd end up here with you."

I whirled around. "No. I wouldn't wish that on you. We'd have met anyway. So I would wish you never had to go through any of this."

He shook his head. "Isn't it the butterfly effect or something? We change one thing and everything changes?"

I took his cheeks in my hand. "Have you talked to Sam?"

"Thought about it, but I don't feel like using that outlet right now, and I kind of think he is... happily preoccupied. I don't need to mess with that right now."

I shook my head. "What do you mean?"

"Oh you didn't notice it? Yeah, Sally and Sam and his brothers. Pretty sure that is happening."

My mouth fell open. "You think?"

What would that even mean? Would she stay here with

them? It would certainly mean I could actually talk to someone.

"I do." He leaned against the bathroom mirror. "We all need to try to go to bed."

He was right. I lifted an eyebrow. "Do you think you'll be able to do that, because I'm not sure I can sleep."

Phoenix shook his head, slowly. "No. I need to go back to the Hamptons."

I blinked. Okay. That was an abrupt shift. "You do?"

"Yes. Will you go with me?" He chewed on his fingernail.

I swallowed. "Wherever you go, I go. That's the deal right?"

Phoenix tugged me to him. "Yes, but I didn't live up to my end of that deal. You were alone and hurting without me."

I closed my eyes, pressing my forehead against his shoulder. "You had your own pain to face, and I wasn't with you."

"You know it's not the same thing." He sighed. "So yes, you'll come with me. I'm going to assume my brothers will. I'll officially ask, but they'll say yes. Honestly, I think Barrett is about two seconds from exploding being here. And none of us have gotten to deal with our grandmother's death. I need some space from my parents, too. Even this kinder, gentler parent thing they are doing. It's too much. We can't undo all of the years of what has been because they suddenly got... affectionate."

I supposed that was true. I might never really understand the intricacies of their familial relationships. Not ever. I might get close, but I hadn't lived it myself.

He rocked me back and forth as a sound reached me from outside of the room. Finally, I spoke again. "I don't ever want it to be tit for tat with us, quid pro quo or whatever. Maybe they'll be some times when I do more for you guys or you guys do more for me." I suspected it was the latter most of the time. "But we're not keeping track. Okay?"

He nodded. "You know, or maybe you don't know, that one of the things that I struggle with is feeling worthy. I lived when the others didn't, and I spent the next years really drugged up and out of it. One of the things that I was running away from was the feeling of not being worthy. Worthlessness. I mean, why do I get to live this life anyway? Why do I get to have everything when so many people struggle? I'm not special. Anyway, add to that the not dying thing and I... I just struggle with it. So I want to make sure I'm living up to your love. Living up to the end of our unspoken bargain of getting to be yours and have you as mine."

I squeezed him tighter. "No. I hadn't understood that. Not at all. Not even a little bit." My voice hitched. "You are so worthy. You are beyond worthy. You are everything that is good in the world."

He kissed my temple. "I think you might be the only person in the world who would say that or think that. Come on. Bedtime. There are no good conversations to have after midnight."

That was probably true.

There was noise in the bedroom. Someone had climbed into bed. I pulled back from Phoenix.

"Leave in the morning?"

"Maybe by lunch. I'll get Kit to get the plane."

Okay. That sounded fine. That was right. They had a plane. I couldn't really remember it, but they must have brought me in it. "Your granny had to drive to New Orleans and fly from there. It was hours of driving ."

He put his arm around me, and we walked toward the door. "That might be fun under other circumstances, and I'm being totally selfish, but I want to get there so I can see what I need to see."

"Which is what?"

He visibly swallowed. "Where they held me."

It was Julian who was in bed, and he sat up, leaning on the back of his elbows, some of his brown hair falling into his eyes. He needed a haircut. "Are we going to the Hamptons?"

"Unless there is a reason not to, and frankly, after today, I'm in a get-the-fuck-out-of-dodge kind of a mood."

I climbed in next to Julian who rolled me against his side. Phoenix climbed in behind me and wrapped his arms around my waist.

"You don't want to stay here and wait it out?" Julian stared at the ceiling.

"I just remembered what I've been not able to think about for years. I want to go see it for myself. And yes I want to run away. I'm admitting that."

Julian nodded. "Okay, we'll run away with you. Where you go we go. That's the motto we all live by." He yawned.

I sighed. "I'm so sorry you haven't really had the time to mourn your grandmother. This was supposed to be her day."

Jeremy leaned in the doorway. I wasn't sure how long he had been there. "I can't think of anything she would have liked more than to get answers about what happened to Phoenix all of those years ago."

He walked toward us. "Where are we going tomorrow? I missed that part."

Phoenix nuzzled the back of my neck. "The Hamptons."

"Right. I haven't been there in the winter in years. Okay." He squeezed my foot. "Love you, Alatheia."

I smiled at him. "I love you too."

"That's good. Because I am not sure what I'd do if you didn't anymore."

His words were like a warm bath through my mind. They flushed the day away with them. There would be plenty of time to worry about things tomorrow. Those struggles weren't going anywhere.

THE WIND BLEW hard at my head. It was cold even though I had the slightest bit more of fuzz on top of my scalp . Sally stood next to me, and we stared at the lake together.

I swallowed. "And you're sure? Because you could come with us. I mean now that you know you could totally come with us."

She side-eyed me. "I... I know I shouldn't be so comfortable in so little a period of time, but I really like them, and I don't want to leave them. They don't seem to want me to leave either. When I brought it up, they actually got really quiet, and I think upset. Sam said that maybe if I went, they would come too. That seems silly. Phoenix has stuff to do or whatever. You guys need to go. I've never... felt this way before. Maybe I had to go through what I went through to get here? Or is that just fantasy ridiculousness or something?"

I shook my head. "I would be the last person to know how to answer that. This has all been nuts for me. In the best possible way. But I don't think that either of us, or any of us in that place, had to go through that for any particular reason. I don't believe that. It just happened because it happened."

She hugged me to her. "I think we'll see each other again soon. Sam will miss Phoenix. I bet we come see you soon."

I hoped that was true. I had hardly gotten to see her, but I did like the idea of leaving her here. No one was trying to kill Sam's family. Or kidnap them. Or whatever. For Sally, maybe this place would be tranquil and healing.

"If it doesn't work out, you always have a place with me. Okay?"

She hugged me. "Thanks for saving my life."

I blinked. Had I done that? I guessed I had. I'd wanted to save everyone. I had no idea what happened to anyone else. "Do you think... they're all dead?"

She sighed. "Maybe. I mean... I keep thinking I should start googling them, but I don't know what I'll do if I find out they're dead. Who's going to believe any of us? We were branded as bad, you know?"

I did, actually. From the moment my mother died everything about my life had changed. "That seems to be our story, right? Everyone's, I mean. Something happens and the world makes a decision about us and that's that. We're too young to know we should be protecting ourselves when it happens and yeah, that's it."

She nodded. "Yes. But how could we protect ourselves anyway? Even if we did know."

She looked away. "Anyway, I'm glad to be here. Be careful, okay? It sounds like up there... everything is a lot."

That was putting it mildly. I had inadvertently brought her here. What was going to happen to her now was anyone's guess. But she wouldn't get killed by the Lents' worries. They would have no reason to bother with her.

I could keep her safe by leaving. That much I knew.

❧

I COULDN'T REALLY REMEMBER my flight over here. Just the sense of the Lents talking to me as we boarded the plane, but I tried to remember some of it anyway. The whole thing was just a blank. A big old emptiness.

Barrett sat down next to me, snuggling against me. "You okay?"

I chewed on my lip. "I was trying to remember flying here."

He winced. "You were in such bad shape. It's like a miracle you're upright and doing as well as you are right now considering what you just went through and what is happening around us."

I leaned on his shoulder. "Maybe I will fall apart into a million pieces one day and can't be put back together."

He kissed my temple. "I can't see that happening. Not with you. But if it happened, that would be okay. I'd just fall apart with you, and we could be broken together."

I smiled. "I hate flying. This is my, I guess, my sixth flight ever. I only remember three of them. I hate it."

Jeremy slumped into a seat across from us. "What we need to do is take you on vacation. Like a real vacation. On an airplane. And then you can associate it with fun stuff instead of just always being hauled around."

I lifted my head. "What would that be like? A vacation? I mean your vacation is the Hamptons right?"

"That's where we summer. I wouldn't call it a vacation. Or where we summered." He added the past tense. "I liked the summer in the city with you."

Phoenix climbed onto the plane and walked to one of the longer seats. He winked at me before he lay down on it. Okay. He was going to nap. Julian was last on. He walked over and kissed my cheek before he sat next to his brother, yawning.

Yes, they were all exhausted. So was I. But I doubted I would sleep.

"How did it go with your fathers?" I asked Barrett and Jeremy, looking at both of them.

Jer shrugged. "It went fine. They're under water emotionally the same way we are. They have a lot of shit to deal with. And, they have to unpack it. Better they do that without us here. But on the other side they want us around because they are all in this newly rediscovered we-have-to-be-a-family zone and that's hard."

The engines started, and I shivered. Yes, I really hated this. I was never going to feel better about it, no matter how many people insisted it was perfectly safe.

Julian opened his eyes. "I should have gotten you a Xanax from my mother's cabinet."

"We don't need to be giving out drugs, over the counter or otherwise." Phoenix called from where he'd lain down. "My goal is to keep Alatheia away from all that. You remember what happened last time?"

Julian shook his head and closed his eyes again. "She isn't going to get arrested for drugs on this plane from one pill that no one has to know she ever took. But point taken. I was just worried about the fact that she is scared."

The plane took to the air right then, and I forced myself to breathe. Okay, that part was done.

"I can distract you." Jeremy groaned. "With something I've been keeping to myself. But it is distracting."

Even Phoenix sat up with this announcement. I looked between them. The other three had no idea what he was going to say. That was different for sure.

"What is it?" I met Jer's gaze.

He leaned back. "Murial Monk is texting me daily. I kept it from you. Why bother you with it? But, she's becoming increasingly pushy about it. The Monks want to see you."

And in a world where the Lents ruled almost everything they touched, the Monks actually outranked them. It would be hard to keep the Monks from getting to me if they really wanted to push the issue, even for the Lents. The guys would fight them, for me. I knew that with everything in me. The question was how difficult did I want to make this for everyone?

I sighed. "Did you tell her that I don't have hair?"

"Yes. I mean, initially she understood you'd had your hair shaved. Why?" Jeremy shook his head.

He didn't get it. That was okay. Jer lived in rich world but this was girl world. Girl world and rich world colliding. As had been clear in the city, he really didn't understand that world. Not at all.

"She isn't going to want me around looking like this." I rubbed my hair. "Take a photo. Send it to her. Just text not ready yet. Or something like that."

Jer rubbed his eyes. "I am absolutely not going to say anything disparaging about how you look. You are gorgeous. End of story. And your hair is fuzzy. It's everything I can do not to not rub my hand over it all of the time."

Barrett snorted and then outright laughed. "I would love to see you try to do that. Just rub her head."

With a smirk, Jeremy shook his head. "I am controlling myself. The point remains. I will not be saying she doesn't look good to Murial Monk. Fuck that."

Phoenix lay back down. "Tell her to wait. Just because she is bored with her life doesn't mean that she gets to interfere in ours. Cousin or no cousin."

Julian who kept almost falling asleep shook his head. "She is a Monk. Whether we like it or not. Maybe Alatheia would like to see her cousin. We can't just assume she doesn't. Do you want to see your father's family?"

I shuddered. "Not yet. Maybe not ever, but I don't suppose that is possible. So no. Not yet."

Julian nodded. "We need to at least ask." He snapped a picture of me. "I'm texting her. I'll say as you can see she isn't feeling ready for New York yet. Talk soon."

Jeremy groaned. "You realize you just opened the door so she can text you too. Actually, why am I complaining? It gets her off my shit."

"If you want, I can text her myself."

"No," they both answered together, and I smiled. My ears popped and the engines made a noise. I closed my eyes tightly.

"It's just the engines slowing after lift," Julian supplied, and I shook my head.

"Don't tell me, okay? I feel like that makes it worse."

Barrett kissed my cheek. "Jer's right. We need a vacation. A big one. For many, many reasons."

Despite my terror, the turbulence was minimal, and I actually dozed on Barrett's shoulder. He smelled familiar, and the plane was quiet, filled with the sounds of the guys breathing and the airplane traveling through the sky toward the Hamptons where we would go to collect the rest of Phoenix's memory and maybe let my hair grow in for a while before I had to be a Monk.

It was hard to imagine that could actually happen. I wasn't a Monk. I wasn't even sure that I could be a Lent. They had to be so constantly on to not have their truths exposed. I didn't know if I'd be any good at it or make it worse for them. But I wasn't giving them up. I could potentially avoid taking ownership of being a Monk. But I would be a Lent because I needed them like air.

I jolted as the feeling of descent struck my ears. Barrett read a magazine that had cars on it, and he looked up at me when I woke.

"Hey. You're okay. We've just started our descent."

That was what I figured. "I'll work out how to be a Lent. And not be embarrassing."

"You could never be embarrassing. You're everything. You're all the whys."

I wasn't how Barrett saw me. But I loved that he did.

❧ 17 ❧

I hadn't expected the beach to look so quiet, so impossibly still. The cold had swept across the sand like a hush, leaving everything dusted in white—snow clinging to the rooftops, the paths, even the edges of the bay. I walked toward the house, wishing I had boots, my sneakers pressing deep into the packed sand, my breath fogging just enough to feel the bite in the air. The house loomed in a way it hadn't in summer—less like a backdrop and more like something ancient and watching. Or maybe I just felt that way because I knew what was coming. Phoenix was going to remember. It would be dark. Like the estate looked right now. The windows were dark in the main house, and the little houses—their g ranny's and the guest house—closer to the trees looked almost shy, tucked into the snow like they didn't want to be seen.

Like we didn't want to be seen. The staff had come in and set up the guest house for us. The last time I'd been here I had stayed in their granny's house. But now no one wanted to go inside of it. Her death was too close right now. Like setting foot in her place would overwhelm us with it. We'd eaten dinner and climbed into bed quietly, hardly saying anything after we arrived. With the guys still asleep, I had crept outside to watch the sunrise over this scene. I couldn't sleep. Everything was just... too much.

Inside, there'd be silence. No slamming doors or music bouncing from the kitchen where the chefs were working. The fridge was stocked, but we were left to cook it, which was fine by me. Still, it was strange to be here in all of this nothingness. Just the echo of empty rooms and the trace of summer still clinging to the curtains like memory even though it was months ago. I hadn't spent much time here, having been thrown out before summer had really gotten started. But, I'd thought of it like that. The Hamptons. This place. Their granny had hated it here. Still, she'd come every summer to be with her family. The guys were okay with not doing that anymore. I might be too.

This place was terrible in its beauty.

I stood at the bottom of the porch, unsure if I wanted to step inside or stay here a moment longer—this quiet, frozen version of the house that only existed in the off-season. It was beautiful, in a lonely sort of way.

Julian came through the door, staring at me for a long second. "If you're going to go walking in the snow, you need to at least wear a coat and a hat. Some better shoes."

I did have clothes. I hadn't packed myself, but someone had. My bag lay unopened on the living room floor, surrounded by the others. Inside, it smelled like the fireplace. Someone had lit a fire.

"Which one of you knew how to light a fire?"

I stepped toward Julian's open arms and let his warmth fill my body. He was right, of course. But I wasn't feeling like being smart about the weather. "I just wanted to see it. For a moment. In stillness. Or something."

He pressed our foreheads together. "You couldn't sleep because I was snoring, right?"

"Not that. I don't even hear the two of you snoring anymore. It just sounds like home to me."

He rocked me with his laugh. "Love you. And to answer your question, apparently Phoenix knows how to make a fire. He doesn't remember how he learned, but he knows how to do it."

"Yeah, I'm slightly concerned that there are going to be a lot of things in my life like this. Like I know something but how I know is a bit of a blur."

Julian let go of me, and I hugged Phoenix. "Well, that has to be weird. But I am really glad you made this fire."

"Me too." He nodded. "It's going to start to snow again, so I'm going to wait to go on my let's-find-where-they-held-me quest until tomorrow when I think the weather report is better."

That sounded like a plan. I didn't see Jeremy or Barrett. Maybe they were both still sleeping. "What got you two up?"

"Cold where you were supposed to be." Julian sat down on the couch; he patted the spot next to him, and I sat on it. They had been who I had been cuddling with the night before. "I'm sorry. I just... needed to see this place in the winter."

Phoenix threw himself down next to me. "That's okay. You aren't trapped in bed because we happen to be asleep. Although, wait, what am I talking about? I completely want you trapped in bed."

I laughed, throwing my head back, which made them both grin. The fire crackled in the fireplace. It flickered quietly, its orange glow painting soft shadows on the wooden walls. This house had less stone everywhere than their granny's had. In the hush of early morning, the world outside that I'd just traipsed through to get a look at things, felt miles away—snow whispering against glass, the cold nowhere to be found in our little room. They'd built the rooms smaller in here than the other houses too. There were more of them and they were each tinier in size. How had they made these decisions? Would that be in the diaries?

I watched the flames twist and climb. The crackle and snap of burning wood filled the silence between us. Julian played with a piece of my hair, tugging it as he too stared at the fire.

Phoenix sighed. "Other situations I might be scared to wake up and find you gone but I know, at least for now, no one is here who would want to hurt you." He rubbed his chin. "Then again I guess I am going to have to get over myself. You went around New York with no trouble. In fact, half the time I didn't know what was going on, so I couldn't have helped you even if you'd needed help. And you got sent away because of me, which just illustrates the point so, yeah, go ahead and do as you like. Ignore me. "

I shook my head. "Phoenix, you also saved me when I got hit by the PI and chased him down and threatened to hit him with your skateboard. So, you showed up a lot for me, too."

Julian frowned. "I need to be more heroic."

"You are plenty heroic. What you need to be doing more of is writing." I smiled at him.

"No, Baby, the person who needs to be writing and creating is you." He leaned toward me. "Time to pick back up the *Poor Relation*?"

Now there was a thought. With everything... I just hadn't. But should I?

"Hey," Jeremy called down to us from the top of the stairs. "Why didn't anyone wake me? I don't want to miss fireside chats with Alatheia." He was half asleep. I could tell from the way he ran his words together. "Is there coffee? Who made the fire?"

I got up. "I'll make it."

The guys weren't particularly wonderful in the kitchen. It came from years of not having to be. No one had ever taught them to cook, and probably they would go their whole lives without having to do it. I blinked. Would I be with them the rest of their whole lives?

"I can make it." Phoenix yawned.

He could. Truthfully, they could all use the coffee maker. That much they could handle. And probably I could teach them some basic meals. They'd all attempted things like eggs and easy things for me.

I rubbed his arm. "I'm more awake than you. I'll make it."

"That's what happens when you don't sleep." Julian sighed.

Jer came downstairs the rest of the way. "She didn't sleep?"

"Not much, " I answered. "Don't stress about it. New place. Lots on my mind. Whatever."

I fiddled in the kitchen, eventually making coffee and turning on the oven to cook bacon. If they wanted something else, I would make it. I heard footsteps before arms came around me from behind. It was Barrett. I leaned against him.

"Morning." I smiled. "Coffee is almost ready."

He nudged me. "You obviously didn't sleep okay."

"Does anyone sleep okay? Ever?" I raised an eyebrow.

"Probably some people do. I mean, I don't really know any, but yeah." I lifted my mouth to kiss his chin.

"Move so I don't accidently burn you if I spill this." I paused. That had sounded more pushy than I'd meant it to. "Please."

He had already let go by the time I said please, and he winked at me. "Might be worth it to get burned to get to hold onto you."

Barrett was so sweet. I doubted anyone outside of our household would know that, but he really was. I poured coffee and turned to him. "Hey, when you are a little bit more awake, can you play the piano? You haven't been playing since we got back together." There had been a piano in the other house, but he hadn't used it. In Manhattan, when he wasn't busy, he tended to just be on it playing quietly in the background of every day, like he lost himself in the music.

He blinked, taking his coffee cup when I offered it. "Sure. I... I guess I sort of lost it when they took you away. I haven't wanted to play since. I'm not some kind of great musician, as you know. I just like it. I want to help real musicians."

Well... there he was. This was the Barrett who had been missing since my return. He had been too busy taking care of all of us to talk about what he wanted. "I think you don't give yourself enough credit."

He leaned over to whisper in my ear. "The fact that you could even think that is such a gift."

Phoenix came in. "Hey—oh is that mine? Thank you—" He picked up his coffee cup. "Let's register for school. Want to?"

I stared at him. "Like in the public school here?" Was there one? I had no idea. I supposed there had to be. People did live here all year round.

"No." He shook his head. "That's not a terrible idea, but I don't want you out in public until you're feeling better about things so that if it gets back to someone we don't want seeing you yet that you're out, you can withstand their presence. I mean, unless you really want to? I meant online. We could go to school online."

I picked up my own cup. "I don't have a strong desire to be seen in front of others right now. Just us. Warning, that might last forever. We could be locked away forever." I winked at him. "You guys can tell me when it's enough."

Jeremy laughed as he came into the room. "They'll make documentaries about us. The hermits in the house in the Hamptons. But whatever. I'm good with that, truly."

I put out my hand. We had never settled the photo issue. "Phone please."

"You have one." He yawned and took his coffee as his brother dragged himself into the room and leaned against the counter.

Yes, I did. "I need Murial's phone number. I'm going to take over communicating with her. Relieve you of this burden."

He stared at me. "Really? You want that?"

Phoenix slid his computer toward me. "Enter your info. I'll register us. Or you know what? I'll just do it for you. You don't need to deal with this."

It took me a second to realize he was still talking about school. There were a lot of various conversations going on at the same time. The sound of music wafted into my ears. The easy light sound of piano playing. I guessed maybe that wasn't fair. Sometimes piano playing could be intense, dark. But it wasn't right then. Barrett was feeling joyful.

Jer finally passed me his phone. I took a photo, not letting myself look at it at all because I might hate it and then want to take a better one. The worse the better right now. This was the second time she would be seeing how awful I looked. Hopefully this time she would realize it wasn't an easily fixed problem.

I attached it to a message and typed before I could overthink it.

Hey, this is Alatheia. I know we have a lot to talk about, but this is what I look like right now. Still recovering from where I was. I'll be in touch.

I hoped that would be good enough. "Let me know if—when—she answers, it requires more."

Jer frowned. "I like that photo of you. It's you, having taken a walk, looking brisk, bright and beautiful."

I shook my head. "Liar. I see that picture. We both know

I am not yet looking like any of that, if I ever did." I kissed his chin. "We can get you some glasses. I'm sure there must be an eye doctor somewhere."

He groaned. "Alatheia..."

Phoenix cut him off. "She's stunningly beautiful. Even when she was in the hospital. We are in agreement. But we both need an elective. What looks appealing? I'll go ahead and take whatever you want."

"You did not have the slightest interest in the same elective as me when we were at Pullman." I stepped toward Phoenix. "Like, is there a writing class? Or something? You won't like it."

He shrugged. "I need to pass. That's it. Get out of school so the parents are satisfied I have a high school diploma. No one is actually expecting me to go to college. The three of them? Yes. You? Yes, you should go. Not me. So, I just need to do whatever to get out of there. I'll take what you take so we can do the process together."

Julian pointed at Phoenix. "Look at him being pragmatic."

"Fuck off, big brother." Phoenix grinned at Julian, which negated the harshness of the words.

Jer's phone dinged and I looked over at him. He winced. "She agrees with you. She thinks it's three weeks until you can be seen by her but says one way or another she will be seeing you then."

I sighed. "Tell her I'll come into the city and meet with her privately. How's that?"

Phoenix clicked on his computer. "We're both registered for art appreciation unless you hate that."

"Perfect." It really was. I was going to finish high school. That seemed like exactly what I should be doing. I nudged Phoenix, "Aren't we here so you can find where you were held and make peace with it?"

He leaned back. "I don't know that I am ever going to

make peace with it. But, we are here to find it. Once we find it, maybe we stay. Just stay and finish things and then figure out what to do after that."

We hadn't discussed that. Not at all. Phoenix had just sort of thought we'd stay here? The piano playing stopped, and Barrett rose to come over to us. The twins were staring at him, rapt attention on their faces. I wasn't the only one who noted what Phoenix had just said.

Okay. I had to speak first. "You hate it here. I spent less than a week the last time I was here. I... I don't know if I'm ready to commit to making this full time."

Was that fair? I hoped I wasn't being a bitch. Or ungrateful. Or problematic.

"I don't want to hate it here anymore." Phoenix sipped his coffee. "Was there bacon? Anyway, I'm working on not hating it here."

Yes, I could walk to the fridge. "So you want to stay to... prove something? To show the world or whatever that you aren't afraid of this place?'

"I hate that word. Ooh, maybe that's something I should talk to Sam about. Afraid. Look at you making connections I wasn't making. Love you so much, Red. Um, yes, that." He drummed his fingers on the counter. "Don't make bacon. I have to run out. Actually, three of us have to run out."

I turned to look at him. "What?"

"I have to run out." He started again. Yes, that I had garnered. I interrupted him. "Where do you have to go? Three of you?"

Julian walked over and put his arm around me. "We have a surprise for you. Phoenix, Jeremy, and Barrett are going for a drive. They'll be back. I am staying here with you." He kissed my cheek. "I won the coin toss."

Phoenix grinned before he groaned. "But... but I was kidnapped. I need to stay here with Alatheia. I need it."

Jeremy tossed a napkin at him. "Sorry, that isn't working today."

Phoenix grinned broader. "A guy has to try."

"Hold on. Where are you going? What surprise?"

Jeremy leaned against the wall. "If we told you then it wouldn't be a surprise, now would it?"

If Jeremy was going it was a present they were getting. He was the absolutely official master of gift giving.

I swallowed. "Guys, I don't need gifts."

"Sure you do." Barrett stretched. "We all need gifts, and I think giving you gifts is the best thing in the world. So you do."

I fingered my ear lobe. There was still phantom pain from when I had to take off the sapphires Phoenix gave me, and I looked for my pearls all the time that Jer had gifted me. "What if someone takes whatever you give me? When that happens... I..."

Julian kissed my cheek, lingering there. "No one is taking anything from you. Not ever again. And... I don't want to get your hopes up..."

"Jules." Jeremy interrupted. "The point of not getting her hopes up is to, you know, not get her hopes up."

What was going on? Phoenix laughed. "We are a pathetic bunch. Now she knows there is something we're not telling her. It's a good thing. Both your present and this thing we're not talking about are good things. So don't worry. If that is possible."

As the other three exited the room, grumbling at each other, Jules shook his head and squeezed my hand. "Want me to tell you? He doesn't get to tell me what to say or do. Even if he thinks he does. Jeremy is not in charge. You're in charge. Want to know?"

I swallowed. "If it... No. But do me a favor, if it's something that isn't going to happen, like you know for sure that it isn't going to happen, tell me then what it was?"

I wasn't even sure I had said that coherently, but Julian nodded. He must speak and understand Alatheia. I was grateful for that. More than grateful. As the front door closed, indicating that the three of them had gone on an errand to buy me something they just thought I had to have because they loved me, I smiled at Julian.

We were alone. I was so rarely alone with any of them—and I wasn't complaining—but I wanted to take advantage. I leaned over to kiss him. Jules caught his breath. He hadn't anticipated I was going to do that.

"Wow." His voice was low. "I love when you kiss me. When you spontaneously kiss me."

I took his hand, leading him over to the couch. "Maybe we can do more of that."

"Kiss? Yes." He took over dragging me against him when we sat down on the couch to really kiss me. He had so much more experience with this stuff than me, and that was fine, I wasn't going to think about it, particularly right then, but he could kiss like he had been born to do it. And if I was being romantic—and right then I was—I might think that he had been born to kiss me.

I was going with that.

His lips were smooth and warm. I sighed against him, and he deepened our embrace. Julian would never push me on anything physical, which was wonderful, but it really left it to me to take things to the next level if that was what I wanted. And it was what I wanted. Right then.

I pulled back to look at him. Maybe it wasn't what he would want. I was pretty beat up still, quasi-bald, and a mess. Still, there was nothing I could do but ask.

"Julian Lent." I had no idea why I started this exchange by saying his full name. Well, sort of his full name.

"Alatheia Winder." He lifted an eyebrow. "Sorry. You did it, so I thought maybe that was something we were doing."

I loved him so fucking much. "Actually, what is your middle name? That's not the point of this conversation, but I realized I don't know. I don't know any of your middle names. Unless your parents weren't middle name people."

He touched his chest. "I'm Julian Emerson Lent." He smiled. "Very literary. I know. My mom just liked it. But maybe it made me a writer. My dear twin who thinks he is in charge is Jeremy Nathaniel Lent. After Gran's oldest husband. Barrett Heath. Some actor Mom liked. Phoenix Alaric. That's from some show about vampires? That was on at the time." He kissed my mouth, gently. "And you are Jayne Alatheia Winder."

"So weird. Never knew that I was Jayne." I grinned. "We sort of match, don't we? Julian and Jayne."

He leaned back. "Love it."

"Okay so back to the main point?" I swallowed. "Maybe I'm nervous."

"To talk about something with me? I hope not. Come on, Baby. Whatever it is, just say it, I love you and your every thought."

"We're alone. Maybe we could... get naked together and see how things go. That is if you have a condom." There I said it. Badly. But I did.

He smoothed my hair off my forehead. "Sounds like a great idea. You. Naked. Seeing how things go. And yes I do but there's no rush to that if you don't want to..."

I shook my head. "I want to. With you. For my official first time. If you're..."

He kissed me. I guessed he was.

⚘ 18 ⚘

I managed to talk in between his kisses. "I have very little experience with this, so you are going to have to lead this show."

"It's not a show." He kissed my neck, and I shivered. "It's just me loving you. And you have no idea how incredible you are. Don't have any nerves. You want to stop? We stop. Okay?"

I nodded, hardly able to think through what he was doing to my neck. "I know. And same by the way, if you want to stop, we stop."

He laughed. "Thank you. I can pretty much guarantee I won't want to stop."

Still, he should know he had a say too.

Outside a sight caught my attention. It was snowing. It had the night before while we were sleeping, but now I could see it. I bit down on my lip. "Jules, should we go upstairs? I mean, I know we're all in this kind of unique relationship, but I would rather your brothers not walk through the door right in the middle."

"Me too." He nodded and jumped up before I could

imagine what he would do, scooping me up in his arms. I made a sound—something akin to an oomph. He grinned. "In my head, I was better at that. I will just have to practice doing it."

I shook my head. "I loved it."

"Good. Still going to practice. Be aware." He smiled before he winked at me. "Or don't be aware. It's more fun to surprise you."

He carried me up the stairs and went into one of the bedrooms we hadn't yet used. They were all empty of any character, matching, as they were purely used as guest rooms for anyone staying with the Lents. There were no small touches; they just looked utilitarian, which led me to believe that the Lents didn't want guests staying very long.

Knowing them, that was absolutely true.

The bed was comfortable enough. Someone had taken the time to make that happen. They were all king sized and soft but not too soft. It didn't matter right then. Not when I had Julian leaning over me.

He was so strong; he was in a plank position over my body, and it didn't bother him at all. He smiled down at me, and I bit down on his lower lip. He closed his eyes and sighed. Yes, that was a good sound. Okay. That worked.

Maybe I wasn't entirely inept at this seduction thing. Or maybe he just loved me.

That had to be it because I knew exactly how bad I was looking right then.

He opened his lids, his blue eyes so clear and bright I had to catch my breath to look at them. "If this is a dream, don't wake me up."

The same went for me. We could share this mutual unbelievable moment together in disbelief. That worked.

His fingers brushed over the fuzz on top of my head before coming down to cup the side of my face, lingering for a moment as if memorizing me with his fingertips. The room felt suspended in time, as if only we existed within the space of these walls. Even the faint hum of the heat being pumped in faded into the background. It was just the two of us, breathing each other in.

He kissed me again, softer this time, a gentle reassurance that everything here was real despite its dreamlike quality. I pressed closer, needing more of what I had asked for and what he was offering me.

When he finally pulled back, he looked at me with a kind of reverence that belonged to only him. This was a Julian look, and I was lucky that I got to see it. To the rest of the world he was Julian Lent, untouchable, rich and unknown past the external. In his gaze I could see his soul. "You know," he murmured, "I never thought I'd find this. How could I? With what and who we are? But you're here and you want this. With me."

I swallowed, feeling every unspoken word between us settle softly in the air. "Neither did I," I admitted, tracing the outline of his jaw with my fingertips. "But I'm not letting go. And I'm the one who has to consider who and what I am. Not you... you're perfect. Don't argue."

Julian smiled. "The fact that you know I would is enough. You're the perfect one here."

We undressed each other. Maybe the time for words had passed. I didn't know. I was new to this. Every time I'd gotten naked before it had been different. With Jules it was silent, and I loved it.

Finally, when I was completely exposed to him, I forced myself to meet his gaze. "I didn't think I'd feel shy."

"But you are." He nodded. "I am too."

I shook my head. "Are you lying?"

"To you? Never. No, I am. You matter, Baby. Like nothing else, or anyone in the universe."

He slipped a finger inside of me before he leaned down to suck on my nipple. I bucked beneath him. Wow, I was sensitive. Really sensitive and wanting more. I wasn't sure what I should be doing right then. In our position, I could kiss his shoulders and run my hands around his back, so I did just that.

His skin was soft and firm. Jules tasted clean and smelled masculine like the citrus scent of his soap only enhanced the very essence that was Jules. He lifted his head. "I am so excited. You can probably feel that. I will be better at this next time. If it goes too fast. You can count on that."

Was he worried about that? "Jules..."

He winced. "Told you I was also feeling shy and insecure."

I would say adorable, but we'd leave that alone. Instead, I just kissed him and held onto him, knowing that this was Julian and everything would be beautiful.

And it was.

⚜

I LEANED ON HIS CHEST, listening to Julian breathe. What a week it had been. We had lost his granny, discovered Phoenix's abductors and what had happened—or at least some of it—to him, flown to the Hamptons, and now I had done that. Ups and downs in the most extreme ways.

I smiled and kissed his chest. He responded by kissing the top of my head. "I love you."

"I love you so much."

I could feel him smile, his mouth on my temple. "It's snowing, isn't it?"

Had he just noticed? Yes it was snowing. It had started before we had. I sat up, slowly. "Should we be worried about the others?" I had been really preoccupied, not thinking about the fact that they were out there driving.

He joined me. "Barrett is a good driver and hopefully had the sense not to use his own car today." Their oldest brother had a thing for older cars. Beautiful but maybe not perfect for the Hamptons in the snow. Julian grabbed his phone and looked down at it. "They're fine. See?" He held up the screen. "I mean they're not as good as I am right now. But they're coming back. About twenty minutes away I think."

That was good. I was a bad girlfriend. I should have thought of it earlier. And now I had to not think about what could go wrong in those twenty minutes on snow and ice. The guys really didn't drive enough.

"Hey," he nudged me. "Come on. We're getting in the hot tub."

I raised an eyebrow. "Jules, we were just discussing the snow."

"Best time to get in the hot tub. Trust me." He rubbed his eyes and then with remarkable energy considering just seconds ago he had looked tired, he got out of bed. I followed him. I needed a bathing suit, but I didn't have one with me. Or maybe I did. Presumably I had a bathing suit somewhere —they'd packed all of my stuff to bring to Louisiana. But I had no idea where it was, and even though we'd packed everything again when we left, we hadn't unpacked anything since coming here.

So, I had to make do. I grabbed the shirt I had been wearing and decided it would do for the hot tub right then. Julian put on his shorts and stayed shirtless. We were going to be freezing. Maybe Julian was kidding around with this?

But no, after shoving our feet in sneakers, we both rushed outside to the hot tub which was on. "How?" I kind of pseudo-shouted at Julian.

He grinned at me. "I should say magic but it's a button in the house that turns it on."

Heat in the form of steam released upward, hitting the

snowflakes that came into contact with it and immediately bursting them into nothingness, like they joined into one thing instead. As though the heat from the tub took over the snow itself.

I sort of pseudo hopped in after Julian, the warmth replacing any cold the frigid air brought to my body. I shrieked. He was right. This was fun.

"Sit back." He smiled at me. "Relax. The cold can't get us in here."

I sank deeper into the bubbling water, letting my shoulders slip beneath the surface until only my head remained above. This made me giggle. In my whole life I could never have imagined doing something like this. The sensation was surreal—warmth enveloping me while the world beyond the rim of the tub was being bathed in white. The snowstorm danced, sending flakes sideways, piling up around the deck where the tub sat and clinging to our sneakers, which we had hastily abandoned at the edge. Our shoes were going to be soaked. I would deal with that later.

Steam rose from the water, before being whisked away by the wind. I reached out and caught a snowflake on my palm. For a fraction of a second, it perched there, fragile and perfect, before dissolving instantly against my skin's heat. The contrast was incredible. I wished I could capture this someday in something I created for *Poor Relation*. Yes, today had really brought my desire to create. For many reasons. My breath fogged the air, mingling with the steam, making the whole scene feel strangely unreal.

Julian leaned back, eyes half-closed, tracing lazy circles in the water. I followed his lead and let myself float, muscles loosening, heart slowing. The tub seemed like a secret haven, a pocket of summer dropped into the middle of winter's fury. I hadn't loved it here in the summer. Maybe I was a person who wanted to visit summer and live in winter. Maybe I was overthinking it. Every part of me that remained above the water felt the bite of cold, but the rest—immersed—was safe in the heat.

We laughed together, both of us starting almost at the same time. I didn't know why he was but for me it was the absurdity of it, the way we'd shivered just moments ago and now reveled in despite the fact that we should absolutely be inside. The wind howled, rattling the branches of the nearby trees that would lead to the bay if we decided to venture that way, but inside this small circle of warmth, I felt untouchable. Even the sky seemed closer somehow; the blizzard's darkness made the hot tub feel like the only true thing left in the world.

I closed my eyes for a moment and simply listened—to Julian's quiet humming, to the fizz and pop of the jets, to the distant rumble of the wind. I thought about how rare it was to feel both exposed and protected at the same time. But then I did sort of know that well. And the Lents lived that way constantly. Dangerously exposed but also protected by who they were. And I knew, right then, that I'd remember this—this heat, this laughter, this wild, impossible comfort— forever.

"Alatheia, can you tell me about my granny? Something I don't know."

I blinked. Yes, I could. I absolutely could. "You could wait to read the diaries. I mean, I will tell you whatever you want to know, Jules. But you could."

He shook his head. "This is going to sound narcissistic. Terrible. Like I'm the worst fucking person ever..." His voice trailed off on whatever it was he was going to say.

"I doubt that. You are maybe the least narcissistic person I know."

He sighed. "But her death keeps hitting me. Like I'll be in the midst of something, like being in this hot tub, and I'll remember she's dead. But ten minutes ago I wasn't thinking about it."

"And you think you're all the things that you just said because you aren't thinking about it 24-7? I mean, I don't really know how grief works. But maybe that's just how you do it."

He stared at me a long moment, only the stars and the snow hearing our conversation. "How was it when you grieved your mom?"

I swallowed, a lump forming in my throat. "Maybe I'm the narcissist. I don't know if I ever did. I don't know that I ever could."

"You're not..."

I shook my head, cutting him off. "This isn't about me. Um, okay, your granny? Her red walls. She did it to get a rise out of your grandfathers. They weren't getting along so well then She wasn't getting pregnant. " I hadn't actually gotten to the part of the story where she would, yet. "And they weren't letting her come to work. So she painted the walls red."

He grinned at me. "And she just kept doing it?"

"She totally did."

A whoop caught our attention, and we both turned around in the tub as his shirtless brothers ran outside into the snow. They'd spotted us and they were joining us. I grinned. Barrett emerged first, towel thrown over one shoulder—we had totally not thought about towels—I was glad to see that he had. His hair already turning white with the snow that drifted in lazy spirals from the roof. Phoenix followed, barefoot and grinning, his teeth as white as the drifts piling up around the property. Then Jeremy—last, as always—hunched into his hoodie, clutching a small canvas bag to his chest. The three of them stepped out into the blue hush of the night, exhaling plumes of steam.

Barrett tossed the towels onto the railing and shivered

theatrically. "It's so much colder than it looks," he said, but his voice was amused. Phoenix rolled his eyes and hopped straight in, sending up a surge of hot water and a hiss of vapor. Barrett slid in after him, his toes curling against my own, and Jeremy set his bag carefully beside the tub before lowering himself onto the edge.

"Brought something," he said, tapping the bag and meeting my eye with a crooked little smile. The snow kept falling, collecting in the hollows of his hair, but he didn't seem to notice. The hot tub was suddenly crowded, limbs brushing under the water, the air thick with breath and the faint scent of whatever chemicals they used to clean the tub. For a moment, I watched them—my odd, beloved collection of Lents—blinking snowflakes from their faces, laughter bubbling up to fill the empty spaces. The world felt warmer than it ought to, out here in the night.

Jules frowned. "You brought it out here?"

"Don't want to wait." He smiled. "Alatheia, we had to run that errand because we all got you something when you were missing. Something we wanted to give you because we wanted you to know how much we missed you."

Barrett sighed. "You're blowing this."

Jeremy shoved his shoulder. "I am not."

"You are." Phoenix grinned. "But that's okay because Alatheia loves our imperfections. Julian, do you want to do the honors?"

I was starting to worry. What the heck were they talking about? What was in that bag?

"Guys, what is going on?"

Julian grabbed the bag, looking at Barrett. "Did it turn out like the pictures?"

"Yes." Barrett nodded. "I'll do it. Give it to me." He grabbed the bag from Julian. "I drove through the snow. I'm saying I get to do it." He kissed my cheek. "Alatheia, don't panic"

I wasn't but maybe I was close. "Surprises haven't been friendly to me lately."

"This is, we promise." Phoenix nodded fast.

"Okay. So, we want you to marry us. You know this. But we get that we are all too young to do that. Or at least," he sighed, "we know that you might feel that way. We'd get married tomorrow."

Phoenix interrupted Barrett. "But the point is that we know that it's too early. Probably legally too. So, we're going to give you this." He opened the bag and pulled out a bracelet. "It has four diamonds in it. We each picked one. We had to agree on the size. It's the only thing we agreed on. None of us would try to outdo the others in the carrot size. Otherwise, we each picked out a diamond for you and it's in the bracelet. When the time comes to get engaged, we'll take the diamonds in this bracelet and make you a ring with all four diamonds present."

I stared at him. We were all in a hot tub, in the middle of a snowstorm, and they were giving me diamonds? I opened and closed my mouth.

Tears flooded my eyes. This was really beautiful, but I could hardly think. "Guys..."

Julian kissed my cheek. "We know you're worried about something happening to jewelry after what happened to the other two gifts. We didn't know that before we ordered this to be made. But the thing is that it's an act of faith, right? It's saying that we are sure that nothing will happen now. That the bad is behind us and that this is all of us agreeing that there will be nothing but blue skies in the future for us."

Jeremy grabbed the bracelet from Julian and held it out where I could see it.

I looked down at the bracelet, trying to make sense of the

four diamonds set side by side. I wasn't an expert on diamonds—far from it, these might be the first ones I'd ever really looked at up close—but even to my untrained eye, they were nothing alike. The first stone caught the light from the porch with a crisp, icy brilliance, nearly colorless and so clear I could see the reflections of the snow swirling outside right through it. Next to it, the second diamond was a little softer somehow, almost as if it glowed from within—a gentle warmth, not overtly yellow, but something mellowed and sweet, the sort of glimmer you'd find in candlelight.

The third was the boldest, set just off-center. It drew my gaze again and again—a touch of rose shimmered deep in its heart, like a secret captured. I had never seen a diamond with a pink undertone before; it was delicate and strange and felt a little magical. The last stone was the most dramatic, with more surfaces than the others, scattering light into tiny rainbows. It looked impossibly intricate, like I might never understand all of it.

They were all set in a simple row, each held in place by slender gold prongs, just touching but not crowding each other. Not quite matching, not quite clashing—like us. I almost didn't want to touch it because it was so beautiful. But they'd given me this and it was... a promise.

I lifted my head to stare at them and forced myself to be able to speak. Even though it seemed impossibly hard. "Thank you." Their grins were huge. Okay. I had to say something else. "I... I want this too. I do. What you're describing. And I will take such good care of this. I promise. No one will hurt it. Ever."

Jeremy squeezed my hand. "We love you. It's more about no one and nothing hurting you. Not the diamonds. But they represent that."

"I just can't believe you love me this much."

Barrett nodded. "We know that you feel that way. And

some day you will. We know it, Alatheia. Some day you will be completely sure."

"I am sure of you. Maybe it's just me I'm not quite sure of yet."

Phoenix chewed on his bottom lip. "Okay, so we'll work on that. See? It's a good thing we came back here. Or we would have had to have it shipped to Louisiana and Barrett would have worried about that."

'He's right, I probably would have."

Julian met my gaze. "Do you know who picked out which? It's okay if you don't. I'm just curious. We can tell you if you don't want to guess."

Did I know? I stared down at them again.

" This one? The first one?" The one that had shown the snow in its icy reflection. "That is you, right, Jules?"

He let out a happy sigh. "Yes."

"And this one?" The softer one. "That is Barrett?"

"That is it." His smile lit up the night. Wow. It was good I was getting this right. But I wasn't done yet. "The pink one? Is this you, Jer?" He did love to give me pink tinted things. My pearls that the school had destroyed when they ripped it off my neck had been pink tinted.

He squeezed my knee under the water. "That's right. Yes."

"And that would make this last one " —the one with the multiple top surfaces— "yours, Phoenix."

"I love that you did that. That you just knew." He closed his eyes. "There. That's done. And she loves it. I told you guys she would love it."

Jeremy laughed. "You didn't know that she would love it any more than we did. You were just as nervous. Maybe more."

"I'll never admit to that." Phoenix opened his eyes and winked at me.

They had worried about that? "I'm in this too. If fate can

be kind to us, some day in the not-too-distant future, I want you to turn this into a ring. I mean, it's going to be a huge ring. I'm not sure I won't get robbed wearing it. But yes, please. Make it a ring."

"Let's put this on you." Barrett gently grabbed my wrist, and after messing with the clasp, slipped it onto my wrist and closed the clasp. It was beautiful. Like they were beautiful.

My voice, when I finally found it, was hoarse. I made myself speak. "I will never be able to thank you enough for this."

"Don't ever thank us." Barrett put his head against mine. "For anything. We completely don't deserve you but we are keeping you."

I wanted to be kept. By them. Forever.

I SAT in the living room, only a small light illuminating the room. Everyone was asleep. Sound asleep. Except me. I was wide awake like I had just woken up from a nap. I grabbed their gran's journals. I wondered what Dina would say about today. Her absence was an ache. My conversation with Julian had pointed out I had never really mourned my mom. Was I actually mourning Dina or was I sticking that wherever I put pain never to be seen again?

HELLO, readers,
    I think I am leaving my husbands.

I BLINKED. What?

❧ 19 ❧

A noise upstairs jarred me, and I looked up, pulling my attention from what Dina had just written. What was that? Dina's journal entry hadn't been dated. She had gone from *we were working hard and I'm not pregnant* to *I'm leaving my husbands*? I rose. I would deal with that in a second. I wished she was there to ask.

The door to the bedroom opened, and Phoenix came out. He was dressed, which was strange because he hadn't been when we went to bed. Outside, the snow fell. It was starting to really pile up, to stick on the ground.

"Phoenix, you okay?" I rubbed at my arms. I was wearing pajama pants and a t-shirt, but there still was a little bit of a chill in here. I didn't know if the main house or Gran's house did better in the winter. It seemed like maybe this one was really designed to be comfortable in a warmer climate.

He didn't answer me, coming downstairs. His eyes were practically squinted. I grabbed his arm. "What's going on?"

"Alatheia..." His voice trailed off. "Gotta go. Not here. The beach. Back there. The door."

I stared at him, my mouth falling open. Phoenix wasn't on

any substances that I knew of. But he was really not with it right now. He pulled out of my hold and headed toward the door.

"No." I grabbed him again. It was too cold out there. He didn't even have a coat. "Phoenix." I shook him just a bit. "Come on. Are you on something?"

He blinked, staring at me. "I know you don't understand, but I have to go now."

His brown eyes were so faded, so distant. And he wasn't really answering the question I'd posed. Yes, he was on something. I was sure of it. We could deal with that tomorrow. He turned, once more pulling out of my hold, and I made a snap decision. If he was going, and it seemed he was unless one of his brothers could tackle him or something, I was going with him, and he was going to put on a coat.

"Here." I ran to the coat closet and sort of half handed him, half dressed him in his winter jacket.

In the meantime, I shouted upstairs. "Barrett." He always woke the easiest. I shouted it twice, and the sound of feet hitting the floor and the door swinging open echoed in the quiet.

"Sweetheart?" He sounded groggy. "What's going on?"

"Phoenix is leaving. He's not really with it, and I'm not sure what's going on. Says he has to. I'm going with him."

"What?" He practically shouted, but I didn't have time to answer him since I was going with Phoenix, and he was walking out the door. I grabbed my shoes and my jacket, which I only had half put on as I sprinted after him into the snow. My sneakers were still wet and soggy from getting soaked during the hot tub fantasy I'd gotten to live in.

Anxiety made my chest tight. What if I hadn't been awake? Would I have woken up or just sort of thought that Phoenix was going to the bathroom?

I chased after him.

The wind lashed against my face while it whipped snow in wild circles across the frozen lawn. Phoenix moved ahead of me, his silhouette blurred almost somehow like a phantom in the storm, his winter jacket flapping against skinny jeans that he'd dressed himself in. I hadn't noticed before but now I was pretty sure they were Jeremy's and not his. Not that it mattered right then. I slipped my arms fully through my own sleeves and ran after him, hoping I didn't face- plant in the attempt.

"Phoenix!" I called, my voice snatched away by the wind. My sneakers squelched in the snow, my toes already numb. The snow wasn't just falling—it was swirling, angry, stinging my cheeks and stealing my breath. House lights glowed faintly behind us, a golden haze dissolving into the storm. I could barely see the outline of Phoenix, let alone the driveway or the distant curve where the road met the edge of the Lent s' property.

Phoenix didn't pause. He just trudged on, shoes crunching, leaving a trail through the drifts. I caught up to him as we reached the scraggly dune grass where the yard, in better weather, became the manicured haven that led toward the beach. You really wouldn't know that now. I reached for his arm, fingers clumsy with cold because I hadn't thought about gloves and neither had he, and he half turned, eyes wide and unfocused. For a moment he looked past me, toward the dunes, as if something was calling him from someplace else. Maybe some other time. I just didn't know.

"Wait, Phoenix, please—" But he just shook his head, lips parted, breathing hard. His hair was already dusted with snow. I imagined mine was too.

We kept running. Or as best we could considering things. It was more like trudging quickly. This was dangerous. I knew that. The world shrank to whiteness and my heart beating too fast. My lungs burned. I could barely hear anything above the howl of the wind, but then—like a miracle—I picked up the rumble of a car engine.

Headlights sliced through the storm, slow and searching, casting monstrous shadows across the snow. Phoenix faltered, squinting against the glare. We were maybe fifty yards from the house, the beach close, just over the last rise of snow-blanketed grass.

The car pulled up fast, tires skidding slightly as it stopped at the edge of the road. The doors flew open and, in a rush of voices and bundled figures, Barrett, Jeremy, and Julian poured out. Barrett reached us first, panting. Considering things, he had gotten here fast. I was grateful. More so than I'd ever be able to say. He took in Phoenix's bare hands, the snow covering my wet and useless shoes.

"Are you kidding me?" Julian yelped, voice sharp with panic. "Get in, you idiots, it's freezing!"

Barrett caught Phoenix by the shoulders, steadying him, while Jeremy wrapped a blanket around both of us, his arms strong. I let myself sag against them, every muscle trembling with cold, adrenaline, and something dangerously close to tears. The storm swirled around us.

Phoenix grabbed his head. "I have to go. You have to let me go. The kids are there waiting for me."

He didn't sound like himself and not because his teeth were chattering but more as he must have sounded as a little boy.

"Shit." Jeremy clapped his hands in front of Phoenix's face. "Are you on something? What the fuck is going on?"

"I think he is." I was amazed I could talk at all. "But I think we need to let him go. I think... I think he's remembering where he was kept. We're here for that."

Julian shook his head. "He can't go wandering out there."

"No, obviously not. Maybe we could drive there." I put

my cold hand on Phoenix's face. "Could we drive there or do we have to walk on the beach?"

He stared at me and blinked slowly. "I think we can drive. But we have to get to the kids."

"I don't love that either." Barrett pounded his hands on the steering wheel. "None of this is safe."

Julian frowned. "It's not. But what if he can't remember where this is tomorrow? Don't we kind of at least need to find it now?"

"Fuck. Okay. Everyone buckle in. Phoenix, whatever this is, you're a dead man tomorrow."

Barrett put the car in gear, tires crunching over the snow as we lurched onto the icy road. We all needed to learn to drive; it wasn't fair that Barrett always had to do this. The SUV felt cramped, the heater blasting stale warmth that didn't quite touch the nervous chill that had taken over my whole body. Nobody spoke. Phoenix sat hunched in the front passenger seat, his breath fogging the window, fingers kneading his knees as if he might spring through the glass if we took too long.

"Which way?" Barrett said as we reached the end of the driveway.

"Left." Once again, Phoenix sounded so young. I stroked my cold hand through his snow-melting hair.

"This could all be just an elaborate nothing." Jeremy shook his head. "He's not necessarily even seeing what we think he is seeing. Or remembering. He might be just totally out of his mind."

That was also possible. "This doesn't seem like Phoenix on ketamine or anything I've seen him on before."

"Well unless he's been possessed by a demon or something he has certainly done something tonight." Jeremy glared ahead at the road in front of us.

Julian popped him in the back of the head. "Not helpful."

"Not trying to be."

Headlights tunneled through the darkness, catching the flakes and the vague suggestion of trees beyond the ditch. Every few hundred feet the SUV slid, a gentle fishtail that made us all catch our breath, but Barrett kept us steady. The only other sound was the faint shudder of Phoenix's teeth and the steady tick of the hazard lights. Thank the universe that Barrett was such a good driver. Like most things he did in his life Barrett did this really well.

Two miles never felt so far, but that was roughly how long we drove with Phoenix giving us directions before he told us to stop. In the distance, a house finally appeared, rising out of the storm like something conjured: three stories, black shutters, a wide porch buried in drifts, and all its windows blank and dark. The driveway ate the car nearly to the axles, but Barrett forced us through, the engine whine echoing against the massive, silent house.

We sat for a moment, breathing, waiting for someone to make the decision to move. Phoenix finally seemed to stir. He opened his door, letting in a bitter blast of snow, and stepped out without looking back. I dashed after him, Julian right behind me. We were all going to die of frostbite or lose a toe or whatever happened in these situations. Seconds later, Barrett and Jeremy were with us, too.

Phoenix didn't hesitate. He walked around the side of the house, past the porch and the sagging snow-laden hydrangeas, his feet sinking with each step. We trailed after him—Julian glancing back at the house, Jeremy swearing under his breath, Barrett with his arm around Phoenix—and I pressed my hands to my lips to keep them from shaking. No one would believe what the Lents went through regularly. They seemed like such a polished, perfect family in New York City.

My head was freezing. What little hair I had wasn't getting it done for me right now.

At the edge of the property, where the manicured lawn ended and the woods began which would probably lead to the beach if we kept going, stood a large, weathered garden shed. The padlock hung open, the door slightly ajar as if someone had left in a hurry last fall. Phoenix pulled it open with a whine of old hinges. Inside, the shed was empty except for the faint scent of gasoline. He stood in the doorway, silhouetted against the weak spill of the SUV's headlights, and we crowded behind him, silent, waiting, as the snow filled in our tracks and the woods loomed black and endless behind us.

"This is where they're supposed to be."

I stared at the shed. It was huge inside. Probably had felt bigger when they were little especially if they were terrified.

Yes, this was where they had been held. I stared at Jeremy. "I don't think he's hallucinating this. How would he have known it was here?'

He nodded. "I agree. Okay. We've found it." He put his arm around Phoenix. "You got us here. The kids aren't here right now. That isn't your fault and it never was. Come on. We're going home and tomorrow after we figure out what is going on with you, we will come back. But we're getting out of this snow. Alatheia is freezing. She is in pajama pants, and I don't know why it's taken us so long to notice that but we are all going to die if we stay out here. So come on. You don't want to hurt Alatheia. I know that."

Jeremy didn't give Phoenix the chance to answer. Instead, he put his arm around him tighter and dragged him back to the car, which I could see thanks to the headlights still being on. Barrett had been smart to leave the car on.

I hadn't been thinking about my legs but Jer was right. It was a problem. Barrett dragged me against him. "Do you want me to carry you?"

I laughed. "I don't think that would help anything."

We'd no sooner gotten into the warm car that Phoenix

put his head against the window and fell asleep. We all stared at him.

I really didn't have a clue what was going on. Not any. But we'd just found that place. All those years ago before everything that had happened since, Phoenix had managed to break out of that shed and get home. Thank goodness he had.

My teeth chattered. "Whose house is this?"

"No one we know." Jeremy and I cuddled together in the backseat. He was warmer than me, but then again, he was actually wearing jeans. "I think they live overseas. It's always empty. Makes sense they'd use this place."

Why hadn't anyone found it? All those years ago? I didn't know and my guys had been children too. The people to ask weren't here. And they might not know either.

I shivered. Now that it was over I couldn't think about anything other than the cold. "Think we should get back in the hot tub?"

Jules laughed. "Well, it isn't a bad idea."

☙❧

IN THE END, we didn't go back to the hot tub. Instead, after Barrett pretty much carried Phoenix inside, helped him undress and put him to bed, the rest of us managed to do the same. I was sandwiched between the twins and they were warm enough to unfreeze me pretty quickly.

"There were bound to be setbacks." I was talking about Phoenix, and I was sure that the three who were awake would know that. I mostly wanted Jeremy to hear me say that since he seemed the most angry about what had happened tonight.

He stared at me in the darkness. "What would you have done if Barrett hadn't woken up?"

I blinked. That seemed kind of a random response to what I'd said. "I don't know. He did wake up. Why?"

"Because if you had run out there after him without us you would both be in big trouble. Maybe dead. Or at least at risk for it. So, yeah, I'd like to know what the plan was."

Julian sighed, loudly. "Jer."

Oh, I quickly understood. Jeremy was mad. At me. He couldn't be angry with Phoenix, currently, as he was asleep, but I was wide awake.

"I don't know if you've ever been mad at me before." I spoke aloud what I was thinking.

Jeremy didn't move. "I'm... Fuck. I'm not really mad right now. I was scared. And I don't like anything about tonight."

"Well, we share that in common. Although I did like how you guys showed up with the car. That was really awesome, actually. To answer your question, if Barrett hadn't woken, and thank you Barrett for being a light sleeper, I would have run up the stairs and then run down them. I'm pretty sure that is what I would have done."

"Okay. Then at least I don't have to obsess anymore about you two dying out there while I slept in here." He paused, and in the quiet I could hear the wind outside—wind I was very glad not to be out in. "Sorry."

I was sure we were going to fight sometimes. Didn't everyone? But I squirmed. "I'm sorry too. I guess I shouldn't have gone after him? Or found a way to stop him? Or..."

Julian shook his head. "Don't let Jeremy get in your head. We're not mad."

"I'm really glad that I woke up." Barrett yawned. "But now I'm going back to sleep. And if Phoenix goes wandering because of whatever is happening, I'm going to lock him in a room somewhere for the rest of the night. Yes, I think that probably his relapsing was to be expected. I wish I knew more. I'll find out more tomorrow."

Jeremy cuddled down against me. "I don't do scared very

well. Not when it comes to the people I love. Where would he even have gotten any drugs?"

Phoenix was breathing. For now that was all I needed to know. Barrett must have been on the same wavelength because I watched as he reached over on the bed to put his hand on his brother's back.

Tomorrow we'd figure it out.

I let my finally thawing out eyelids close.

◊❧◊

I WOKE to the pale hush of late morning, sunlight pooling weakly at the edge of the drawn curtains. The room was quiet —too still, a kind of emptiness that pressed in around me as I registered, slowly, that I was alone. That was pretty unusual for me in the morning. I was usually the first up and they were all still with me or I knew where they were. The chill that had clung to me from the blizzard seemed to have settled into my bones, heavy and unwelcome. My throat prickled with the rawness of sleep, and my skin felt clammy, as if I had come through a fever and hadn't quite escaped its grip.

Shit. I was sick. When was the last time I had been sick? I didn't even know. It was a good thing I didn't get sick much because no one would have taken care of me. This was different than the hospital when I had to come off the drugs.

For a moment, I lay there, hoping the grogginess would dissipate, but it only deepened, draping itself over my limbs like a wet blanket. The ache behind my eyes pulsed in time with my heartbeat, and my breath tasted stale, tinged with the tang of having slept badly despite having slept long. I tried to stretch, to summon some sense of normalcy, but my muscles protested—stiff, as if I'd run miles in my dreams. Or maybe it was the way I'd chased Phoenix through the snow and trudged around in it wearing my pajama pants and a t-shirt under my jacket.

The air in the room was cool, but no longer biting, and yet I shivered. I remembered the wind from the night before, the endless shuddering cold. Now, even bundled in layers and tucked beneath the covers, it felt as though I'd lost something essential in the night—a piece of myself that would only return with time and maybe some cold medicine.

I listened for voices—the comfort of someone else awake, bustling, moving through the house—but all I heard was the distant groan of pipes and the soft creak of the floorboards settling. My head spun a little as I sat up, and I pressed my fingers to my temples. Yep. This sucked.

I didn't feel well, not in any dramatic, feverish way—more like I'd been chilled and my body decided to remind me of its limits. I pulled my knees to my chest and rested my chin there, uncertain whether I wanted to move at all. Even the thought of standing sent a wave of nausea through me, and I resolved to stay put, at least for now.

It was late—later than I'd meant to sleep. Where were the guys? What had I missed? A faint, sour taste lingered at the back of my throat. I tried to conjure the memory of laughter, of voices in the next room, but the house seemed emptied of them, as if I'd been left behind, a castaway. No. That wasn't true. They hadn't done that. This was just me not feeling well and letting those intrusive thoughts I always had into my consciousness.

I just didn't feel well. Not at all.

I closed my eyes for a moment, listening to the silence, letting myself be tired. I really had no choice.

The door opened and Jeremy stood in the entrance. He frowned at me as he entered. "Hey, I was just coming to check on you."

I lifted my head. "I didn't hear anyone. I thought maybe I was alone."

"Barrett took Phoenix to look at the shed. Now that the snow stopped. Are you okay? You don't look well."

I shook my head. "I think I am a little bit sick. Not the flu but like I am being punished for being stupid last night."

He sat down, drawing me to him into a big hug. I groaned. "No, you're going to get sick."

"If I'm going to catch it, I already have. We were snuggled all night." He kissed my forehead. "You do feel warm. Hold on." He rose. "I am going to take your temperature." Jeremy frowned. I rubbed at my eyes. I needed to focus. It was like one thing was happening after another and I couldn't really focus on any of it. "I don't know where the thermometer is here. I know where it is in the big house. Wait here. I'll be right back."

I hated thinking of him venturing out into the cold. "Jer, you don't have to..."

He shook his head. "Yes I do. Julian," he shouted while he left the room. "Alatheia is sick. Come sit with her. I'm going to get the thermometer."

Julian appeared a second later, concern evident all over his handsome features. "You're sick?"

"I guess I'm not tough enough for running around in blizzards."

He groaned, sitting down where Jer had been before. He rubbed my back. "I am so sorry. We'll call Eric. He'll tell us what to do. If we need to find a doctor, we'll go do that."

I hoped I didn't need to go to a doctor, although I had health insurance thanks to Kit putting me on the family's plan since I worked for his mother. Unless that changed because she was gone? I chewed on my lip. "I probably just need some rest." A thought dawned on me. Barrett had taken

Phoenix to look at the shed. "What was Phoenix on last night?"

Jules shook his head. "Would you believe he took a sleeping pill? One he found in the cupboard. Just an over the counter sleeping pill. We now know Phoenix can't take sleeping pills. And he is horrified and embarrassed. Jer read him the riot act, and Phoenix called Sam. I think that's all the information I have to fill you in on."

A sleeping pill? "Why did he do that?"

"Said he just wanted to pass out. Just not to think last night." Julian kissed my cheek. "Feels like what went on between us was a week ago and not yesterday."

He was right about that. "I loved it."

"So much." He kissed the end of my nose. "I love you."

Jeremy ran into the room, carrying a thermometer. "Got it. Let's see how sick you are."

He rubbed it over my forehead, and it beeped. I felt like the last time I had my temperature taken it was with an ear thermometer. Then again I couldn't remember doing that at the hospital.

Jer stared at the readout. "Yep. Just over 101. You're sick."

This sucked.

❧ 20 ❧

Jeremy called Eric and returned with instructions to give me fluids and medicine as needed. Now, I was watching television—not a show I recognized though. But I was thinking about the *Poor Relation* and when I reached over to grab my laptop to work on it, Julian nodded before he did the same with his computer. I didn't know what he was working on, but I was glad he was writing.

I made the character move, to look at the watchers straight on. "Just when you think things can't get worse, they can. But they can also get better."

Was that cheesy? I looked at Jules. "What is going on with *Ghosts*?"

"I sent it, actually just yesterday, to a contest that could get it made in a small theater. Anyway, not likely I'll win, but I'm trying. I meant to tell you yesterday but " —he smirked at me— "I got distracted." My cheeks heated up and not because of the fever. "Let me ask you, because I have wondered and now I need to know, why did you start writing? How did you start making your stream?"

I rubbed the back of my neck. "I needed something. I was

so lonely. My aunt had called me the poor relation when she spoke to my aunt Tricia on the phone. I heard that. I had just moved to Chicago. I didn't know anyone. I was watching streamed videos, and I thought... well, I could do that. I could try to do that. And no one would have to know. I just thought it was for me. No one else. I didn't expect anyone to actually watch."

"But they did." Julian nodded. "I hate your family."

"Me too," Jeremy said as he walked in the room carrying soup. "You are both creating. That's a good sign. I hope. For Alatheia. But if you need to sleep, do that. Eric said rest is the most important thing."

I nodded. "I will. I promise. Who took care of you when you were sick? All the years you lived without your parents."

He shrugged. "Guess it is a good thing we don't get sick very much. But, Barrett is actually not a bad caretaker. He would hand us cold meds. And Eric would show up when we needed him. I don't know. It's not like..."

A sound banged downstairs. Jer turned toward the door. "That has to be Barrett and Phoenix. But..." His voice trailed off. Instead of finishing his thought, he walked to the doorway and stared down.

Nerves assaulted me and I rubbed my arms. What was happening here? It was just Barrett and Phoenix, right? Except why weren't they coming up the stairs? No way they wouldn't come here to see me straight away. I knew that because they all spoiled me with that kind of love. And Phoenix would want to apologize for last night.

Julian rose and Jer whirled around, his finger against his mouth in the universal sign for quiet. His twin nodded and then stared at me. I mimicked his head movement. I got it too. This wasn't Phoenix and Barrett. And whatever was happening or whoever the twins thought was down there had them very concerned.

Jules grabbed his phone and sent a group text to his brothers and me.

Someone in the house.

My heart hammered against my ribs, each beat echoing in my ears as if it might give me away. I wasn't even sure what was happening yet, but I knew that they were scared and that made it even worse in my head. The twins didn't get scared. I'd never seen it. Jeremy eased the bedroom door shut, his face pale, eyes wide but his jaw set and determined. There was a lot going on in his head right then. Julian didn't say a word, just jerked his chin toward the closet. I understood—hide, now.

I moved as quietly as I could, though the effort sent a spike of pain through my head and made my throat burn worse than it already was. This would have been bad enough if I hadn't been sick. I shivered. Jeremy helped me up, one hand pressed warm and steady at my elbow. My legs were heavy, feverish—more so than before—and I wished for the thousandth time that I was well—strong, not whatever this was that was happening to me in the worst possible time.

Julian slid open the closet door and motioned us in. He followed, phone clutched in one hand, his other fist balled so tightly his knuckles gleamed. Jeremy pressed himself behind the coats, trying not to breathe too loudly. I crouched on a pile of shoes, biting the inside of my cheek to suppress a cough. My breaths came shallow and ragged. I pressed my sleeve to my nose, willing myself quiet. Now was not the time to have a coughing fit. Not at all. Seriously. It would be very fucking bad.

The phone lit up. I didn't have mine, but I saw Barrett's name pop up on Jules'. He was answering us. I hoped they would stay away. Whatever this was I didn't want them either walking in unaware—which fortunately Jules had prevented—or charging in if Jeremy thought we were in this much danger.

Julian answered Barrett. I saw the words *not good*.

We had hidden in a closet before. Well, no Jules hadn't. When Jeremy, Phoenix ,and I had hidden in a closet to steal my birth certificate folder, Jules had stayed downstairs and distracted the doormen by talking about sports. I caught Jeremy's gaze as he stared at the closet door. What would they do if someone came in here?

Downstairs, footsteps paused, slow and deliberate. This house creaked. We were lucky or they'd have gotten us completely with no warning. Whoever it was. I mean... was someone trying to just get out of the snow? Someone was moving through the house, not in a hurry, but searching. The silence in the closet was thick, stifling—punctuated only by Julian's thumb flicking across his phone, typing updates to Barrett and Phoenix.

Was the person in the house a stranger, or someone worse? I squeezed my eyes shut, head pounding, and tried to listen for anything that would explain what was happening. Why hadn't I grabbed my phone? I could at least know what Jules knew. And whoever this was didn't give a shit that we might be here in the house. That was really even more concerning. Nothing to lose...

A floorboard creaked beneath weight, much nearer than before. They were coming up the stairs. Julian's hand gripped mine, tight and reassuring. I swallowed my anxiety, or I pretended to, wishing I could disappear, wishing we could all be safe. But wishing had never solved any of my problems. Not ever. The footsteps climbed the stairs, slow—one, then another—each step heavy with menace.

Or maybe not. Maybe I was overthinking this. This was a friendly neighbor who had come to see if we had survived the snowstorm okay. I had to stop questioning myself. If I thought that something was wrong, scary, then it was. I wasn't making up my concerns and clearly the twins thought this was bad too.

"I know that you are in the house." A male voice sounded. It was scratchy, rough, like the person had either been shouting or had smoked too many cigarettes in his life. "And if you're hiding, then you are smarter than you used to be and certainly smarter than your parents." He laughed, the last words slurring together. "I've been watching the house for days now. I know at least two of you are here."

Okay. Okay. What did we learn? He knew them. He watched the house. Smarter than they used to be?

Jeremy winced. Why was I not surprised he knew who this was? He was fast. Incredibly intelligent.

Julian texted on his phone. Maybe he knew who it was too. Or he was just telling the other two that this person who wanted to hurt us—and I was sure that he did—was in the fucking room with us.

A door slammed downstairs and a shout sounded.

"Alright, Daryl, you piece of shit. You get away from my family." That was Rosalind. Their mother was here? The twins looked less surprised than I felt . Daryl stormed out of the room and Jeremy grabbed the closet door, pulling me out with him when he did.

Julian rushed past us and locked the bedroom door behind Daryl and then the bathroom door. There was shouting downstairs.

"We're not safe in here." Jeremy looked around. I heard their fathers and Rosalind shouting. A gun shot sounded and Jeremy ran to the door and unlocked it. "Come on. Good thought. But we have to get out not hide in here. We'll go through the other room and then out the window."

Out the window? What?

"Yes." Jules nodded. "Come on." A second shot was fired, and I jolted. It was so much louder than I had ever pictured gunfire, and considering how many school shooter drills I had done in my life, I had pictured it a lot.

Jeremy yanked me forward, his grip tight around my wrist as we darted through the bathroom to the entrance to Barrett's room. My lungs burned; each breath felt like icicles scraping the inside of my throat, fever sweat prickling at my forehead despite the chill. I really could pick the worst moments to get sick. It would be comical if it wasn't terrifying. Julian moved ahead, his fingers flying over the handle before he threw the door open. The shouts downstairs echoed up the steps—frantic, furious, closer than I would have liked. Who had the guns? Who was firing at who? Was anyone hurt? We had to get out to find out.

We didn't waste a second. Jeremy nudged me toward the room that shared the bathroom with the room we'd been sleeping in. We hadn't really designated whose room was whose since we had gotten to this place. My bare feet slapped against the cold tiles, then the carpet, and I winced every time. My body just hurt. Julian was faster than both of us, already shoving the window open. The snow outside glowed in the pale late afternoon light, a thick blanket covering the yard and the branches of the tree just outside the window.

"Thank God this elm didn't dry. Didn't Granny say that most of the elms in this area died?" Julian whispered to us.

"I don't remember, and I don't care right now." Jeremy scooted past Julian. We were going to use this tree to get down, but it was covered in snow. Nothing about this was going to be easy.

"Are you sure about this?" Barrett shouted up to us. He and Phoenix were on the ground. Gun fire boomed in the house, and we all jumped, us inside and the guys on the ground. How had they known we were going to do this?

Jules answered my unspoken question. "I'm texting them."

Jer nodded. "Yes."

I hesitated, coughing hard, and Jeremy half-lifted me by the elbow. "Now!" he whispered, urgency sharpening his voice. He climbed onto the sill first, his shoes crunching against the icy wood. Julian followed, swinging his legs out and clutching the tree trunk, neither he nor I were wearing shoes. What was the matter with me? Why could I never be appropriately dressed for the situations I found myself in?

The air outside hit me like a slap: cold and biting, stinging my eyes and throat. I clambered after the others, hands shaking, feet already numb. The bark was slick with snow; I almost slipped, and for a second, panic flared—would I fall? Jeremy reached over, steadying me, and Julian guided my hand to a sturdy branch.

I had never done this before. How did I shimmy down a snow laden tree? But necessity bred competence or at least not being totally and completely inept.

We scrambled down as quickly as we could, Jeremy leading the way—his footprints pressing clear and certain into the snow below. Julian gritted his teeth, his socks quickly soaked through, but he never looked back. I felt every inch of the climb, every ache in my chest. My fever burned, but the fear of what was happening in that house was stronger.

Phoenix grabbed me around the waist, pulling me against him before I got to the ground. "Got you. Wow, you are hot."

Was I? Because right then I was freezing. I shivered in his arms, but I didn't know where we were going when he carried me around the side of the house. Their gran's old house was lit up, and they ran, Jules still in his socks.

"Are you okay?" Barrett put his hand on my forehead. "Yes, you are hot."

Phoenix set me down on the couch. I had to say something. "What's happening?"

"Well, I think that Daryl is going to die. I think my mom is going to kill her brother, if she hasn't already." Phoenix took off his coat and wrapped me in it while Julian stripped his socks and then grabbed mine, pulling them off. Barrett grabbed blankets and wrapped all of us in them.

The reality of what we had just done struck me. We could have died going down that tree.

Jeremy touched my cheek. "She's hotter than before. The stress. We need Eric. Is he in that house?"

The door swung open and Stephen rushed in. He was out of breath and flushed. "Thank god. You're all here. Okay. An ambulance is coming. Kit got shot. Don't panic. Eric says he will be okay. But he's hurt. And Daryl is dead. I need towels. I came to get some because I don't know where they are in the other house."

His words spurred action. My guys didn't shout, they ran. Phoenix grabbed a towel and sprinted outside, his brothers on his heels. I didn't have shoes, and I wasn't moving so fast. But I got to my feet. What was I going to do? I really, really couldn't go outside barefoot. I needed to be there, but I couldn't be there as I was.

Barrett rushed back. He picked me up, wrapping me in a blanket. "Stay with me. Okay? I'm going to carry you but when we get inside don't leave my side."

Barrett carried me toward the house and once again the cold struck me hard. I was really getting tired of this. Maybe we should move somewhere warm someday. But in the meantime, we had to focus. Their father was hurt. The main room was chaos. Or maybe not. At first glance it had seemed that way but actually everyone was organized. Daniel and Rosalind knelt down next to Kit where he lay stretched on the floor, a crimson stain blooming across his shirt. Where was he shot?

"Boys. Don't be scared. My brother assures me that I will survive this. And it was my fault. I didn't move fast enough." Kit was talking.

Eric was beside him, holding a towel and pressing down on Kit's shoulder, his bag open and spilling gauze and instruments onto the carpet. Did he carry that everywhere? Phoenix knelt opposite, holding Kit's shoulders with a gentle firmness that kept him from twisting away. I saw how calm Phoenix was—his voice low and soothing, his movements quick but deliberate as he counted Kit's pulse and relayed numbers back to Eric.

"I really am fine."

Rosalind ran a hand through his hair. "Stop fussing and let Eric do what he does. You're hurt. We're going to help you. You were very brave."

I deliberately didn't look across the room. Daryl was dead. Someone had thrown a sheet over him. Probably Stephen who was pacing from the dead body to his brother.

"Don't faint," Eric called up to him.

Barrett set me on a stool. "We need you, Kit, so you're not allowed to go anywhere. Okay? How would we function without you? I'm serious about that."

"I know you have things to say to me, Barrett. If you want to, I am not moving right now."

A siren sounded in the distance.

Barrett gave a short, trembling laugh, the kind that held back tears. His hand was on my shoulder. "Good. Because you're not off the hook yet but I am not going to do this with you right now. I am going to major in whatever I want. You are just going to have to deal with that."

"Sorry to be this person right now, but should we hide this body?" Jeremy called out. "Or are we telling the police we killed someone?"

"Let me worry about the police." Stephen shook his head. "Daniel and I will handle it. Nothing will happen because of this. Making crises go away is something I'm good at. Even if it's usually Kit's foray."

He laughed, the sound full of pain. "At least you are all willing to admit I am good at something."

"Lots of things." Rosalind kissed his cheek. "Many, many things."

I hoped he was right because the ambulance was here.

The guys couldn't lose Kit. Their family dynamics didn't always make sense to me but that much I understood. They loved each other.

৩১১১১

AFTER SO MUCH CHAOS, the house seemed too quiet. Barrett and I stared at the blood stains on the floor. "We should try to get it out."

"I think there are companies that could do this for us." Barrett sighed. "I know how that sounds. I'm doing my favorite rich boy thing again, but I really, really don't want to scrub the floor right now. I just don't."

"What do you want to do?" I stared at him. I shivered. Maybe he was right. We shouldn't be scrubbing anything.

He tugged on the end of my hair. "Feel okay to sit up for a while?"

"I am standing, so I think I must be able to sit." I shook my head. "I think I might have actually reached a point where I'm not even noticing how sick I am."

Barrett walked me over to the piano. He sat down on the bench, his legs spread. "Come sit here. Almost like you're on my lap. I want to play music and not think about today. I want to play you the song I've been writing for you while you sit here with me. And then you are going to drink some bubbly sweet soda and go lie down. Sound okay?"

I did as he said, leaning against his chest. My breath was short but not from sickness. "Are you serious? You wrote me a song?"

"It's probably terrible. But yes."

He flexed his fingers above the keys, pausing for a moment as if letting the silence fill up with possibility. The first note was soft, uncertain, like a question he didn't know how to ask out loud. I closed my eyes and let the music wrap around me, the melody meandering at first, then blooming into something gentle and bright.

Barrett's chin brushed my hair, and I could feel the vibration of the piano in his chest. For a little while, the world shrank down to just the notes he played and the warmth of his arms around me. He played with more confidence as he went, the song shifting from hesitant to hopeful, from apology to something like love.

When he stopped, the absence of the music left my heart aching. The weight of the day pressed in again, but softer now, blurred around the edges by something beautiful. I turned enough to look at him, my voice barely above a whisper. "That was not terrible."

He let out a shaky laugh. "Yeah?"

"Yeah," I said, the word lingering between us, holding back everything else I was too tired to say. Finally, I found my voice. "I loved every second of it."

We sat there for a minute, listening to the echo linger, and I let myself believe, just for tonight, that the song could hold us together after the day we'd just had.

The door opened and Phoenix came in. He had left with the twins to go see Kit in the hospital. As I was running fever it was just better that I not go and possibly infect anyone in there.

He walked toward us. "What was that? I could hear it outside."

I smiled up at him. "Something Barrett wrote for me."

"Amazing." Phoenix dropped down into a chair. "It's beautiful."

"Thank you. How is Kit?" Phoenix kissed the back of my neck.

Phoenix smiled. "Pretty pissed. He doesn't like being holed up and not able to do anything he wants at any time. But pissed is better than anything else, according to Eric." Phoenix stared at me a long moment. "I am so sorry about what happened with my sleeping pill. You aren't feeling well and that is probably because you were running around in the cold."

"Cold doesn't make us sick." I leaned against Barrett. "But your apologies are accepted."

I could hear Barrett's heartbeat. I closed my eyes. Kit was going to be okay. We were all okay.

Barrett squeezed my hand, warm and steady. "We've had worse days," he offered, his voice a low thread. "Daryl is dead. You are sick but going to be okay. Trust me, when Phoenix went missing it was worse. When you went missing it was worse. Granny dying was worse. This is an all and all okay day. Considering the ending."

Phoenix gave a half-laugh, rubbing his thumb along the groove of the chair's arm. "Somehow we always make it through. You two—" He shook his head with a fondness that softened the shadows under his eyes. "You keep surprising me. You write love songs. You climb down snow draped trees. I mean... fuck."

The room felt small, safe despite the fact that someone had broken in and died in there earlier. I glanced between them—Barrett's gentle steadiness, Phoenix's open apology—and let a slow breath fill my chest.

"Tomorrow will be easier," I said, not sure if I believed it, but wanting to. "Maybe this is a twenty-four hour bug and no one will try to kill us."

Barrett leaned closer, his shoulder a gentle weight against

mine. "We'll write a new song for tomorrow," he said softly, and that I decided to believe was a promise he could keep.

I let my eyes drift close listening to his heartbeat. I could just stay right there.

I woke up in the middle of the night, between Barrett and Phoenix. I didn't remember getting here which I knew meant Barrett had brought me in here. The twins were back, each asleep in the other bed. I wasn't better. That much I knew. And that sucked. I coughed and Phoenix adjusted, drawing me closer to him. I was going to make all of them sick.

"Feeling sicker?" Barrett's steady voice had me turn to him.

"Little bit."

He nodded. "Let me get you something. Stay here."

I watched as he rose and exited to the bathroom, coming back with two pills I knew would lower my fever and some water, which I happily took. He lay back down next to me. "Do you think there are people who don't live like this? Who don't live from one crisis to the next?"

"Yes. And we will be those people someday." He ran his thumb across my brow. "I love you."

"Do you think there is meaning to anything? To any of it?"

Barrett smiled at me. "That is the fever talking. Feels deep, but it's nothing right now. I do think that there is meaning to everything. How else could I explain that you exist? So yes, I think there is meaning. And right now, I think you need to rest because we have to figure out what's next as soon as you're well." He kissed my forehead. "I love you, Alatheia. I always will."

❧ 21 ❧

My cold lasted days. I was finally feeling slightly better as I sat on the couch between the twins. Barrett played Mozart on the piano. Julian was writing his next play that I didn't get to know anything about until he was finished—I knew what that was like for sure—and Jeremy was working on a project he wanted to show Stephen about an investment opportunity.

Phoenix had been quiet for the last couple of days. When I'd asked him how he felt seeing the shed he'd told me that he didn't feel different being there than he had anywhere else. He could remember now but the actual vicinity to the place did nothing for him. I wasn't sure if that was disappointment in his voice or not. He had been talking to Sam a lot on the phone about why he had taken the sleeping pill.

When he spoke, stopping the quiet of the room, it wasn't to say anything that I could have expected. "When I was helping Eric with Kit, it felt really right. I mean I knew what Eric did for a living, but I hadn't really thought about it. Not really. I wouldn't want to do what he does but I might like to do something similar."

I wanted to make sure I wasn't misunderstanding him. "You want to be a doctor?"

"Sounds crazy, but yes, I think that is what I want to do. How he knew what to do? How he could save lives."

Eric was his father. They never discussed those things, but he was, and I'd seen how much he wanted Phoenix to confide in him. He was going to love this.

"I think you should speak to your father. You'd be great at whatever you did."

Barrett turned around on the piano bench. "So finish high school. Let's start with that. But yes, speak to Eric. And we'll see about you actually going to college, which you always said you weren't going to do. Also, if you're doing that, I am teaching music. Everyone can kiss my ass."

Jeremy didn't look up. "Be a doctor. We obviously have things like gun shots happen in this family. Eric is going to need someone to take over. And yeah, teach music. I'm going to be a lawyer."

Julian grinned. "I always assumed I would do whatever I wanted. I don't know what is the matter with the rest of you."

I couldn't help my smile. This was so typical of what it was like when the four of them were together. Still, we had hardly discussed what had happened. Or maybe they had. I was just so sick and out of it for the last several days that I hadn't heard any of it if they had.

"I mean should we have a conversation about what happened?" I swallowed. "Or is it pointless and we all just do better when we don't bring things up?"

Jer lifted his head. "Oh you mean how Barrett burned rice tonight and none of us are going to be able to cook except you, ever?"

I rolled my eyes at him. "Sure, that's exactly what I meant."

"I will conquer the rice." Barrett laughed.

"We can talk about it." Jeremy sighed. "I mean we probably should. A guy with a gun came to kill us. Same guy who took my brother and killed some kids. It's really bad. I am not even sure how to begin to process it. How about the rest of you?"

The door opened and closed. We all jolted. Had anyone else heard a car arrive? We needed to get a little bit better at paying attention to things. Otherwise, there was always the possibility of another guy with a gun coming in. Or maybe I was just really, really paranoid right now.

Eric, Rosalind, and Stephen came in. The latter winked at us and walked past us into the kitchen. "Did you burn something in here?"

Barrett laughed. "I can't cook."

"That's okay, sweetheart." Rosalind walked over and kissed Barrett's cheek. "We can get you someone to do that if you want."

He held up his hands. "I want to be able to do basic things so Alatheia isn't always thinking she has to do them because we are otherwise incompetent."

"I don't think you're incompetent." I hadn't known he felt that way. "There's no need for you to worry. I like doing things around the house. I mean I might not like to be picking up constantly but anyway, I'm rambling."

I tended to feel like an idiot in front of their family. I tried not to but there it was. The rambling discomfort rearing its ugly head. It might be better if I just stayed quiet like I used to do.

Rosalind bent over the couch. "Don't pick up after them."

"Can I talk to you?" Phoenix rose, addressing his biological father who startled before he nodded. "In private?"

"Sure." Eric ran a hand through his hair. "Let's ah... go into the back of the house."

Rosalind stared at them, her face unreadable. She waited

until they had stepped back before she turned to the rest of us. "What is that about?"

"Don't worry." Jeremy smiled at his mother. "We all know he'll tell you in the car. How is Kit?"

She clapped her hands together. "He is getting to go home, and we have decided to go back to the city. Eric really needs to get back to work, and it'll be good for all of us. I hoped that you would all come." She looked over her shoulder. "I know you are avoiding Alatheia's family, but they aren't there currently, I don't think. Do you hear a car?"

Barrett got to his feet. "We really need to get some security cameras in here. Gran's place had it and the main house does. Why don't we have cameras in here?"

"Why would the guest house need security?" Daniel stepped into the house. "Who's here?"

Rosalind shook her head. "I don't recognize the car."

I turned toward the window, heart thrumming—I really didn't want strangers here right then—and caught sight of the black car as it glided up the gravel drive. The paint was so glossy it mirrored the sky, each raindrop scattering across its polished hood in silver beads. Some of it even looked like it might be changing to snow. Even from a distance, the low, predatory shape and the subtle growl of the engine spoke of money—old money, the kind that didn't flash but whispered. Meanly. Chrome trim winked as the car slowed, tires barely crunching. It was the sort of car you saw in magazines, never expecting it to actually pull up to your house, unless, of course, you were the Lents, and I realized I was holding my breath as it stopped just beyond the porch.

"Shit." Rosalind swore, the word sounding contrary to her sweet, genteel accent. But nothing about Rosalind was exactly what it seemed. That might be her best quality. "It's Murial Monk."

It was a good thing I was sitting because I wasn't sure if

my quaking knees wouldn't have given out just at the sound of her name. "How did she find us?"

"Who's here?" Phoenix came back in with a smiling Eric.

"Murial." Jules stood. "Come on. She doesn't catch you sitting. Power move. On your feet."

"It's her cousin." Barrett crossed in front of me to the door.

"Sure. But even vipers have cousins." Jeremy sighed.

I blinked. No. I couldn't get caught in that thing Jer just said. I had to focus on that and not wonder if vipers had cousins.

The doorbell rang and Barrett pulled the door open. I wouldn't want him to ever look at me with as much disdain as he just sent Murial Monk.

"What a surprise." Rosalind stepped forward, her smile bright and her gaze wary. I sort of expected that was the case with my cousin and a lot of people. For her part, Murial stared around the room, slowly, as though she had no reason to hurry and could simply stand and make people wait for her as long as she wanted.

I'd been with her twice in my life. The first was when I'd gone to her party and she had brought me upstairs—probably to threaten me—and hadn't because I had known something about the art on her walls and she had decided that I was more interesting than she had believed I would be. The second time had been in an art museum when she had brought Jeremy and me to see them authenticate a painting her uncle had bought to see if it had been stolen from a Jewish family during the Holocaust. I blinked. I guessed that man was my uncle too.

This was the first time I was seeing her without Davis, our other cousin. There had been four brothers and my late father as the missing one.

Her hair, dark and shiny, was always perfect. She never

even had any bumps in it when it was pulled back, as it was now. My own—currently fuzzy—hair didn't look that way when it was long. Not even close. How could we related at all? It was bizarre to me.

Yet there she stood and when her gaze finally reached me, she tilted her head. "Hello, Cousin."

I tried not to look at the floor in submission to the sheer power she had just by existing. She was a mean girl. Complicated. But mean nonetheless.

"Hello. What brings you here?" She had ignored Rosalind, but maybe she would answer me.

"Well, we heard you had a break in. That was when we realized you must be in the Hamptons here. I think the Lents would admit we have been patient. Letting them play hero instead of handling our family business ourselves. Now that we know that you are one of us, Darling, you are our business. So I came to see you for myself. Granny is so concerned."

I rubbed my arms. "Yes, there was a break in." The fact that the break in had been Rosalind's brother was left out of the story the police had given to the press. "And thankfully their father will recover from his gunshot wound he got protecting all of us."

Wow. I really could lie like a Lent. I could protect this family's secrets too.

"Thankfully." Rosalind nodded, meeting my gaze.

"Good. I wouldn't want anything to happen to you ever." She looked over her shoulder. "Here comes Davis." Aha. So they weren't separated even now. He held a package wrapped in brown paper.

"Hi, everyone." His grin was fake. It always was. And it used to give me the creeps. Just because he wouldn't be hitting on me anymore—I hoped—didn't mean that it didn't still have that overall effect on me.

Phoenix groaned. "Davis."

"Oh, you love me, and you know it."

Murial turned her head slightly. "Put it down and go back to the car. We're almost finished here."

We were? What had she come here to do? Just stare at me across a room?

"Alatheia, we need to proceed now in a manner that befits you. You were taken and that was awful. Your mother's disgusting family will be found and dealt with. I can promise you that. It's already being handled. As for this, which one of them are you dating? The nonanswers you give to that are not going to fly. If you won't tell me you will tell Granny. I assure you, you want to tell me."

I hadn't been prepared for this. What was I supposed to say? I gripped the side of the couch.

"Me." Barrett spoke fast. "She's dating me."

"Excellent. You're easier to handle than your brothers?"

What did that mean? "Don't talk about them like that."

Her smile was slow. "I like loyalty. Good. You and Barrett will be back in the city before the thaw. Got it? Don't make me come back and get you. That's for you." She nodded toward the package. "A reminder that there are benefits to being us. Goodbye, Lents."

She turned and left as quickly as she had come. We stood, no one talking.

"Wow." Daniel shook his head. "I really fucking hate them."

"It had to be me. You know it was always going to have to be me. When you're all done being mad, you know that." Barrett turned his back on us. "It's always the oldest brother."

"God forbid we do something different." Jeremy's tone was cold, unpleasant. "What is in that stupid package? I really can't stand that we have to deal with them.

Rosalind closed the door to the house. "It's for Alatheia. Open it when you're ready."

I was never going to be ready, but I walked over, knelt down, and tore up the brown packaging. What I saw made my heart skip a beat. No. It couldn't be. That wasn't possible. Was it?

"Red. " Phoenix's voice was low. "What is it?"

I swallowed. "I think... I think it's a Rembrandt."

I AM LEAVING MY HUSBANDS. I don't think I can handle it anymore.

DEAR READER,

Since I wrote that so much has changed. They came and got me. Found me. I couldn't believe it. They are so sincerely sorry for all the tension lately, all the unhappiness. They are committed to me. And I do love them. I'm not sure who Dina is anymore without the Lent brothers. They hold my soul.

PLUS A MIRACLE HAS HAPPENED. I'm pregnant. Why. How. I don't know. But I am. As I write this I am crying. This time with happiness.

DL

END NOTE

Thank you so much for reading Lilies! I hope that you enjoyed it and you'll consider giving it a review. Please take a look, Violets is either on pre-order of for sale right now (depending on when you are reading it). --RR